SURVIVAL INSTINCT

JANIE CROUCH

Dedication

This book is dedicated to Tia.
You have the heart of a warrior and a true survival instinct.
I will be your trooper always.

Chapter 1

"Remember that time you were about to be beheaded in an unofficial Iraqi prison and I led the team that saved your life?" Zac Mackay mentioned the situation so cheerfully it was like he was talking about a long-ago frat party or prom date.

Shane Westman groaned, shifting the phone more securely between his cheek and shoulder as he used both hands to carry a packing box across the room to the door. He swallowed a chuckle, because laughing now would only spell disaster for the cause of resisting whatever favor his friend and ex-Special Forces teammate was calling in.

"I'm sorry, you must have the wrong number," Shane said. "I'm just a pizza delivery guy. Never been in an Iraqi prison, of either the official or unofficial kind."

Zac didn't even try to hide his own laugh. "It's understandable that you might not remember. You'd been beaten to within an inch of your life, and I had to nearly carry your sorry ass all the way back to the neutral zone. I even heard they did some sort of mind-control testing on prisoners to make them think they work at Pizza House for the rest of their lives."

"Did you want pepperoni or olives on your pizza?"

Zac's bark of laughter made Shane smile. "How's the packing of your grandmother's stuff going?"

"Hard. You know how it is. Some of the stuff in this house seems like it's been sitting in its exact position since before the Revolutionary War. Getting rid of it feels like a crime." Boxing up the memories of the woman who'd raised him, his Grammi, was much harder than Shane had thought it would be. He'd spent the entire day yesterday just going through her closet.

For someone who had spent the last twelve years unflinchingly fighting some of the most dangerous enemy combatants in the world, it was surprising how difficult boxing away one small woman's clothing had been.

"Have you decided to sell the house? Rent it out?"

"I haven't made any decisions yet. It's completely paid off, so it's no hardship. This has always been my home." He might be moving to Cheyenne, Wyoming, in a couple of weeks to begin his civilian career at Linear Tactical with Zac and some of his other former army brothers, but Black Mountain, North Carolina, would always be his home. "I just wish I'd returned sooner. Gotten home last Christmas like I told her I would." Before his Grammi had died of a sudden heart attack.

"That tough old bird knew you loved her. That's the most important thing."

"Yeah, I guess." He hoped she'd known. He'd always tried to tell her, but for the last few years he'd been around less and less. "So, Mackay, you only bring up busting me out of the Iraqi prison—which I would've gotten out of just fine by myself, by the way—when you want to ask a favor."

They both knew Shane wouldn't have gotten out of that prison without Zac and the team's help, as well as that Zac didn't have to lord the rescue over Shane to get him to help with whatever Zac needed. If it was in Shane's power, he'd do it. Just like Zac would do the same for him.

"Yeeeahh." Zac dragged out the word in the most annoying way possible. "Linear Tactical has a job for you."

Zac had formed a company with three of their other Special Forces buddies once they'd gotten out of the service. Linear Tactical trained others in tactical awareness, small-arms safety, wilderness survival, and self-defense. People from all over the country traveled to their compound in Cheyenne. People who wanted to learn from the best.

"This can't wait until I get out there in two weeks? I know you miss me, Zac, but I want to enjoy not being snowed in for as long as possible."

It was only September, but the Wyoming winters were damn long.

"You know, for someone with the nickname Avalanche, you sure don't like cold weather."

Shane began loading up another box, knickknacks of Grammi's he wouldn't be able to keep if he wanted to fit anything else in the house. "Yeah, well, I didn't get the name because of my snowboarding ability."

He'd gotten it because of his ability to completely shut down his emotions. To pull ice around him, distancing himself from a situation to obtain the best tactical advantage, regardless of the horrors going on around it. A saving grace many times when he'd been a soldier, people dying all around him. When he'd been forced to make decisions as team leader that cost others their lives. He'd frozen his emotions to get the job done.

Unfortunately, now he couldn't seem to thaw.

"Job's not out here," Zac continued. "As a matter of fact, it's right in your backyard."

"North Carolina?"

"Yep. It's a side job."

They both knew that type of job for Linear Tactical tended to be much more dangerous than the work they did in Wyoming. Their home base was for training and teaching about weapons and situational awareness. Their "side jobs" tended to involve the *actual* weapons and situations. Kidnap and ransom assistance, bodyguarding, even guns-for-hire if the situation was right.

"I've been out of the field for more than six months, Zac. I may not be in peak shape."

Zac's eye roll was evident even over the phone. "Whatever. I'll take you in not-quite-peak over most people at their very best. Plus, this is a pretty low-risk job, which can help ease you back in to American civilian life, and it'll get you on our payroll."

"I'm already on it."

"Whatever. Get you *more* on our payroll."

Shane stacked another box. "Fine. What is it?"

"There's a television show, *Day's End*, that does all its primary shooting near you in North Carolina. They're having trouble with some sort of stalker. Most of the stars have their own bodyguards, but the studio is looking for someone good—and discreet—to send and help coordinate the security teams. To look around, see if they can figure out who the stalker is."

"I'm not a detective, Zac, nor an investigator."

"Yes, but you are more observant than anyone I've ever known."

Shane wiped a hand over his eyes. "That wasn't enough to keep my whole team from getting killed."

Zac didn't even stop for a breath. "You were cleared of

that. You made the best decision you could with the intel you had. Everyone agreed."

Shane didn't respond. Being cleared didn't bring back the dead.

"Avalanche, listen. I need someone I know personally. Linear Tactical got the call because the show's creator is Adrienne Jeffries's sister. She helped us out last year with that kidnapping case, which would've gone to hell in a hand-basket without her."

"The Bloodhound lady."

Zac chuckled. "She still doesn't like to be called that, but yep. Adrienne was concerned about her sister, so she made sure the studio contacted Linear Tactical to get the security support the show needs."

Shane rubbed his eyes. He didn't want to do this. Didn't want to be in charge of someone else's life again. "Send one of the other guys, Zac. I'm not the right person for this. I agreed to work for you because I thought I would be doing training. Teaching civilians how to defend themselves or handle their Glock."

"You'll have plenty of time for that. Trust me, a year from now you'll be begging me to send you back out in the field for some action." Zac's voice got serious. "I need someone I can trust one hundred percent. What Adrienne did for us with that kidnapping case? I can't do anything but give her someone I trust completely to help with her sister. We need the best."

"That's not me, Zac."

"Just give it a couple weeks. If you still feel like you can't handle it, then I'll find someone else. I know you've been on your little stroll for the past six months, but I have zero concerns that you've let yourself slip in either fitness or mental acuity."

Shane rolled his eyes. His "little stroll," as Zac put it, had been a demanding hike through the Alps, one Shane had taken because he'd needed to be away from everything and everyone while he'd tried to come to grips with losing his team. And while Zac was right—the time had made him stronger and more focused—it sure as hell hadn't brought him many answers.

Shane was going to argue more but stopped. What was the point? It wasn't like he was going to say no. When a brother asked you to do something, you did it. "Fine. Give me the details."

"Like I said before, the show is *Day's End*. It's about all these different paranormal creatures who attempt to stay alive while being hunted by a sort of human mafia."

"Yeah, it's been shooting around here for three years." The wilderness of western North Carolina had provided a beautiful backdrop for the show. "My grandmother mentioned it, but I've never watched it."

"It's one of the most popular shows on television, so you should probably check it out. Chloe Jeffries is the creative force behind the whole thing. It's her baby. She leads all the writing and some of the directing too. She's supposed to be this amazing, ingenious visionary."

Great. In Shane's experience, creative tended to mean flighty. Unaware of what was going on around them. "How long do they need someone?"

"Two weeks tops. Threat assessment and coordination of security. See what you can spot and make any changes you need to. You might have to do a little people watching for a few days, but those needing watching include Alexandra Adams. She plays the lead role, Tia Day."

Shane might not know the show, but everyone knew of Alexandra Adams. The show had catapulted her straight into the role of America's sweetheart.

"Yeah, I know who Alexandra Adams is." Not that it

mattered. This was about loyalty to Zac and the others, not about who he'd be guarding. "I'll do it, Mackay."

"I knew no red-blooded male could resist the thought of being near Alexandra Adams."

Shane rolled his eyes. "Two weeks. If they still need someone after that, it's more than just threat assessment; it's long-term containment. That's not what I'm in for."

Going in and assessing the holes in the security would be bad enough. Shane definitely wasn't interested in holding someone's life in his hands again.

Been there. Done that. Failed miserably.

Being a soldier was the only thing Shane knew how to do. He was glad to join his friends at Linear Tactical, but he wanted to teach, not be back out in the field. He was out of that game. And he particularly didn't want to be guarding people involved with some crazy zombie, vampires, and faeries show.

"Got it. Two weeks tops." Zac turned serious. A rarity. "Thank you, Shane."

"Don't thank me yet. You know I don't tend to play well with others."

Zac laughed. "If you're not nice, they'll just dress you up like one of the zombies and put you on camera. Wouldn't take much makeup the way you scowl. I'll let you go finish clearing out your Grammi's house. Your house now. Shane, thank you. I promise not to bring up your near-beheading for at least another four months."

Shane smiled. "Mackay, do you remember that time I carried you six miles over my shoulder in the Afghanistan mountains when you fainted?"

"*Fainted?*" Zac let out a blistering string of curses. "I was shot in the damn head."

"You were grazed and faking the whole thing because you

were too lazy to walk. I'm convinced of it." Shane couldn't stop the grin spreading across his face.

"Damn it, Westman, go protect some movie stars before I fly out there and kick your ass myself. You obviously had your brain tampered with while you were in that Iraqi prison."

"You want extra cheese on your pizza?"

Chapter 2

Chloe Jeffries's smile was a bit too cheerful considering all the blood on the walls.

Fortunately, none of it was real, just a mixture of corn syrup and food dyes used by most movie and television shows to emulate blood. It was definitely just as sticky and gross, so Chloe was sure not to touch it as she walked across the wraparound porch of the house that was one of the primary locations of *Day's End*.

Everybody was talking and listening at once, without really doing either, just the way Chloe liked it. It was beautifully cacophonous. And part of keeping *Day's End*—a television show with a mix of paranormal, drama, and a little romance—one of the country's hottest.

All the noise and bluster also helped drown out the voices in Chloe's head.

Most people joked about hearing voices in their heads. For Chloe, they were a part of her daily life, and had been for as long as she could remember. She'd long since learned to ignore them, unless they were helping her write a scene. One thing about having the whole world's thoughts in your head

. . . it meant you never had to worry about running out of ideas.

"Seriously, we're going to need more guts coming out of this zombie," Chloe said to Nadine MacFarlane, her personal assistant, cowriter, and best friend since they were eight. "It got into a fight with a vampire, so that would leave some pretty heavy-duty carnage."

Nadine nodded, smiling, and made a note on the tablet she carried around everywhere with her.

"What's on today's schedule?" It was Monday, normally the day they mapped out the week. As the creative director of the show, Chloe was involved with every aspect of its production, from writing to filming to the guts coming out of zombies lying on a wraparound porch.

She loved it. This was home. Or the closest thing to one Chloe had ever had.

"The usual," Nadine said, checking her tablet. "Writers this morning in the Pit, director and crew this afternoon. Putting out whatever fires are about to cause the most damage in between."

Chloe grinned at her friend. "Sounds about usual."

Nadine's big-boned five-foot-ten-inch frame dwarfed Chloe's much more petite one—the two of them had always resembled David and Goliath—but Chloe was more aggressive and protective of Nadine, who was naturally reserved and gentle. They'd been that way since the day Chloe had beaten up a boy nearly twice her size when he'd pushed Nadine down and tried to steal her lunch money.

Reserved and gentle, Chloe was not.

They'd become friends in their group foster home and more than twenty years later, despite being opposites in almost every way, were still as close as sisters.

Chloe also had two biological sisters whom she'd gotten to know as adults. But she didn't see them as often as she would like, since they both lived on the West Coast and *Day's End* was shooting here in North Carolina.

But now it seemed like her close-as-a-sister wasn't quite looking Chloe in the eye. Nadine wasn't normally one to lie. "What, Nadine? Just spit it out."

The other woman grimaced and peeked up from her electronic tablet. "I don't want to tell you."

"What? Budgets? Alexandra again?" The actress was a constant pain in the ass. "That secondary location isn't going to work out?"

Nadine shook her head. "The stalker."

Chloe forced herself not to curse out loud so she wouldn't have to put a dollar in the jar.

"Did we get a letter again? Please tell me there wasn't another weapon."

The letters had been coming pretty regularly for the last three months. They'd started out with a general theme: *Day's End* is evil and must cease to exist. That had gradually grown to: all who are involved with *Day's End* are evil and must be stopped.

Everyone had pretty much ignored the notes until they started showing up attached to knives with instructions for the people involved with *Day's End* to kill themselves or be killed.

Three days ago, another sicko note attached to a knife had arrived. Except this one was covered in blood. Real blood, not the corn syrup and food coloring type.

And it had been in Alexandra Adams's dressing room.

Yeah, the curse jar had been plumb full of money that day.

Alexandra had thrown a fit, of course, and within the hour had three extra security guards. The big behemoth guys had barely been out of the camera shots, Alexandra had wanted them so close.

Figuring out how the stalker/letter-writer/general sicko

was getting onto the set had been the topic of much discussion. But *Day's End* had hundreds of people on the set every single day between the cast and crew. And the knife had shown up on a day when they'd been shooting a large scene with even more extras than usual. So narrowing it down had been tough.

"No, nothing else from the stalker. But the studio is sending a security expert. We're supposed to give him full cooperation."

Chloe rolled her eyes. "Seriously, Alexandra doesn't have enough muscle surrounding her?"

Nadine sighed, and Chloe knew it wasn't going to be good. "This new person isn't for Alexandra. He's going to be in charge of all security for the entire set and surrounding area. Full access to everything."

Chloe held out her hand. "I'm going to need to borrow a dollar. Maybe five."

Nadine laughed. "Just give him a chance. It's someone Adrienne recommended when she got word about what was happening. Because yes—don't give me that look—I told her. She's worried about you. We both are."

But Nadine's concern didn't have to do with the stalker on the set. "Don't change the subject to get out of trouble. Tell me about security."

"He's from Linear Tactical, that group Adrienne worked with to help find the kidnap victim for last year. Adrienne said Zac Mackay and his group are the best. That whoever they sent would be laid-back, fun, and completely fit in to the madness here."

"But full access? You know how I feel about having strangers around poking their noses into everything."

Nadine wrapped an arm around her and kissed her on the top of the head, one of probably, oh let's see . . . *one* person in the world who could get away with doing that without Chloe ripping off a limb.

"This is the home you've built for yourself with your own two hands. I know that," Nadine said. "You don't want anyone messing with your house. But you're going to have to let this go, because you have other things to worry about."

"Ahem, why don't you just come right out and call me a control freak already, Nadine?"

Nadine rolled her eyes and gave Chloe a smile. "Oh, honey, you go way beyond that. But you'll let the security expert in to do his job, because, if not, we're going to end up with a bunch of cops around here, and once the press gets word of what's going on, it will be a free-for-all. And I know you don't want that."

"No fair. You're just trying to get me to have to put money in the curse jar," Chloe muttered. She had gone out of her way to become friendly with the townspeople of Black Mountain over the last three years, including Sheriff Linenberger. And since the stalker hadn't hurt anyone, none of the antics had been officially reported, although Chloe had let the sheriff know what was going on, since he'd heard about it through the grapevine.

Chloe and Nadine walked down the steps of the porch, getting out of the assistant director and lead camera operator's way. They were discussing tomorrow's shot down near the lake that took up a couple of acres of the five-hundred-acre property the show rented. It would be a pretty exciting scene.

Which was saying a lot given the nature of the entire show.

"Okay, I won't kill the security guy," she told Nadine, taking a deep, calming breath in the chaos going around and around in her mind. "I'll try to avoid him altogether. Maybe if he fits in as well as my sister thinks, I won't even notice he's here."

"Good." Nadine nodded and gave Chloe a side glance. The same kind she'd been giving her for the past three months. The making-sure-you're-not-about-to-collapse side glance.

"I'm fine, okay?"

"Nothing happened today? Nosebleed? Headache?"

Chloe rolled her eyes. "No, Mom. I'm fine."

Nadine's spiel about Chloe's need to rest and figure out what was happening was interrupted as the two other writers joined them at the bottom of the stairs.

Travis Oakley slipped his arm around Nadine, since they'd been dating for a few weeks, but his eyes stayed on Chloe.

"Justin and I think we've worked out next week's scene where the hunter closes in on Tia," Travis said without any other greeting, which wasn't unusual for their inner group.

"Did you have to move around the mob scene?" Nadine asked.

"We're not idiots," Justin grumbled.

Chloe automatically situated herself between Justin and Nadine as they all began to walk toward the large luxury trailer that served as the offices for the creative team, what they affectionately called the Pit. Justin was a brilliant writer, but he didn't play well with others and was often hostile to Nadine. He was sick a lot, prone to having to take a few days off for his health every few months. He'd even gotten fired from another writing gig because of it. Chloe had snatched him up.

Maybe he was a jerk because of being in pain and sickly all the time. Justin wasn't ever going to be someone she went out of her way to spend time with, but his creative talent couldn't be denied, and *Day's End* was better for it. Which was all that really mattered to her in the long run. She could take his sickness, his surliness, as long he helped her create a great program.

"I'll read over what you've done tomorrow, okay?" Nobody was offended by Chloe's words. At day's end, *Day's End* was her baby. She had final say on just about everything.

"Also, boss, check this out." Justin pulled a newspaper clipping out of the folder in his hand. Who even read a printed paper anymore? "I saw this last week and meant to bring it up, but then the whole crazy-stalker knife thing happened. It's not often that a headline looks like it was ripped from one of our episodes."

Chloe stopped and looked at the article Justin was holding.

Killer Hunting Psychics.

She caught Nadine's panicked glance at the topic of the article. Only Nadine knew about Chloe's voices. Travis and Justin had probably heard rumors, but Chloe had never confirmed them one way or the other when either of them, particularly Travis, had asked.

According to the newspaper, someone was killing self-proclaimed psychics up and down the East Coast. This latest murder had taken place in Greenville, South Carolina, which was less than two hours from the set.

"I was thinking we could add a couple psychics into the show," Justin continued. "I mean, we have vampires, shapeshifters, and zombies. Might as well throw some psychics in too. Our show would be *just like the news*. Never thought I would say that."

"I'm not sure." Travis was shaking his head, obviously finding the idea of it distasteful. "They're so tame, you know, compared to the other creatures. Not very strong. Plus, the people who were killed obviously weren't real ones."

Justin chuckled. "Not psychic enough to know that someone was about to kill them, that's for sure. Idiots."

Travis and Justin continued to argue the pros and cons of adding the new characters as they walked toward the Pit. Chloe and Nadine kept out of it. Chloe never referred to herself as a psychic, never mentioned her abilities to anyone at all, but the fact was, she could hear people's thoughts.

People tended to freak out when they knew that.

"It's a solid idea, you guys," Chloe finally said. "Let's flesh out the plot and see if we can fit it in. Also, the studio is sending in a security expert to coordinate all the . . . security stuff around here and to investigate our friendly neighborhood stalker. We're supposed to give him access to anything he needs. I've been assured that he will fit in just fine and will not hamper our creative energy in any way. We won't even know he's here."

"Like that guy walking toward us who definitely doesn't scream I'm-a-Navy-SEAL or anything?" Travis's eyebrow was raised so far it looked like it had found a new home in his hairline.

Chloe stared at the man in question. She couldn't turn away from him even if she wanted to. His long legs were encased in perfectly creased khaki pants; his collared light-blue shirt was tucked in—also perfectly—at the waist. His broad shoulders were covered in a tailored suit jacket under which Chloe was willing to bet all of this year's salary lay a shoulder holster for a gun. His posture screamed military. The way he carried himself—the set of his shoulders and lift of his chest.

Alert. Deadly. Ready.

But impressive as his body was, it was his face that drew her more. There was nothing pretty about him. His face was rugged to the point of being harsh. His jaw was already holding some stubble even though it wasn't even yet lunchtime. And she had no doubt Mr. Military Man shaved this morning, unquestionably during his perfect morning routine. His dark hair was cut close to his head, as if he couldn't quite decide whether to keep it military short or go for a more relaxed style.

His eyes were hidden behind aviator sunglasses, but Chloe knew he saw everything. Knew he saw her and that if she stopped him right at this moment, blindfolded him, and asked him to tell her where everyone was, he'd be able to do so with astounding accuracy, even though there were more than a dozen people milling around that he hadn't looked at directly.

This man was the epitome of cool, calm, and collected. She could feel the former radiating off him. She wanted to close her eyes and sink toward him. Her brain, always under such constant onslaught with the thoughts of others, and particularly the one voice that had been searing through her mind so agonizingly lately, wanted to bask in this man's ice. She wanted to douse herself in it.

But she couldn't. Because while she had no doubt this man would be able to organize the hell out of security and unquestionably catch the stalker and freeze him with his ice beams after leaping tall buildings in a single bound, there was no way he wasn't going to hamper the creative energy of the set. Energy that Chloe relied on not only to make *Day's End* the greatest show on television but to keep her own sanity.

He was already sucking in her energy, and they hadn't even spoken yet.

Ten seconds later he was standing directly in front of Chloe with his perfect hair and jaw, his perfect shirt tucked into his perfectly pressed pants.

"I'm Shane Westman with the Linear Tactical. We've been hired for security," he said, taking off his sunglasses. Chloe wasn't a bit surprised to find he had perfectly icy blue eyes. "I need to know who's in charge."

17

There was no way this Shane Westman could stay. No possibility Chloe could allow it.

He was too perfect. Too distracting. Too *everything*.

And he was very definitely not laid back.

She looked over at Nadine. "I have a feeling I'm going to need to borrow a bunch of dollars for the curse jar."

Chapter 3

Chloe had put a week's salary in the curse jar by the time she got off the phone with the studio and then Adrienne a few hours later.

Shane Westman was completely trustworthy, competent, and thorough. The studio had run a background check on him as soon as Linear Tactical had said who they were sending. The man had a stellar military record and was well respected by everyone in the known universe and their mothers.

As if Chloe couldn't tell all of that by the perfect creases in his khakis.

She wasn't worried about whether he could get the job done. Any idiot could see that he'd accomplish everything he put his mind to.

She was worried about her ability to get anything done while he was around.

She'd gotten more and more upset as the studio had asked her very logical questions: Had Shane done something to offend her? Or make her think he was incompetent? To worry her or someone else?

It didn't take long for her to realize that trying to explain to the logical studio executives that Shane Westman's presence might hamper her creative force made her just sound like a nutcase.

And she was a nutcase. But she knew having that man around was going to change everything about everything. Chloe didn't like change. She liked the chaos she'd built around her because it was *hers*, and *she* controlled it. Having Westman around threatened that.

It wasn't that she didn't want everyone safe—she did; *of course she did*—but couldn't they find someone a little less . . . commanding? Forceful? Sexy? Damn it.

She hung up with the studio, knowing that the only way she was going to get rid of Shane was to either boldface lie about him or threaten to walk out herself. She wasn't prepared to do either, particularly when the studio was starting to suggest that it may be time to bring in law enforcement also. The only people she wanted around less than Shane were law enforcement. They would just muck up the creative energy even further.

She felt the coolness pour over her mind just before she heard him speak.

"That's quite a mouth you've got on you there, peanut." He was leaning against the doorframe of her office, looking cool and comfortable.

Peanut. Of all the motherfuc—

Maybe she needed to worry less about whether he would distract her from her work and more about whether she might spend the rest of her life in prison for murder if he stayed.

She didn't say anything, knowing the words that would come out right now would just prove him correct about her language.

He was twirling his sunglasses by the stem. "You're

lobbying pretty hard to have me gone given we've spoken less than a dozen words to each other and you don't know me at all."

"What have you been doing for the last few hours?" She'd told him not to make himself comfortable as she stormed off, but he'd evidently ignored her.

"Looking around, getting a lay of the land. Trying to look for weakness in your security."

"And?"

"In the two and a half hours I've been here, I've spotted at least a dozen places someone could infiltrate the set with the intent to inflict damage."

She raised an eyebrow and leaned back in her chair, pulling from some of the coolness he still had radiating from him, and he had it in spades. God, the cool felt so good to her brain. All the writers—yellow-bellied cowards that they were—had bailed as soon as Shane had returned to the trailer.

It didn't surprise her that there were so many holes in their security or that he was able to pinpoint them so quickly. She wasn't even surprised at the military-precise terms that he used.

"I see you're twirling those glasses with your left hand," she observed, trying to match his cool. "Undoubtedly so you can use your right to do a quick draw from that shoulder holster under your jacket if we're attacked suddenly by violent criminals or drug-running aliens."

She'd surprised him; she saw it in the slightest flaring of his nostrils. He gave a nod. "Very observant. Get many drug-running aliens around here?"

She shrugged. "With this show, more than you might think."

"Look," he said, those blue eyes still seeing way too much. "I'm here as a favor to a friend, not because I have any desire to hang around a television set."

That, she believed. He looked like someone who belonged on a battlefield actively fighting. A soldier, not a guard.

"Rather do something more active? Go around shooting people and chasing bad guys? Is that what you normally do for Linear Tactical, Mr. Westman?"

"Shane. And actually, I'm just starting with the company, although I'm close friends with all the founders. I'll be doing training, simulations, and private-citizen instruction for them."

"You don't strike me as a *training and simulation* sort of person."

He'd stopped his twirling and was now just studying her with those eyes. "I'm here because you need me. People you trust asked people I trust to get a job done. So are you going to let me do it, or what?"

She really didn't like him. She really didn't like the way he was all logical and calm when she was being unreasonable and contradictory. It made her want to put more money in the jar. That fact that she knew she was being unreasonable and contradictory.

Her computer dinged, and the email she'd been waiting for popped up. It was the abbreviated version of the background check the studio had done.

She printed the paper and began walking as she read.

Thirty-five years old, no criminal record. Went to college and then joined the army. Stayed for twelve years. Received all sorts of medals and awards whose meaning she didn't understand. No mention of what he did while he was in, but she had no doubt he'd excelled, no matter what it was. Honorably discharged six months ago.

"Anything interesting?"

She looked up after the last sentence. "You're from this area."

The twirling began again. "Yep. Raised by my grand-mother. Left before this show ever came to town."

For just a second she did what she rarely ever allowed herself to do, even when she wanted to. She tried to pick out Shane Westman's voice inside her head to see what he was thinking. She didn't do it very often, because it was a gross invasion of privacy; plus, it just generally tended to creep her out.

She sat back down, staring at him to try to get a fix on his thoughts, and he calmly stared back.

Nothing. She couldn't hear him at all, which might mean he was empty-headed, but she didn't think so. She could feel that damned coolness where his thoughts should be. She felt her eyes drifting closed because the crispness just felt so good against her mind.

"You okay there, short stack?"

Her eyes flew open, then narrowed. "Are you trying to get me to fire you after only being here one afternoon?"

He wasn't ruffled. "It didn't sound like they wanted you firing anybody."

Chloe knew she could fight. Could throw a fit, and the studio would get rid of him to keep her happy. But she wasn't going to.

"I've got your file right here." She tapped her computer screen. "Background check the studio did. Tells me all about you."

He didn't look worried. "I doubt that."

"Says you're a local boy. Then college. Army." Something caught her eye in the report. "*Avalanche*. Was that your call sign or something? Like Iceman or Maverick?"

Why was she even saying that? No doubt he wasn't going to get the reference. She stood up. He was here; she wasn't going to use her clout to get rid of him; she might as well stop acting like she was. She would show him around, dump him on someone else.

"Call sign?" His eyebrow raised high. "No, because I wasn't a navy fighter pilot. And my friends and I rarely ripped our shirts off and ran down to play beach volleyball or buzzed the tower. But yeah, it was a nickname. Still is, I guess."

He did get the *Top Gun* reference. So maybe his pressed pants, chiseled jaw, and aviator sunglasses weren't everything to him.

Or maybe he just had good taste in eighties movies.

She wanted to know why his nickname was Avalanche but didn't ask, afraid he might tell her. She needed to know as little about this man as possible if she wanted to keep her focus. She smiled.

"Okay, Avalanche, you're in. Because you're right; I don't want to go ten rounds with the studio when you seem pretty qualified to do the job. And because anybody who can throw a *Top Gun* reference back in my face can't be so bad."

"I'm relieved I meet your qualifications." His tone was dry.

"My only qualification is that you are as least distracting as possible. We're a family here. We try to keep a creative vibe flowing here. And before you roll your eyes at me, I'm not talking some kumbaya rainbow gathering, okay? I'm referring to an imaginative, expressive flair that allows the artists here to do their best work."

"Well, your artistic flair is going to have to take a back seat to personal safety. That's why I'm here."

"Can't it be both? That's all I'm asking. Can you just try to respect the creative atmosphere here?"

Now he did roll his eyes. "I'll do my best."

Chloe doubted it.

"Fine, let's go. I'll show you around."

She brushed by him in the doorway—damn it, why was her body so aware of him when he hadn't done anything except piss her off and point out her lack of height since the second she'd talked to him?—and he pushed off from the frame to follow her.

"There's an underwater submersion stunt scene being filmed the day after tomorrow," she told him. "A lot of people are prepping for that. We do numerous stunts around here, but everyone wants more. They beg me all the time to write in scenes where they get to blow stuff up."

"Sounds like some of the guys I knew in the army."

"Yeah, actually a few of our stunt guys are ex-military. Have you ever watched *Day's End?*"

"No, I'm not a big television watcher. I'm more of a reader."

Chloe loved to read too, so she would only hold that against him a little bit.

They walked out of the trailer and down toward the lake. Shane positioned her to his left, and she wondered if he did it consciously to keep his shooting arm free, or if it was just ingrained in him. She didn't want people with guns hanging around, distracting the creative team from the work they had at hand. Alexandra's bodyguard had been bad enough, but now she had three. And a couple of the other actors had gotten some too.

Too many people were feeling an ugly and more panicked vibe. Chloe just wanted to get back to writing the show she loved that had become her very lifeblood. Her home. A possible stalker threatened that, but all the added muscle didn't help.

Case in point: Shane, aviators back over his eyes, studying everything. Assessing. Weighing.

"Look, I want to be honest. I'm not sure these stalker threats are even truly dangerous. I mean, completely cuckoo, sure. But we've had crazies before. Our show seems to bring out the crazy in droves."

"Leaving a knife dipped in blood on someone's chair is beyond just cuckoo."

Chloe shrugged. "Yeah, but I heard it was cow's blood."

"Regardless, my job is to assess the threat and make your location as safe as possible. I know you don't want a crackdown, because you want your free-spirit writing creative voodoo clear. But there are no free spirits if people start getting hurt or worse. So I'll do my best to keep your vibe the way you want it, but I can't make any promises."

Why did his complete and utter calm make her blood pressure skyrocket? And knowing she was being unreasonable didn't help, so she sucked in a breath and counted to ten.

"Where do you want me to show you?" she finally asked, at least sounding like a rational person.

"I'll look around myself. It will be better that way. I'll be able to study things more easily. People pay attention to you, but they won't to me."

Looking at him—that granite jaw, wide shoulders, and a body ready for all sorts of action—she found it very hard to believe that anyone could ignore him.

She had to get away from him right now. And stay away. Shane, as good as he might be for the set of *Day's End*, was going to play hell with her equilibrium. And she couldn't have that.

"Fine, explore all you want. I'll make sure the security force knows you've been hired. Just stay away from me and my creative team, and we shouldn't have any problems.

She could feel his coolness beating against her back as she walked away.

Chapter 4

Shane spent the next two days observing as much as he could about the people, the location, and the general atmosphere of *Day's End*. He went unnoticed as much as possible—everyone had a job to do and generally didn't care about one lone stranger in their midst, as long as Shane didn't get in their way.

Except for Chloe. Her whiskey-colored eyes had pretty much glared at him every time she saw him and the few times they'd talked. No doubt she would punch him if he made one more joking reference to her height, but surprisingly, he couldn't seem to help himself.

Teasing and joking were not Shane's normal MO. Everything about his interactions with Chloe had been slightly off from his norm.

He couldn't quit looking at her. Maybe it was because she never stopped moving. He'd grown up in this area of North Carolina, knew the normal, slower pace people tended to keep here. Chloe Jeffries moved twice as fast—maybe more—than others around her. She was a sexy Energizer Bunny.

Although sometimes concerningly pale. Especially when

he'd seen her first thing both mornings. She looked like she was recovering from the flu or something. A weakness that belied her tough attitude.

Yet after ten minutes in his presence she was back to feisty—paleness completely gone—and both times he'd wondered if he'd imagined the weakness.

God knew his normal MO—keeping remote and detached—hadn't been working so far. Since the moment he'd walked in on her talking to the studio, trying to get him fired, using obscenities that would've impressed even the most battle-hardened soldier, Shane hadn't quite been able to keep his distance from Chloe.

Not that he truly cared if she and the studio decided to bring in someone else instead of him. But damned if watching her head nearly fly off her body in frustration wasn't the most entertaining thing he'd seen in possibly ever.

Yeah, her push to preserve the artistic energy or whatever woo-woo stuff she was talking about above all else had been problematic. Was having a hit show so important to her that she would put a *creative vibe* over the safety of the people on the set? That was going to lead to some real fights between the two of them, not just ones where he was poking fun of her short stature.

But after the last two days hanging around, he'd realized the beautiful little spitfire was protecting the home she'd built. Her demands weren't about the ratings, or at least weren't *just* about them. This set was her home. These people were her family, the ones she cared about. Yes, she wanted their physical safety but also their emotional safety.

She viewed Shane as a threat to her family in the latter sense much more than she saw the stalker as a physical one to those same people. And she had lashed out because of it.

He could respect her reasoning and vowed not to disrupt the creative woo-woo here, give them room to film where and when they wanted. But he would also make sure this was a safe place. Security here was tricky. Difficult. It was easy to see how someone could wander around unnoticed. Shane had been doing it for two days.

Chloe was by the lake, talking to Nadine, and, like everyone else, getting ready for the big underwater stunt coming up soon. He saw her look up and glance at him, and gave a little salute, chuckling as she flipped him off.

It really said something about him that he was turned on by a woman who hadn't said a single nice thing to him since they met and might be using some sort of voodoo doll to hex him at night.

"So you're the new security guy?"

The man—roughly thirty-five years old, sandy-blond hair, medium height and build—was part of Chloe's creative team. Shane had seen him with Chloe and Nadine but didn't know his name. "I am. Name's Shane Westman."

"I'm Travis Oakley. One of the writers." He held out his hand, and Shane took it, noticing the odd-looking scars running down the man's wrist and hand. They were relatively recent ones; Shane had enough of his own to know.

The man looked at his own arm. "Lichtenberg figures. I got struck by lightning not quite a year ago. Lucky to be alive, for sure, but the strike left some crazy scars."

Shane nodded, studying the unique treelike patterns for a minute since Travis seemed to have no problem with it. "The alive part is what matters."

Travis nodded, and they both turned to look out at all the people preparing for the stunt. "I hope you can catch whatever idiot stalker is behind these threats. Chloe thinks it's just pranks, but either way she doesn't need the stress. She has enough on her plate."

Shane shifted so he could glance at Travis. The man was protective of Chloe, although Shane had seen him with

Nadine. Maybe the other man considered the entire creative team as part of a family, like Chloe did.

"Yes," Shane agreed. "Chloe seems to stay pretty active."

"She does. We all do. We're a team. Let me know if there's anything I can do to help catch this guy and get things back to normal as soon as possible: tight and close-knit. We like to keep a creative vibe around here."

Meaning, get rid of the stalker and thus Shane as soon as possible.

Shane dipped his head at the other man. "So Chloe told me. Thanks for the offer, Oakley. I'll let you know if I need backup."

They nodded at each other and walked in opposite directions. Travis wasn't going to be a problem, not unless Shane decided to address this attraction between himself and Chloe.

So in other words, Travis wasn't going to be a problem. Shane was here for a job. Emotions weren't a part of it.

He spotted Alexandra Adams, or at least the three hulking bodyguards surrounding her, and made his way in that direction. She was the starting point for the investigation, particularly since the latest threat had been found in her dressing room.

He introduced himself to the head guard, Markus Templeton, and was relieved when the man had seen him around and had already called it in to make sure Shane was legit. That was definitely the type of diligence they needed. Markus had been Alexandra's private security for years, even before the stalker incident.

Shane felt even better after talking to the man for a while. Markus had been in the security field for more than twenty years and had been in the navy before that. He was obviously in top physical shape, even for a man close to fifty years old. Shane had served with soldiers like Markus: alert, focused.

Those were the type of people you wanted to have your back.

"Markus, sugar. Who is this?" Shane felt a hand touch his arm softly. "Is this the new security liaison?"

"Yes, ma'am." Markus's eyes never stopped looking for potential threats as he spoke to the woman who'd come up behind them. Shane glanced at her, then couldn't help but almost do a double take.

Alexandra Adams herself.

She was already in full makeup for her part in the scene they were about to shoot, but it was clear that even without cosmetics she would still be gorgeous. Porcelain skin, full lips, big green eyes.

She wasn't one of the most loved actresses in the country for nothing.

"Yes, ma'am, I'm Shane Westman. I'll be coordinating security until we get the situation handled."

Alexandra laughed, the sound almost musical. She was famous for it—that sweet laugh that had made her America's sweetheart.

But all Shane could think was that it wasn't as real and gutsy as the laugh he heard from Chloe when he made the joke about *Top Gun* that first day.

"Now sugar, I'm not going to be able to let you call me ma'am. Markus here insists on it, but I don't think there's any way I'm going to allow it from you."

"Alexandra, then."

If possible her smile turned up another hundred watts. "Or Lexi—that's what the people who are really close to me use."

Although the man never said a word and his stance didn't change, out of the corner of his eye Shane saw Markus's eyebrow raise. Evidently the *call me Lexi* offer didn't come up very often.

Alexandra continued to chat, talking about how nervous she was after the stalker had left the weapon in her dressing room. How glad she was the studio was taking the threat seriously, since Chloe thought it was some sort of prank. How glad she was that they were sending someone as obviously qualified as Shane.

Markus's eyebrow had basically found a new home at the top of his head by that point. Alexandra continued to talk with her melodic voice and angelic smile, her hand only leaving Shane's arm when she made some sort of statement and touched his chest to emphasize it.

Shane didn't discourage her. His nickname may be Avalanche, but nobody was cold enough to ignore Alexandra Adams when she turned on her full charm.

Finally, a kid in his early twenties with a headset that looked like it was permanently attached to his ear, who'd been flittering around from person to person since Shane and Chloe arrived, came up to Alexandra.

"Miss Adams, we are ready for you. We just want to get some primary shots of you in the car with the same lighting before the stunt woman takes over."

"Sure, Noah, sugar." Alexandra turned her smile to the younger man, but her hand didn't leave Shane's arm. She turned to Markus.

"I'm going to have Shane walk me down to the shot, okay, Markus?" She didn't wait to see if her head of security would agree; she just linked her arm with Shane's. "It will give him a chance to see everything up close."

Markus didn't get huffy. "Good idea. But I'll come with you." Markus's eyes met Shane's. "No offense."

Shane gave a half shrug. "I rarely get offended by people doing their job well."

He walked with Alexandra down to the water's edge until she was swarmed by the costume and makeup teams, all trying to ensure she was perfect for the upcoming shot. Shane stepped back next to Markus as the crew peeled off the robe Alexandra had been wearing.

The shirt she had on under the robe was completely ripped down one side, exposing her entire shoulder and the upper curve of her breast. Lots and lots of creamy skin.

A six-inch prosthetic gash ran along her chest.

"Don't worry; it didn't hurt." Alexandra winked at Shane as she handed her robe to Noah and stuck her breasts out so the makeup crew could continue adding the finishing touches to her wounds. Finally, she headed off in the direction the minions were leading her, in no way self-conscious by her state of half-undress.

"A chance to see everything up close, huh?" Shane muttered.

Markus chuckled. "North Carolina is a long way from LA. A girl gets lonely. Fresh meat starts to look mighty tasty."

Shane's eyes sought out Chloe. She was still standing over with Nadine, looking out at all the happenings and chaos around her as if she were a hostess and this was a party she was throwing. Which it kind of was. He found her much more compelling to watch than Alexandra, even with the actress's state of half-undress.

"Believe it or not, I don't think I'm interested in being Alexandra's fresh meat," he told Markus.

And if that didn't make him an idiot, Shane didn't know what did.

"Well, we won't tell her that, because that will just make Alexandra want you more."

Shane couldn't help but wonder, what would make *Chloe* want him more?

And as opposite as they were, why the hell would he even want that?

Chapter 5

Nadine pressed a wet washcloth into Chloe's hand from where they had set up to watch the big water stunt just behind the director and assistant director's station, so they would be able to see the footage as it was being shot.

Chloe immediately put the washcloth to her face, relishing its coolness. "Crap, is my nose bleeding again?"

Nadine's features became even more pinched. "No, but there's some dried blood, so I know it was earlier. Does your nose start bleeding without you even realizing it now? Chloe, you've got to do something about this. Maybe it's a tumor."

Chloe did her best Arnold Schwarzenegger voice. "It's not a tumor."

Nadine didn't budge. "You can't be sure of that, Chlo. I know the voices have always been part of your brain, but this one is different. I've been reading about how people with brain tumors sometimes feel like they hear—"

Chloe squeezed Nadine's hand. "It's not a tumor, okay? I had a CT scan a couple of weeks ago. A full neurological workup."

The two women stared at each other for a long moment. Nadine knew just about everything there was to know about her. Chloe might have two biological sisters whom she loved very much—and who were just as weird as Chloe when it came to their own mental gifts—but she'd lived most of her life without Adrienne and Paige around.

Nobody knew why three six-year-olds, whose mother had died and had no other relatives to speak of, were separated into different foster situations. It would be unheard of now. Maybe it was because all three of them had "special" needs: Chloe hearing voices no one could, Paige seeing auras no one could, Adrienne feeling evil no one could. Once they grew into adults, they each came to understand that their abilities made them unique. Different from others. But when they were six years old, that difference must have seemed an awful lot like trauma or emotional scarring to would-be foster parents.

So Chloe had lost her mother and sisters in a very short period of time. If it hadn't been for Nadine, who had no other family and had come from a pretty traumatic situation of her own, Chloe might have shut herself off completely. It was a testament to Nadine's innate kindness that Chloe had any tenderness at all. Growing up, Chloe had the mettle, the spunk. Nadine had the compassion, the warmth.

Chloe didn't know what she would do without her friend.

She squeezed Nadine's hand again before pulling the other woman—a sister in every way but blood—in for a hug. "The neurologist didn't find anything. I promise."

Nadine pulled back. "Why didn't you tell me? I would've gone with you."

"I know. But I needed you here with the show. The only way I could let myself take the time away was to know you were here to handle anything that might happen."

Nadine didn't make Chloe feel bad about the decision.

They'd been friends long enough for her to know what was truly important to Chloe. That Chloe cared more about *Day's End* than she did her own health.

"And no tumor?" Nadine whispered.

"Nope. My brain looked fine. At least from what their scans could show."

"Then what is happening to you?"

Because they both knew Chloe was dying. Like, literally, not the dying-only-to-be-reincarnated-as-something-else kind that sometimes happened on the show.

The debilitating headaches, nosebleeds, and full-body muscle seizures seemed to be happening to her more and more often over the past few months. And in the last three days, they had gotten even worse, especially at night.

Chloe had always heard voices in her head and had generally ignored them. But this one she couldn't ignore. It was like someone had turned his volume up as loud as it would go inside her mind.

Not his voice, but his emotions too. His obsessive thoughts burned through her brain like someone was stabbing the inside of her head with a hot poker.

We'll be together.

You're the one.

His thoughts were always short like that. Bursts of focused obsession. The man, whoever he was, was in love with a woman. Or maybe love wasn't the right word. He was *consumed* with her. His need for her overwhelmed him. And therefore, Chloe.

We're meant to be.

I'm coming for you.

Soon.

Chloe had taken to calling him Conversation Hearts, since the emotions he blasted into her head reminded her of the saccharine phrases written on the tiny Valentine's candy.

They might have even been considered sweet, in an excessively engrossed stalkerish sort of way, if they didn't burn like agony through her brain every time she heard them.

His thoughts weren't about Chloe, or if they were, it wasn't because the guy was nearby. Most of the time his emotions bombarded her head when she was completely alone. Her brain was just picking up the frequency of some whackjob's thoughts—just like she did everyone else in the world—but for some reason his volume was at an intolerable level.

Literally, as in, her body shut down when it happened, almost like a seizure.

"I hadn't seen you in pain on the set the last couple of days, so I thought maybe it was getting better," Nadine said.

Chloe always tried to hide it if she was having some sort of mental "attack" by Conversation Hearts while she was with the cast or crew. But Nadine was too perceptive.

But it was true, while Chloe had been working the last couple of days, there hadn't been any attacks. "I think I've been so focused on the pain in my *ass*, the pain in my *head* didn't have a chance to break in."

She glared at Nadine, daring her to say something about Shane.

So, of course, Nadine did. Grinning, no less. "I'm just wondering when he's going to pull your pigtail so you can chase him around the playground, *peanut*."

By the time Chloe finished her sentence concerning her feelings for Shane Westman, where he could go and what he could do to himself and his mother, she owed Nadine another five dollars for the curse jar.

Nadine just ignored her rant. "He is super sexy, isn't he? I mean, I'm happy with Travis, but Shane looks like something they pulled off a sexy soldier wall calendar."

Chloe forced herself to stop staring at Shane. Again. Just

like she had for the past two and a half days. It was like he had some sort of homing beacon she couldn't escape.

And now he was standing with Alexandra Adams, who had evidently decided to paste herself to Shane as soon as he'd gotten into her general vicinity.

Shane hadn't tried to get away, not that Chloe could blame him. Who in his right mind would try to with Alexandra Adams? With all her perfect skin, megawatt smile, and huge boobies?

She'd talked with him right up to the point where she was needed for the scene and had once again attached herself to his body now that she'd finished the hour's worth of shooting it had taken them to get the ten seconds she was on screen.

The way everyone applauded, one would think Alexandra had truly saved the young boy in the back seat of the car from drowning in icy water as the car they were in submerged lower and lower. In reality, they'd said their lines with the car sitting on a platform well above the lake as temperature-controlled water was sprayed on them.

Okay, unfair. It had been a harder scene than usual. Alexandra had needed more emotion since not only was her character, Tia, in danger, she had someone else's life on the line too.

And all the water being sprayed in the actress's face couldn't be comfortable. So Chloe should cut her some slack for running straight to Shane after she finished her scene and dried off.

Chloe reminded herself that she had met Shane only a few days ago and she did not care what he did, or who he allowed to leech off him. As a matter fact, they had a scene coming up in a couple of weeks about a character who offered his blood as payment for protection against the hunter mafia. They still hadn't cast the role. Maybe they should see if Shane was interested . . .

If they could drag him away from Alexandra, who was once again laughing sweetly at something he'd said, looking up into his aviators as if he were her personal hero.

Chloe was disappointed in him.

It was ridiculous; she knew it. She had no reason to be upset because he was paying more attention to the beautiful, world-renowned actress who was flirting with him rather than doing his job and focusing on what was around him.

She was disappointed because he was a man, responding to a beautiful woman. How ridiculous was that? Just because Chloe wanted him to respond to her that way instead. Fat chance if Alexandra had set her sights on him.

It didn't matter. He wasn't what Chloe wanted or needed. She refused to look at him again as she watched Alexandra's stunt double get into the car that would be submerged.

The rest of the team was getting set up, the safety scuba diver was already in the water, and the camera crew was in place. They would only have one good chance to get the shot right.

The stunt double would stay in the car until it was completely under the water. She'd then roll down the car window, allowing water to fill the inside of the vehicle. Once the car was full of water she would be able to swim to the surface.

Normally shots like this would be done in a pool, but the entire cast and crew had wanted to do it in the lake because it was such a central aspect of the story of *Day's End*. Not to mention they were all a bunch of daredevils.

Chloe wasn't worried about safety. They had some of the best safety crew in the country. The stunt double, Suzie, had her own private supply of oxygen if she needed it, not to mention the other scuba diver ready to assist.

The question would be getting the shot.

Chloe walked down so she was close to the water one last time to take everything in. Forget Shane Westman. She had an award-winning show to create.

Soon Noah, the intern, headset attached to his face, was moving all noncritical personnel away from the lake's edge. Chloe moved back to the monitors. It was time to start.

Everything was going like clockwork, just the way the creative and stunt teams, as well as the directors, had mapped out on paper. The front of the platform holding the car was lowered slightly with hydraulics, which on screen would make it look like the car was sinking engine first. Soon the car was completely submersed in the murky lake water.

This was going to be some fantastic footage. A grin she couldn't stop covered her face as they all huddled around the monitors showing the different footage the digital cameras were catching.

"I know," Nadine said, grinning also, as if she were the one who could hear voices. "I can already smell another Emmy."

And then the laughter started.

Chloe spun around, trying to figure out who would dare laugh so loudly and potentially ruin such an important shot. But everyone was studying the scene intently. No one was laughing out loud.

It was in her head.

It wasn't a chuckle, a giggle, or any sort of sound meant to express actual joy.

It was a laugh of pure evil.

Chloe took a step away from the monitors, closer to the water, trying to break the sound in her mind. What was going on? Whose laughter was stuck in her head? Someone far away or here on the set?

Inside the submerged car, Suzie was doing her part for the scene. The car was slowly filling with water, and she was using a metal pipe to look like she was cracking the window. In reality, the window was made of a special breakaway material.

"Okay, give Suzie the signal that we are good for her to break the window." The director said into a walkie-talkie. The signal would be given to her under the water by special camera operators who were trained to get the shots needed while wearing scuba gear.

The laughter in Chloe's head got louder.

She watched the screen as Suzie mimed a motion of hitting the inside of the car window with her pipe. It immediately broke away, as it was supposed to, and water began flooding the car in earnest. Even knowing there were safety measures around her, it was still jarring to watch. Especially with some crazy person's maniacal laughter providing a soundtrack in Chloe's head.

But Suzie was a professional, and they had planned the stunt meticulously. She pulled on her seatbelt, jerking just a little when it seemed not to come off—also planned—then finally escaped the belt. Suzie constantly looked over her shoulder at the child the audience would assume was still in the back seat based on clever editing.

Suzie didn't panic, just like Tia Day wouldn't on the show.

Until there was a sudden lurch in the platform—definitely not planned. The director cursed and immediately got on his walkie-talkie as multiple members of the crew began talking at once.

"What the hell happened?" the director asked the stunt coordinator. "Please tell me this was just something you decided to slip past me."

The stunt coordinator shook his head, already communicating with his own team.

The platform was sinking lower. Now, instead of being seven or eight feet under the water, the car was slipping past twelve. And still moving.

They could all see it on the cameras. Everything was sinking. This very definitely shouldn't be happening.

"Get Suzie out," the director said. "Cut the shot and get her out."

Everyone was moving frantically now. The underwater cameramen were backing away from the scene, no longer trying to keep to the scheduled shots, although all of them kept their cameras running.

Suzie's features, so much like Alexandra's, were definitely pinched. She still had to wait for the car to finish filling with water before she could get out. But now the car would be much deeper than she'd expected. She grabbed her oxygen canister and had it in her hand.

"Okay, she's almost completely submerged," the assistant director announced, obviously being given feedback from under the water. "After that, she'll just swim through the window."

It'll be too late.

The words were clear in Chloe's head. Then more laughter.

Evil is so easily distractible.

Chloe closed her eyes and concentrated on that one particular voice in her head.

They're going to miss it. They're going to miss it.

The words were sing-songy, almost childlike. Chloe could envision someone jumping up and down and clapping his hands with joy, like a kid on Christmas.

This was the stalker.

"Suzie is out of the car," the assistant director was saying. "She just gave us a thumbs-up. It looks like we're all clear."

Going to miss it. Going to miss it. Going to miss it.

Chloe left the director's area, walking closer to the lake. Everyone was running around a little chaotically as Suzie swam toward the lake's dock and the underwater camera operators began to make their trek toward shore.

Even the costume and makeup crews were giving off a panicked buzz. Everyone was caught up in the mania. Normally, Chloe would love something like this; it made the noise in her head even out. But right now, she was trying to find one specific voice.

What were they missing?

Someone ran past her at a full-out sprint and dove into the water.

Shane.

It only took her a moment to realize where he was going. About twenty yards out was the scuba safety diver, floating facedown.

Chloe didn't waste any time. She yelled for help, then kicked her shoes off and ran into the cold water of the lake after Shane. He was stronger and faster and had already reached the unconscious man and was swimming back toward shore by the time Chloe caught up.

Silently, she grabbed for the man's other arm, taking some of his weight from Shane.

"Hang on." She'd been scuba diving enough times to know that getting the diver's weight belt off would help move him faster. She dove under and unhooked the belt from the man's waist, then just let it fall.

She and Shane worked together silently to get the man back to one of the docks. Help was pouring out by the time they were close. Medics pulled the man from the lake out onto the dock.

Chloe just held on to the dock, trying to catch her breath as the medics began performing CPR on the man. Shane moved next to her in the water.

"Are you okay?" he asked.

"How did you know that guy was there? Hurt?"

"That's my job. Not just to watch the obvious, but to watch everything."

Her teeth were beginning to chatter. She heard the medic yell that the diver was breathing again. Then Shane called to get them assistance. A few moments later he helped hoist her from the water as someone else grabbed her arms and pulled her up to the dock. A blanket was wrapped around her as she watched Shane pull himself up.

"You were already walking toward the water before I passed you," Shane said. "Did you see the diver?"

She shook her head. "Not until you ran past me."

"Why weren't you focused on the car scene and malfunctions?"

Because the voices in my head were pointing out there were other problems.

Attempting to explain to straight-laced super-soldier Avalanche that she heard voices in her head would not go over well. Nobody else on the set would care. They'd all probably heard the rumors about Chloe. But weird stuff happened in Hollywood all the time.

Chloe had learned the hard way multiple times over not to try to tell people about the voices she heard. Especially to someone like Westman, for whom everything was so black and white. Logical.

"I just thought maybe something else was going on. I don't know why."

Shane stared at her, the two of them wrapped in their blankets, for a long moment. She could tell he didn't believe her. Knew there was something she wasn't telling him.

He'd have to learn to live with it.

The medics were taking away the diver in the ambulance. She and Shane made their way back to shore from the dock and were immediately bombarded by people.

"Thank you," Chloe said to him as different people fluttered around them, replacing their soggy blankets with towels. "That diver would've died if it wasn't for you. Nobody else saw him. Honestly, I'm surprised you did."

"Because everyone's attention was on the sinking platform?"

"No, because—" She stopped herself. Damn it. Why hadn't she just said yes? *Yes, Shane, because everyone's attention was on the sinking platform.* Perfectly logical and much better than, *because I noticed Alexandra Adams had herself all pressed up against you, and men tended not to notice a nuclear bomb when that happened, much less something in an isolated section of a lake.*

"Because what?" Shane's eyes narrowed.

"You just seemed busy . . . guarding Alexandra. I didn't think you'd have much attention span left to be focused on anything else."

He took a step toward her, the ice in his eyes freezing out everything in her mind except the two of them. She could see all the people skittering all around them but for the first time couldn't feel them in her mind.

Her eyes closed at the blessed coolness.

"Are you all right?" Shane's fingers wrapped around her arm shocked her, returning her to reality. The noise all came flying back into her head. "Do you need a doctor?"

"No, I'm fine."

"Just so we're clear, my job is not to guard Alexandra Adams. She has her own security team for that. My job is to coordinate all security and catch the bastard doing this."

"Maybe this was just an accident. Or a practical joke or something." God, she wanted to believe that more than anything. That perhaps the voice she'd heard hadn't actually meant to truly hurt someone, just cause trouble for the show.

"Joke? Accident? If so, it was one hell of a coincidence. You know what twelve years as an Army Ranger taught me?"

She couldn't seem to look away from his blue eyes. "Besides how to play beach volleyball and buzz the tower?"

He smiled, and her breath actually left her for a second. It softened everything about him. "Of course. But also, fun size, that when it comes to an enemy, there are no coincidences. *Day's End* has an enemy."

Chapter 6

Shane spent the next two days continuing to immerse himself in *Day's End*. The set, the cast, the crew. Familiarizing himself with routines, ways of getting on and off the set, and even the vendors that serviced the show. Made sure he knew everyone and everyone knew him.

Day's End was a huge enterprise and had been shooting here in western North Carolina for years. Even his grandmother had mentioned "that strange television show that shot nearby." Grammi had never had anything bad to say about the cast and crew and their influx into the relatively unknown town of Black Mountain, North Carolina. But it had definitely been a change. One that had brought in lots of money, jobs, and popularity, but also the problems that came with tons of extra people.

Most of the cast and crew lived locally either in Black Mountain or the surrounding areas during the seven months out of the year that they did the shooting. Chloe lived here on the set in her trailer. The stars, including Alexandra, had both luxury trailers on the sets and homes in the town.

The number of people who worked in supporting a show

of this size was staggering. Vetting them all would take longer than Shane could do on his own in a year. He'd already called Zac and, after being put on speakerphone and grilled by all his ex-Ranger buddies on what it was like to breathe the same air as Alexandra—he'd deliberately left out the "call me Lexi" part, knowing they'd never leave that alone—Adams, had gotten Linear Tactical working on the background checks, with full financial support from the studio. If there was someone with a record or history of mental illness in any of the cast, crew, or supporting vendors, Shane would be notified.

But Shane wasn't resting on that. A stalker who was stealthy enough to move around for weeks without drawing anyone's attention probably didn't have either.

Chloe once again was glaring at Shane between sips of coffee from across the large conference table where everyone sat for today's all-hands meeting. She'd been glaring at him pretty constantly for the last two days. But today her glare was tinged with exhaustion. Brackets formed around her mouth, and a tiredness pulled at her posture. Her hands cupped the mug as if it were a lifeline.

This meeting was necessary, but obviously not what any of them wanted to be doing. The director, assistant director, and stunt coordinator sat on one side of the table. Alexandra and five of the other principal actors, their security guards crowding the wall behind them, sat on the other. Chloe and her creative team sat at the far end.

The studio wanted to send in a lot more security, but so far Chloe was holding them off. She'd allowed three extra bodyguards: two of them going to Alexandra, one just as a general presence.

The little rebel wanted nothing if not her creative freedom. She'd kept arguing with the studio there was no actual proof that the stalker had been involved in the lake accident.

Shane didn't think she actually believed that, but she wanted to keep everything as natural as possible, as she'd been fighting for the whole time. Shane wouldn't argue, at least not yet. Right now, they needed to figure out where to consolidate their focus.

The scuba diver had fully recovered and was already home from the hospital. The doctor said that his air tank had been contaminated by a potent mixture with too much carbon monoxide.

It did happen in scuba diving. Not often, but it did. Just like the hydraulic malfunction of the platform holding the car. Malfunctions did happen.

But both happening on the same day? In Shane's professional opinion, that *did not* happen.

And he knew, although he didn't want to discuss this with Chloe until he had proof, the stalker was someone inside the show. Everyone speculated that it was an extra or a crazy fan who had snuck in, but Shane didn't think so. Leaving the weapons and notes had been one thing. Sabotaging a complex hydraulic system and scuba gear so they both malfunctioned within a few minutes of each other? That required someone who had inside knowledge of how the show worked, as well as its people and scheduling.

Someone in Chloe's set family was a traitor. Shane fully intended to find out who.

Shane turned to the people around the table and reported that Suzie the stuntwoman and the safety diver were both going to be fine. No lasting damage. The words were barely out of his mouth before Alexandra took over the conversation.

"It could've been me in that car!" she screeched. "What if the hydraulics had failed an hour earlier? I didn't have an oxygen mask for backup like Suzie. I don't know how to break the window! I would've drowned. This is unacceptable."

The stunt coordinator didn't like to be accused of subpar work. "The hydraulics were thoroughly checked. We don't put our people into unsafe situations."

Alexandra rolled her eyes. "It looks like you certainly did two days ago."

Shane held up a hand to stop a fight before it started. "I believe the stunt was sabotaged."

He could feel Chloe glaring at him from across the table but didn't care.

"By the stalker?" Alexandra asked, her voice an even higher octave. Dogs would soon start howling.

He nodded. "Probably."

Chloe put her coffee mug down on the table. "Don't stalkers have an MO, a pattern, or something? Why would he go from letters and leaving stuff lying around to sabotaging a stunt?"

"Because I believe the stalker's purpose is to shut down the show. I think he was trying to scare everyone with the letters; that didn't work, so he's upped his game. Added the weapons, then decided to take it further when that didn't yield the results he wanted."

"Great." Alexandra threw her hands in the air. "So I'm not safe. Nobody is."

Chloe glared at him further from across the table as everyone began talking at once. The director was trying to soothe Alexandra. If Alexandra decided these weren't conditions she could work under, then the stalker would definitely get what he wanted. The show would shut down.

The stunt coordinator was still defending the safety of the equipment to anyone who would listen. The other actors discussed whether they would be next in the stalker's line of fire.

Chloe just raised a brow and held her hand up as if to suggest he had caused all the pandemonium.

"People." Chloe's brown eyes broke from his as she raised her voice. As soon as she spoke, everyone in the room stopped talking, a testament to both Chloe's place in the show and the respect others had for her. Even Alexandra got quiet.

"Alexandra." Chloe faced the woman. "We're going to focus security around you. You're right; it looks like someone has unfortunately decided to make you the center of their crazy. Not sure how you got so lucky. I'm jealous."

Chloe smiled, and everyone chuckled, the tension easing slightly. She continued. "Westman is right; we need to bring in more security. I've been fighting the studio on that, because I like our family here the way it is, even with the perverted uncle." She winked at the stunt coordinator, and everyone laughed again. "But we'll get what we need to make sure you're safe, Alexandra. To make sure everyone is safe."

Chloe stood. "This is going to get handled. So everyone needs to focus on their jobs and on making *Day's End* the best show it can be. We have a great security team who will handle the rest."

The meeting was over. Nobody announced it as such, but Chloe had addressed the fears suffocating everyone and assured them she would take care of it. And they believed her. A few more things were said, questions were asked, but soon everyone was on their way with a renewed energy. They'd lost a day and a half of production and needed to make that up. There was work to be done. They all trusted Chloe to take care of any other problems.

Shane gave Markus a nod as he left with Alexandra, who smiled at Shane and trailed her fingers along his shoulder from where he sat in the chair. Everyone else filed out also, even the creative team.

Leaving just Shane and Chloe sitting across the table from each other, staring. A showdown.

"What you just did was impressive," he finally said. "I've been in briefings with three-star generals who didn't have as much control of the room as you did just now."

She just shrugged, picking up her coffee mug from the table. "We've all been working together a long time. They know that when I say I'll take care of something I mean it. We trust each other."

"Like you said before. You're a family."

Which was why it was going to hurt her to find out a member of that family—even if it was a distant one—might be the one trying to hurt the show.

"And most importantly, we all want *Day's End* to be the best it can be. We've been successful in that for three years, which is an eternity in television, and we're still going strong. We all want to see that continue. So congrats, you win. I'll call the studio today and tell them to do whatever you say. Bring in as much security as you want." Her lips pursed in distaste.

"I'm not trying to kill the creative spirit, Chloe. Just protect you. Everyone."

"I know. I just . . . don't like change. Especially not the kind that brings a lot of strangers in."

He nodded. He didn't want to make Chloe's life more difficult, but there was no way around it. "We'll focus the extra security on Alexandra. She's had stalker threats before. We're checking into her social media, seeing if there's anyone who's upped their interest in the past few months."

Chloe sat back in her chair. "Someone who's as big a name as Alexandra always has issues with people like this. Crazies. Those who want to scare her, toy with her."

"Markus seems excellent at his job. No one is getting to her without going through him."

"Fine. We'll get the extra security to help him out. But I don't think this stalker really has intentions to kill someone. He's just trying to cause trouble."

She sounded like she believed it, or that she at least wanted to. But she looked away as she said it. She was hiding something. What?

Shane got up and walked to the opposite end of the table near her, sitting on the corner so his legs were almost touching hers. She shifted slightly but didn't move away. He knew he was crowding her personal space and that it was making her uncomfortable. Good.

She needed to tell him her secret.

"So you don't think that diver lying facedown in the water was an intent to kill someone?"

She glanced at him before looking back down at her coffee cup. "Look, I've approved all the security you requested, okay? I just don't want to blow this completely out of proportion and cause a panic. Just in case it was malfunctions during the stunt, or coincidences. You have to admit it's possible."

"Neither of us believe that and you know it, Chloe." He leaned in closer, and she slid back farther into her chair. "Why don't you tell me what is really going on?"

Her eyes darted around again. A poker player she was not.

"Nothing's going on. You just need to accept that our show is about crazy, freaky stuff. It brings out the crazy, freaky people. We deal with it here on a daily basis."

"I don't mind crazy. I just don't like violent."

She sat up straighter. "Fine. You make sure the set is secure and Alexandra and everyone else is safe. I've got a show to run."

He ran a finger down her cheek before he could help himself. "You're tired, peanut."

Now an eyebrow raised. "You trying to say I look like crap, Westman?"

Shane chuckled. "I'm trying to get you to share whatever it is you know so I can help. Like you said, you've got a show to run. Tell me what it is, and let me take that off your shoulders."

He could see her consider it, which only confirmed there was something she wasn't telling him. For a moment, she closed her eyes and leaned toward him, breathing deeply, almost like she was trying to draw something out of him and into herself. But the next moment it was gone. She was shuttered again.

"Believe me, if I had any information that would help with security, I would tell you. This show and the people involved are my first priorities."

She said it with such conviction he believed her. But that didn't mean she wasn't keeping something from him. He stepped out of her way as she stood and brushed past him, her head barely coming up to his shoulders. It was easy to forget how little she was when she had a personality that was so forceful.

He grabbed her wrist gently as she moved past, a little surprised when she didn't jerk away.

"Whatever it is you're not telling me gives the stalker more room to maneuver. You can't carry everything, Chloe."

She shrugged. "I think you might be surprised exactly how much I can carry, Westman. Keep my people safe. If there's something inside my head that will help, I'll be sure to tell you."

Her phrasing—*something inside her head*—was odd, but Shane let it go. She was obviously done talking.

Chloe had a secret she wasn't ready to give up. Shane didn't like it, but for right now he'd have to live with it.

Chapter 7

The pain woke her. For a moment, Chloe panicked when she couldn't see even though her eyes were open, but then thankfully the inky blackness rolled away.

The pain didn't.

She lay still on her bed inside her trailer on the set, hoping lack of motion might ease some of her agony.

The voice and the accompanying pain had been getting worse since the stunt accident. Conversation Hearts was pounding his thoughts out in her head again, his emotions, so putrid and loud.

We'll be together soon.

Every second I'm not with you, I miss you.

You're the one.

Meant to be.

Mine.

She wanted to cover her ears, to turn up the radio as loud as it would go, anything to drown out his thoughts. God, she hoped he got the girl he wanted soon so he'd get out of her head. She had enough to worry about with the set's stalker without having to worry about someone else's.

She felt liquid trickle down the side of her cheek and knew her nose was bleeding again. She gingerly moved her fingers to her face to catch the blood.

This was killing her. She couldn't deny it anymore. Fire was licking her brain, scorching her. There was only so much of this her body could take, she knew.

Her hand reached out blindly toward the nightstand by her bed for the box of tissues, then came up to catch the rest of the blood. She snuggled deeper into the blankets, not understanding how her body could feel so cold while her brain seemed to burn.

I need you.

We are meant for each other.

"Yeah, I get it, jerk-off," Chloe muttered. "You love her so much. So, so, so, so, so, so much. Go tell her, not me."

As much as she wanted Conversation Hearts' emotions out of her head, she hoped whatever woman he was so engrossed with would be careful. Because he very definitely was obsessed. His words were tinged with desperation rather than passion.

And they were painful on all possible levels. Not only because of their volume and intensity, but because of the words themselves. They were the most generic, unimaginative declarations of love she'd ever heard. And all his thoughts were almost completely centered around him, and what she would do for him. Nothing about her.

Chloe eased herself from the bed, wrapping the throw at the foot around her shoulders. She knew she wouldn't be able to get any more sleep tonight. Normally she would work, but the thought of looking at a screen right now had bile crawling up her throat.

She would go sit in the hot tub. That sometimes helped her relax under normal circumstances. Maybe it would chase

Conversation Hearts out of her head. At the very least it would warm her body.

She couldn't be bothered to get dressed. She was in boy shorts and a tank top, suitable enough for a hot tub, especially since it was nearly three o'clock in the morning and nobody else would be around. She stumbled to the bathroom and grabbed a towel, still clutching her blanket around her shoulders. How could she feel so cold when her brain was in agonizing fire?

Slipping on flip flops, she walked outside, gingerly taking steps away from the main sets of trailers to what they jokingly referred to as the hot tub shack. Alexandra had insisted on having it built, saying her doctor had prescribed it for relaxation. The tub was large enough for twelve people but was enclosed on all sides by untreated wood. If someone didn't know what it was, they would think it was an outhouse, thus the name "the shack."

But the great thing about it was that it had no roof. The walls provided privacy—a necessity when paparazzi cameras could take pictures from hundreds of yards away—but you still had a beautiful view of the western Carolina sky.

There was a reason they called it God's country.

Chloe shuffled to the shack, careful to keep her head as still as possible. Halfway there, her nose began bleeding again. Her muscles seized.

Chloe reached the door, holding a tissue to her nose, cursing when she realized she'd forgotten the key to the shack. But another step showed the door was unlocked, the padlock on it, but not closed. Thank God. There was no way she could manage another round trip. She wasn't even sure she was going to make it through the door.

She reached for the padlock with shaky fingers as tremors assaulted her. She needed to get in the hot tub. Try to get her body warm, her brain cool. Try not to panic at the suffocating pain of having someone else in her head she couldn't ignore.

The tremors had her falling against the door, struggling to stay upright. Her leg muscles cramped, followed by her shoulders. Chloe felt like she was possessed. She couldn't stop the sob that escaped her.

She was going to die alone right here. She needed to get back to her trailer, to a phone, to someone, but she had no idea how she was going to manage.

She pushed herself off from the shack doorway and felt something she hadn't been expecting at all: blessed coolness.

Not on her body, but on her mind. She could feel it. The change in the temperature inside her. And with that, her cramping muscles released; the bleeding in her nose stopped.

Shane.

He was here; she had no doubt about it. But all she could do right now was lean against the doorway and let the coolness filter into her. Suddenly, she could no longer hear Conversation Hearts. Could no longer hear any of the voices always present. All she could do was feel the cold, drag it in, and use it to continue to put out the agonizing flames that had tortured her mind.

It truly was like an avalanche the way it poured over her. Her body temperature stayed the same, but her brain felt so much better. Maybe she wasn't going to die. Maybe she would live to see her next birthday. For too long she'd been wondering about that.

Neither of them said anything for a long time but she knew he was coming closer by the way the pain eased even further. She wanted to cry for the absence of it, but Chloe Jeffries didn't do that. She'd never cried even when she was a little girl with no family. She wouldn't now just because Shane Westman was helping her in a way neither of them could understand.

"Out for a midnight stroll?" he finally asked from behind her.

She didn't get up from the doorframe. She couldn't. She just needed a couple of minutes more. "I thought I might get into the hot tub. Couldn't sleep."

"You want to tell me what is really going on, Chloe? Tell me why you were about to collapse a couple of minutes ago? Tell me about that look that comes over your face sometimes when I get close to you?"

Damn him. Those blue eyes saw too much. How the hell was she supposed to keep private things private around him? Things there was no way he would understand. Chloe barely could.

"I have no idea what you're talking about, Westman. I'm just here to use the hot tub." The words to invite him to join her were on her lips, but she swallowed them. That was a bad, dangerous plan for multiple reasons. She took a step toward the tub, farther inside the door, her need to get away from him just as strong as it was to get close to him to feel the blessed coolness.

"Whatever secrets you're keeping aren't just hurting you; they're hurting everyone. I can't believe that's what you want."

"You don't know me at all. Don't try to act like you do." She didn't look at him as she said it. Was afraid to. Afraid he'd see too much. Afraid he'd see that she was so different and think her a freak.

Afraid she'd want to get close to him anyway.

She pressed the button on the outside of the hot tub to turn on the jets. "Just go away. I don't want you here."

She sighed. Now she was just being rude. Damn it. He hadn't done anything to deserve that. If only he weren't so damned observant.

"I don't get scared off as easily as you might believe. And I don't think you're as tough as you pretend to be. Don't be a coward, peanut."

Did he just call her coward *and* peanut in one sentence? Oh *hell* no.

Now Chloe spun around. His eyes widened slightly as he saw her face, which was probably not pretty with the blood and paleness, but she didn't care. She strode toward Shane, who stood his ground a few yards away with his arms crossed over his chest.

"Look, Ranger Rick." Her eyes were narrowed to slits, even though she knew he was egging her on. "I don't know who you think you are, jackass, but I am not, nor never will be a coward." She reached him as she said the last word and poked him in the chest.

He tilted his head to the side. "It doesn't look like it to me. Looks to me like you won't—"

His words were cut off as heat and force, coupled by a loud roar, propelled her off her feet and into Shane. They both fell to the ground, Shane taking all her weight as the shack exploded behind her.

"What the fu—" She tried to look, but Shane rolled her underneath him, covering her head with his arms and the rest of her body with his, as what was left of the shack exploded in a second roar. As soon as the noise died down, Shane's face was right next to hers.

"Are you okay?" he asked.

She nodded, still trying to get her bearings. "Did the shack just explode?"

He rolled off her. "Seems that way."

They both sat up, staring at the burning wreckage of what used to be the shack. "How—How? Did I press the wrong button?"

"Yeah, the *blow-the-entire-tub-to-kingdom-come* button is right next to the *on* button, so you have to be careful."

She smacked his arm but still smiled a little. Then it occurred to her . . .

"I would've been in there."

The small smile on his lips completely disappeared.

"If you hadn't made such a jackass remark about me being a coward, I would've been . . ." She gestured weakly at the burning outline of the hot tub building before rubbing her chest. Oh God, she would've been in there.

Anybody still on the set was rushing toward them now, trying to figure out what had happened, looking at Chloe to tell them. She and Shane got to their feet. She could already tell she would be sore tomorrow.

Not nearly as much as she would've been if she'd been in the shack.

Travis and Justin came running over to her.

"What the hell happened?" Justin asked.

"I have no idea. Electrical malfunction?" she asked.

All three men looked at her with eyebrows raised. Evidently not an electrical malfunction.

"What are you two even doing here?" Shane asked.

"We were writing in the Pit," Travis said. "Justin wanted to try to work that psychic idea in earlier in the season. We both work better at night."

"Miss Jeffries." Noah, the intern, ran up to her. "I've called the fire department. They want to know if anyone is hurt."

"No, no one is hurt," she told him. Didn't the kid ever go home?

She was beginning to shake. Oh crap, she'd almost been in there.

She felt Shane's arm slide around her, pulling her up against him. "Hey, it's okay. Breathe."

"I-I . . ."

She felt his lips against her hair. "I know. But I'm a jackass, so you weren't in there."

61

Unable to help herself, she wrapped her arms around his waist, keeping the blanket tucked securely around her body. "I'm glad you're such a jackass."

It wasn't long before the fire department showed up and had the flames under control. The shack was isolated for privacy, so the fire had nowhere to spread. Shane's arm stayed around her as she answered the questions of the police officer who'd also responded to the call. Noah brought out coffee.

She finally stopped shaking, but she still didn't find herself pulling away from the comfort Shane's closeness provided. Nor did he withdraw it.

She had a feeling it wasn't the norm for either of them—leaning on someone else's strength certainly wasn't for her—yet neither of them seemed to be able to pull away.

It was nearly dawn by the time the fire department had completely extinguished the flames, marked off the scene for the fire inspector to investigate the next day, and left. Everyone else was heading back to their own trailers to try to grab a couple of hours' sleep. The day's production would begin again soon, whether they were exhausted or not.

Shane walked Chloe back to her trailer. She realized she didn't know where he slept. Did he stay on the set? Have an apartment in town?

"Are you always on set at night?" she asked. "We have guards, right? So you don't always need to be here, do you?"

"I have a house on the other side of town. It was my grandmother's, and she left it to me. But I've been staying here at night, trying to pinpoint any holes in security."

"Don't you ever sleep?"

A shadow fell over his face. "Not as much as I used to."

She understood that. Had she gotten an entire night's sleep since Conversation Hearts began blasting his thoughts into her head? She didn't think so.

Evidently, Shane had his own demons. Which, damn it, just made him more appealing.

"Yeah, I get it," she said. "Demons."

He gave a half smile and shrugged. "Yeah. Some of them we fight; others we just snuggle."

She gave a rueful laugh. She completely understood what he meant. Sometimes it was too hard to fight, so you just survived until you could fight another day.

They arrived at her trailer. She needed a shower and then to get to her office. The fire had just added five hundred things to her to-do list, beginning with a call to the studio.

She smiled awkwardly at Shane. She was great at writing, at thinking of creative scenes and witty banter. But she sucked ass at sincerity and attraction, especially in real life.

She held out the hand not holding the blanket toward him, cringing at how awkward it felt. "Thank you for all your help tonight. I was a mess."

He took her hand, but didn't shake it, just held it in his much bigger one. "I think you were fine, all things considered."

She shrugged. "We can talk about all the ramifications of the fire later. After I've had a shower and coffee."

When she began to withdraw her hand from his, he gripped it more firmly and gave her a tug toward him. Not expecting it, she stumbled closer.

Then he let go of her hand and brought both of his up to grab the edges of the blanket that sat around her shoulders, pulling her so their faces were just inches apart.

All she could see were blue eyes.

"We *will* talk later. About the fire. About what you're not telling me. And since we're starting a list, we'll add this to it."

He kissed her.

Chloe had been kissed before, of course. She wasn't a virgin. But men, kissing, and sex just hadn't been a priority in her life. *Day's End* took up too much of her time to try to find someone who didn't annoy her. Plus, the voices had always made a relationship too difficult to focus on the man she was with.

Not this time.

He kissed her with a shattering absorption. As if he couldn't get enough of her. Any voice inside her head, hell, any thought fled at the feeling of Shane's lips on hers as he traced her lower lip with his tongue before slipping it into her mouth.

He pulled her closer with the blanket, and she fisted the material of his shirt, hanging on for dear life as he plundered her mouth with his.

When he finally pulled away, resting his forehead against hers, they were both breathing hard. He kissed her gently, softly once more before stepping back.

She couldn't even form a word as she stared at him, the sun rising majestically behind his broad shoulders.

"Take your shower. Have your coffee. I'll see you in a little while." He took another step back and gazed intently into her eyes. "And yes. We very definitely will talk. About everything."

Chapter 8

"No offense, Sheriff, but this is bullshit."

It was two days after the hot tub building exploded, and the sheriff had called Shane in and handed him the arson inspector's report.

Accident due to faulty wiring and improperly stored accelerants.

The arson inspector had deemed the explosion of the hot tub structure an accident. He said that when Chloe had turned on the jets, a spark from a faulty wire in the electrical panel in the back had dropped onto a rug, catching it on fire. It wouldn't have been an issue at all except that evidently someone had stored a dozen gasoline canisters at the back of the hot tub.

"Now, Shane, I knew your grandmother for a lot of years. She was awfully proud of you and your record with the army."

Shane closed his eyes for a second, regrouping. In a small town, everyone knew everyone else's business. And nobody ever forgot anything.

"You're about to bring up the time you caught Sarah Winslow and me drinking under the high school bleachers."

Sheriff Linenberger leaned back in his chair and smiled. "As I recall, drinking wasn't the only thing you were doing."

Shane shrugged, a smile tugging on his own lips. "Yeah, well, drinking was the only *illegal* activity we were doing since it was Sarah's eighteenth birthday."

"I'm sure her daddy wouldn't have seen it that way. You wouldn't have become an Army Ranger, that's for sure."

Sarah's dad had been the high school football coach—still was, seventeen years later—and would've shot Shane outright, even though he'd been one of the coach's best players, if he'd known how he and Sarah had celebrated her birthday.

"I always appreciated you not telling the coach or my Grammi what may or may not have been going on there that night."

"Hell son, my job is to stop murders, not cause them."

Shane shifted back in his own chair. "We can talk about the good old days all morning, Sheriff, but that doesn't change the fact that this fire inspection report is bogus."

"Not from his point of view. The spark definitely came from wiring in the electrical box on the hot tub. The spark definitely dropped onto a rug that happened to be very thick and pretty damn flammable. Once that caught, all it took was a little bit of gas leakage on the outside of the canisters, and one not closed properly—happens all the time—and you have yourself a nice big explosion."

"Don't you find it a little coincidental that all those things happened to line up?"

Sheriff Linenberger shrugged. "Me personally? Maybe. But the inspector's job is to report exactly what he finds. He found no evidence of foul play. No suggestion that anyone deliberately placed any items or started the fire to begin with. So in the official report it goes down as an accident."

This had Hollywood PR spin written all over it.

"The studio called you, didn't they? Asked you to keep it quiet."

The sheriff shifted in his chair. "Shane, I like you. And you know I loved Miss Betty, God rest her soul; she was my babysitter when I was in first grade. But the people from *Day's End* have been here a while now. They're good for the town. Bring in revenue that we wouldn't have otherwise. Honestly, I'm not sure that the town would've survived otherwise. Too hard for people to live so far away from any big cities."

Shane wasn't going to be deterred. "Did they ask you to keep it quiet?"

"They asked me to report the truth. To not speculate or elaborate if it wasn't necessary. You know how the gossip rags love to report anything that can be blown up into something it's not."

Shane raised his eyebrow at the sheriff's choice of phrasing. "You can't ignore that it's awfully coincidental, John. Especially given what happened last week with the stunts."

"Look, I'm not saying the fire or problems in the lake don't have someone behind them. I'm just saying, in both cases, looking at the events independently, there is no reason to suspect foul play, and that's the way it's written in the official report."

"Because some studio executive is asking you to write it that way."

"Am I the type of person who cares what some studio in California is demanding when it comes to law enforcement in my town? I don't think so."

It may not be someone in California asking him, but someone was. Someone who had more clout with Sheriff

Linenberger than a faceless bigwig in a studio. Damn it. *"Chloe Jeffries* is asking you to write it that way."

The sheriff smiled. "Have you met her? She's a little firecracker."

"Yes, I've met her." Remembered the softness of her lips pressed against his. The tiny little sigh—sexiest thing he'd ever heard—she'd made as she'd given in to the kiss between them, pressing her smaller body to his. "And yes, a firecracker."

"She basically took the town by storm. A lot of people from Hollywood might have just come in here and got what they wanted with their cameras and shots and never really cared about the town itself. But not Chloe. She and her friend, Nadine, have really gotten to know people around here. Almost like she's putting down roots."

Shane knew from the background check that Chloe owned a home in Malibu. "I agree that Chloe isn't your typical Hollywood type, but I don't think that means she's applying for a North Carolina driver's license."

"Maybe." The sheriff shrugged a shoulder. "But the people here like her. Respect her. And she respects them. So yes, when she asked me to keep the report as clean as possible so the press didn't get wind of it, I agreed. She said there was an investigation going on, a security coordinator brought in. Mentioned your name."

Because she knew his name would go further with the sheriff? "It's true. I'm handling what I can. A friend of mine from Special Forces has a security company and asked me to step in since I was already here."

"Then I'm sure Chloe and her needs are in good hands."

"Sheriff, I'm not an investigator. Yes, I have some experience from my time in the army, but it's not the same as having official law enforcement on scene. And if things are escalating, they need to be."

"As soon as Chloe Jeffries wants me there, or a true crime is committed—not just vague letters and what might be a weapon but could be a kitchen tool left lying around—I will make sure she has any and all the support she needs. That would be true of anyone in her situation."

"And if she's not aware of the actual threat? If she wants to hide her head in the sand? If she's asking you to do something borderline illegal by keeping information out of official documents?" Shane's voice was cool, almost cold.

Sheriff Linenberger leaned his elbows onto his desk and steepled his fingers together. Shane felt like he was eighteen years old again. "I am assuming since Chloe has her own personal Army Ranger, and one of the smartest and most tactically aware people I've ever known in my life, working at protecting her and the set, that someone on the premises is aware of the threat. And that same someone will notify law enforcement when there is actionable intel."

Shane scrubbed his hand across his face. The hell of it all was, the sheriff was right. Right now, a strong argument could be made that the *Day's End* set just has piss-poor luck. Just because Shane was convinced otherwise didn't mean there was anything law enforcement could do. Like the sheriff said, actionable intel was what counted here.

"And I will not falsify a document and report for anyone, regardless of how much I like that person. Since your Grammi was such a good babysitter and took me to the swings all the time, I will overlook the fact that you implied otherwise."

"Yes, sir." Shane at least had the good grace to feel sheepish. "I know that. I'm just concerned with the whole situation. I don't like coincidences."

"And Chloe doesn't like unwanted press. She's had enough about her personally."

"Like what?"

Sheriff Linenberger paused. "Personal stuff. Rumors about how she gets her creative ideas. I don't put much stock in it, but I guess some people may."

"I see." He didn't at all, but it would be something he could look into.

"Unless someone breaks the law and the studio wants to report it," the sheriff continued, "I can't force an investigation. Can't force Chloe to accept any help. Can't shut anything down. She's stubborn. Protects that show like a mother hen. She doesn't want her people to get hurt; I know that, and I'm sure you know that too if you've spent any time at all with her. But she also doesn't want to let some would-be bully back her into a corner and stop production."

"She would've died, John," Shane said. "The arson inspector can say it was an accident, and I believe it probably looks that way. But the fact is, if Chloe hadn't turned around to call me a jackass to my face, she would've been in the enclosure when it blew."

The sheriff studied Shane for a long minute. "Then let's be thankful you're a jackass."

Shane gave a short bark of laughter and stood, reaching out his hand to shake the sheriff's. "That's basically what Chloe said. I'll keep you updated and let you know if we need help. My gut says we will."

"I trust your gut. We'll be ready." He walked with Shane to the door. "You planning to stick around? Live at your grandmother's place?"

"No, I'm committed to a job with Linear Tactical out in Cheyenne."

"That's some pretty country out there. Of course, not as pretty as here. I hope you'll think about staying." The sheriff slapped him on the shoulder. "You know Betty would've wanted you to. Did she ever send you the DVD?"

"What?" Shane had no idea what he was talking about. As

far as Shane knew, Grammi had never owned a DVD player. "I don't think she had many electronics."

The older man just chuckled. "I'm sure she left it for you somewhere."

"Left a DVD for me? Of what?"

"Oh, you'll know it when you see it."

There was a lot of his grandmother's stuff he hadn't gone through yet. "Okay. I'll be sure to keep an eye out for it."

Small towns. Had to love them.

Chapter 9

Shane sat in the office he'd commandeered in the security trailer back on the set. He'd returned from the sheriff's office hours ago. Part of him had wanted to find Chloe and have it out with her about why she was determined to have the police term this an accident.

He'd been with her, had held her shaking body when she'd realized how close she'd come to dying. She knew this was no accident. But Shane didn't need to fight it out with Chloe to know why she was doing it. Sheriff Linenberger had said it, but Shane had already known.

Chloe would do whatever it took to protect her on-set family. Fiercely. And right now—despite the explosion that could've taken her life—she felt that making the press aware of the stalker and woes that had befallen the set would do more harm than the stalker himself.

Shane wished he believed the same. He'd spent the entire afternoon talking to multiple people, trying to figure out why those gas canisters had been there. Nobody knew anything. Nobody had any idea why they'd been taken from the supply shed on the opposite side of the set, half an acre away, and placed in the hot tub shack. There was no logical reason for those cans to have been there.

And one very ugly reason why they would: to do as much damage as possible.

It wasn't actionable intel, but it was a step closer to proving to himself that he was on the right track. And he planned to bring it up to Chloe to make sure there was no way she could deny that this was no accident.

A tap had Shane looking up from his desk. Travis stood in the doorway.

"You lost?" he asked. In the battle between him and Chloe, Travis had definitely been Team Chloe. Shane hadn't talked to the man directly since the second day.

"More like here to offer my services. See if there's anything I can do to help."

Shane motioned for Travis to join him in the chair across from his desk. "Where's the rest of the Brady Bunch?"

"Justin went home since we've been working nights so much. Chloe is in the creative zone and kicked everybody out but Nadine. She'll probably write for like twelve hours straight. It's amazing, and a lot of the show's best scenes have been born that way."

"Sounds pretty exhausting."

There was something akin to awe in the other man's voice. "It has to be, but she's bloody amazing."

"And Nadine gets to stay for this creative spree, but nobody else does?"

Travis shrugged. "Those two have been pretty inseparable for a long time."

"What, college? High school?"

"Longer. They both were in the same group foster home growing up. Fast friends who never separated."

"I thought she had a sister." Shane realized there was quite a bit he didn't know about Chloe. Foster homes and whatever secrets the sheriff had been referring to that the gossip rags reported.

Travis nodded. "Two actually. They're triplets. But their parents died when they were young or something, and for some reason they were separated. Chloe went into foster care."

Shane didn't know much about Child Protective Services, but that seemed pretty harsh to separate triplets after their parents died.

And a group home? Suddenly a lot of pieces of the Chloe Jeffries puzzle clicked into place. Why she fought so hard for her misfit family. Why protection was so important to her.

"Have you known her very long?" Shane asked Travis.

"I came on board six months ago, so no. Justin and I both came on at the beginning of this season. This job is a dream come true for me. I never thought I would be on the writing team of a show this caliber."

Shane didn't know much about how Hollywood worked. "Pretty competitive?"

"You wouldn't believe it. Especially for someone like me, who didn't even work in the business, have an agent, or anything. I didn't even write until after my accident." He held out his arm that showed the striking Lichtenberg figures again.

"Struck by lightning, right?"

Travis nodded enthusiastically. "Best thing that ever happened to me besides the almost-killing-me part. After that, I left my job as manager of a bank and decided to use the creative part of my brain that seemed to be overflowing. I entered a writing contest and three months later ended up here. No place else I'd rather be. The creative energy around Chloe is amazing."

The man's enthusiasm definitely wasn't faked. If he was

the stalker and wanted the show to be shut down, he should get out of writing and into acting.

Shane looked at a file on his desk. "And Justin? What do you know about him?"

"Brilliant writer but hard to work with. Seems angry all the time. A loner. But that's not necessarily uncommon when it comes to writing. I also think he has a drinking problem. Sometimes he goes away for a few days. Never during critical writing times, but it's always inconvenient."

Shane made a mental note to have someone check out Justin more thoroughly. An angry loner with a propensity for being gone days at a time? Definitely deserved a second glance.

"You two were together all evening on Tuesday, right?" Shane asked. "The night of the explosion?"

"Yeah, working in the Pit. Justin is all caught up in the psychic serial killer angle. Wants to write it into the show."

Shane vaguely remembered reading about it. "Hasn't something like that been in the news?"

"Yeah. Somebody has been killing so-called psychics. Seven of them, from here down to Florida."

"It does sound like a plotline that could be a part of *Day's End*."

Travis rolled his eyes. "So Justin keeps telling me. A psychic would have to be pretty special—and real, unlike all the victims of that killer—to be a part of this show. But I'm willing to give it a try, if Justin insists."

"So you and Justin were working together the other night. You were with him the whole time?"

"Yes. Although I will admit, I closed my eyes for about thirty minutes or so. Justin was lost in his own head—which happens a lot. But look, he couldn't have done anything, because when I woke up, the notebook he writes in was full of dialogue."

Shane nodded but knew it actually meant nothing. If anything, it was an easy way for Justin to "prove" he'd been working when it could've been done much earlier.

But it was way too early to be singling anybody out. There were literally hundreds of people who could be behind the set "accidents."

Travis leaned back in his chair. "Oh my gosh, you think the stalker is a member of the cast or crew. Not just a random person or extra."

Shane shrugged. "All I know for sure is that these accidents aren't accidents. But yes, if I had to wager a guess I would say it's someone with inside knowledge of what goes on around here. Someone who could come and go without being studied."

"That's a lot of possibilities," Travis whispered. "And it can't be Justin. He may be a jerk, but he wouldn't do that to Chloe. None of the creative team would. Hell, I can't even think of anybody on the set who doesn't like her. I mean there are a lot of rumors . . . crazy stuff, but everybody likes her."

Shane shifted farther upright in his chair. The sheriff had insinuated something similar about Chloe. "Tell me the rumors."

"Take your pick." Travis rolled his eyes. "It's all ridiculous. Psychic stuff again. Some people says she's a mind reader or something. That she hears voices in her head. Some people say she worships Satan, and his dark angels give her all her ideas. Some people say aliens."

"And what do you say?"

"I say she's freaking brilliant. Does she have more going on inside her mind than the rest of us? Maybe. But some people are just like that, you know?"

The admiration for Chloe was clear in the other man's tone. Maybe something more than that. "You and Chloe used to be an item?"

Travis turned beet red. "No! No." He laughed awkwardly. "I'm with Nadine. Have been for a few weeks now. I've never seen Chloe date anyone. She keeps to herself."

Shane nodded. He didn't know if Travis was unaware of the feelings he had for Chloe or if he was just unwilling to admit them, rightfully so, since he was dating Chloe's best friend. Shane wouldn't press. It wasn't pertinent to the situation at hand. Not to mention how much it would hurt sweet Nadine's feelings if it were true.

"Here you are." Nadine entered the trailer, coming around to hug Travis as he stood.

"Speak of an angel." He wrapped his arms around Nadine. Shane didn't know if he seemed a little stiff because of the topic they'd just been discussing, or if that was just how the man normally was. "I was telling Shane I want to do whatever I can to help catch the stalker."

"We both do. Chloe . . ." She trailed off, a pinched expression on her face.

"What?" He and Travis both asked at the same time.

"Is Chloe okay?" Shane asked.

Nadine brought the heels of her hands up to her eyes. "I just don't know."

Travis pulled her closer to him. They were almost the same height, but Nadine folded her head on his shoulder. "Chloe gets like this. You know that. When she's writing and wants to be in her own world."

"I know she does. But . . ." She stepped back from Travis, her words trailing off again.

"But what, Nadine?" Shane demanded. This was part of whatever secret Chloe was keeping; he was sure of it. When Nadine didn't look like she was going to respond, he kept pushing. "You need to tell me. I can't help if I don't know."

"I don't know what it is. Honest. She's . . . she just hasn't been feeling well."

Shane thought of how Chloe had looked the other night on her way to the hot tub before he'd spoken to her. He'd almost thought she was drunk the way she'd been staggering and how sluggish her movements had been.

"Where is she now?"

"In the Pit. She kicked me out."

"Does that happen often?" Shane said.

"Sometimes," Nadine said softly.

Shane stood up. "But not like this, right? This isn't just a creative binge she's on."

"I don't know how to help her." Nadine's voice had dropped to a whisper as she stared at Shane. "I don't even think she knows how to help herself."

"What's wrong with her?" Travis asked. "Does she have the flu or something?"

Nadine shook her head in answer to Travis's question, but her eyes didn't leave Shane's.

"I'm going to talk to her right now," Shane said.

"Are you sure that's wise if she's sick?" Travis frowned. "You two don't get along on her best days."

But Nadine nodded. "I think that's a good idea. She may not actually like you, but you at least distract her from all the crap inside her head. And she needs that. She's not good at asking for help."

Shane was already standing, making his way out of his office. He could hear Travis continuing to voice his concerns but didn't care.

He nodded to one of the security guards roaming the set as he made his way to the Pit. Nadine wanted him to distract Chloe from whatever was going on in her head? He had no problem doing that. If she needed a fight, he could give that to her. They could start with his anger over how she was having Sheriff Linenberger hide important information. Because whether either of them wanted to admit it, that's what they were doing.

He didn't knock on the door as he entered the trailer; the creative team entered freely in and out of here. His fighting words died on his tongue when he saw Chloe sprawled half over her desk, eyes closed. She didn't just look like she was asleep. She looked dead.

He felt like all the oxygen had been sucked out of the room as he rushed over to check her pulse. His relief at finding it was staggering.

She was sitting in her chair with her head on her desk. Face on top of a stapler, for God's sake. That couldn't be comfortable. How exhausted did she have to be to fall asleep like that?

The pallor of her skin was frightening. The only color on her face at all was where a tiny drop of blood had dried just under her nostril. He'd seen dead people who looked more alive than she did.

Obviously, she'd fallen into an exhausted slumber after kicking Nadine out. Just collapsed where she sat by the look of it.

And why had her nose been bleeding?

Shane didn't want to wake Chloe by moving her, but he also didn't want to leave her there sleeping on the stapler. Getting her to the couch seemed like the kindest option. He'd toss a blanket over her and let her rest. They could have their argument tomorrow.

He moved around behind her, then slid one hand gently under her head, moving it away from the stapler. He moved his other arm under her knees and lifted her as gently as he could. He half expected her to wake up, but she didn't. She just turned her face into his chest and nuzzled.

Shane held her sleeping form, just staring down at her for

a long minute. He'd regularly carried backpacks that weighed more than her. She was so feisty, leading her team—hell, the entire cast and crew—with such fearlessness, that it was easy to forget how small she really was physically. But she was obviously working herself into exhaustion. Shane didn't know if that was normal for how television writers worked, or if, like Nadine said, Chloe just had too many stressors piling on her right now.

He was glad to see a little bit of color coming back into her cheeks. Her fretful breathing was evening out also.

Shane crossed to the couch on the opposite side of the room and laid Chloe gently on it. When he shifted away from her to get the blanket from the nearby chair, she murmured fitfully.

"It's okay, peanut." He smiled at the thought of how much she hated him calling her that. "Go back to sleep. You need to rest. Everything else can wait."

He draped the blanket over her body and slid a pillow under her head. Not perfect but definitely better than sleeping on a stapler. He walked to the door, grabbing his phone so he could text the night security guard. He wanted to make sure the team knew Chloe was in here.

He was almost to the door when he heard the noise from her—a cross between a moan and a quiet sob.

"Chloe? Are you all right?"

No answer; she wasn't awake. But she was moving around on the couch, still moaning. Shane rushed back to the couch and crouched down. Was she having a nightmare?

She had drawn her knees up to her chest and wrapped one small arm around her head.

"Chloe, wake up. You're having a nightmare."

She moaned again, and her arm flew out, giving him a view of her face.

A little drop of blood was easing from her nose again. What the hell?

Her sobs were becoming more pitiful, like she was in pain and couldn't do anything about it.

Shane wiped Chloe's hair back from her face. "Chloe? Can you wake up?"

She reached out toward him with her hand, but he could tell she still wasn't awake. He needed to get her to sit up. He couldn't stand the pitiful cries coming from her throat.

He picked her up and sat down on the couch, situating her on his lap. "Chloe, come on. Wake up."

She didn't, but once she was settled against his chest, her distress seemed to ease. She snuggled against him just like she had when he carried her from the desk.

Shane held her there for a long time, waiting to see if she would wake up or if her nightmare or nose bleed would return. Nothing happened. She just slept, her head against his heart, her weight around him like a blanket.

Maybe her subconscious just needed to know someone was here. Nearby. Able to face any danger that might present itself.

Shane knew what it was like to sleep better because a teammate had your back. Chloe's mind obviously needed one. Shane could be that. And very deliberately ignore the parts of his body that argued that she was nothing like any teammate he'd ever had.

Eventually he eased himself down so they were both laying on the narrow couch. Chloe stayed attached to his chest. Normally that would've driven Shane crazy.

Avalanche wasn't known for his cuddling.

But right now, there was nowhere else in the world he'd rather be.

Chapter 10

In the ten days after the hot tub incident, security quadrupled on the set. Chloe's life had been crazy enough before. This was an absolute mess. Everywhere she looked, everywhere she went, everything she tried to do, some sort of security person was around. They were obvious by their uniform: dress pants, collared shirt, tailored blazer, and sunglasses.

Like they all shopped at the same Bodyguards-R-Us store.

And now everyone was required to wear badges. Unless you were on camera, you had one around your neck.

God forbid that you forgot your badge as Chloe had last week when she went into town. She had not been able to get back onto her own set. The guard literally was going to turn her away even after she explained who she was and showed her driver's license. Showed him a picture on her phone of her holding her Emmy award for *Day's End*.

The last straw had been when the man had to get permission from the Khaki Power Ranger himself to let her onto her own set. Shane had arrived at the gate, grinning like an idiot, and calmly told her to please remember to keep her badge with her at all times.

She had to put fifteen dollars into the curse jar that day. And Westman should be thankful she hadn't had a gun.

For ten days, everyone had been walking around on eggshells. Waiting for equipment to break. Or something to collapse. Or blow up. Or a knife with blood dripping from it to arrive from the stalker.

Nothing.

It was like the stalker had never existed. Or maybe he'd just wised up considering the security force on set made it look like the queen would be visiting any day. No stalker in his right mind would try to sabotage something now. Chloe hated the tension around the set, but at least nobody was getting hurt.

Which was good, because it was all she could do just to survive.

The pain from Conversation Hearts had spiked ten days ago. She had sent everyone away from the Pit, even Nadine, under the guise of having a writing spree. But really Chloe had been afraid she was about to have a breakdown.

She woke up the next morning on the couch, with no idea how she'd gotten there, feeling better and more rested than she had in months. She had hoped perhaps whatever had been happening with Conversation Hearts had passed. Maybe he'd gotten his girl.

But by the next day the pain, noise, and emotional cacophony was back. And it had been getting steadily worse. She could barely eat, hardly slept, and just tried to live through the constant pain.

She never went anywhere without a tissue in her hand, because her nose was bleeding more often than it wasn't. His obsessive thoughts provided a continual soundtrack in her mind.

In two days, the show started its five-day break. It was written in everyone's contracts that they would have these days in September off. All Chloe had to do was survive the next thirty-six hours, then almost everyone would be gone. She could use her time to figure out a way around whatever was happening with Conversation Hearts.

You complete me.

Great. Now the creep was becoming Jerry Maguire. She rubbed her forehead, trying to get rid of the ache, as the crew set up for today's shoot.

"Here's some water." Shane held out the bottle in front of her.

She took it from him, muttering her thanks, glad the pain eased as she sipped the water. It wasn't the first time he had offered her something before she even realized she needed it. As a matter of fact, for ten days straight he had pretty much been everywhere she looked. Holding the door open for her. Bringing food by the Pit and forcing her to eat. Ibuprofen in his hand every time the pain became too much to deal with.

Nadine was so thrilled with it she was about to pop with happiness. Chloe had tried to explain that Shane was just doing his job, plus a little extra because he was . . . polite or something. Nadine had just laughed.

But what did Nadine know anyway? She was in love and wanted everyone else to be as well.

"I'll have someone from catering bring you a sandwich."

"I'm fine. Just leave me alone. I'm not hungry." Her stomach chose that moment to growl as loudly as possible, making her both a bitch and a liar.

Shane just stood there with one eyebrow raised. "So. Sandwich?"

She gritted her teeth, wishing a hole would just rip through the earth and swallow her. Or him. "Yes, thank you," she said, then finally tacked on, "I'm sorry."

He took her apology like he did everything else: in stride. He left her to attend to all his other duties, but sure enough, a few minutes later, Noah arrived with the sandwich.

"Mr. Westman asked me to make sure you got some food, Miss Jeffries."

She took the plate from the intern. "Am I ever going to get you to call me Chloe, Noah?"

The younger man smiled. "No, ma'am, my mother taught my sister and me that we were to always be good. Polite to our elders."

She was definitely almost a decade Noah's elder but didn't like to be reminded of it. "Are you from Black Mountain?" A lot of the interns the show had were from Los Angeles, but they sometimes got a few from the local town.

"No, ma'am, but I only live a couple of hours from here. In an even smaller town, if you can believe it. I always wanted to learn about film and television, so this has been a great experience for me."

Shane was talking to the stunt coordinator and caught Chloe's eyes. He mimed for her to eat her sandwich. Bossy.

"Thanks for bringing this for me." She held up the sandwich and smiled at Noah.

"My pleasure." He said it so automatically she wondered if he had worked at that fast food chicken place that used the phrase so regularly. He was gone before she had a chance to ask.

But Shane was still watching to make sure she ate. She made a big show out of taking a bite before he turned back to what he was doing.

His attention both thrilled and terrified Chloe.

There was no doubt Shane was smart, capable, and very good at his job of coordinating the security team. Just because she was chaotic and free-spirited didn't mean she couldn't appreciate organization and leadership in others.

Shane Westman commanded attention. It wasn't something he demanded—it couldn't be—he just had a leadership quality people innately responded to. She had no problem picturing Shane as the Special Forces soldier he'd been.

Calm. Collected. Cool.

Avalanche.

She still felt the coolness wash over her almost every time he was around. She didn't know why it happened but figured it was the tight rein he had on his emotions that leaked into her psyche. The opposite of Conversation Hearts, who blasted his emotions through her subconscious. Ice poured out of him.

Chloe didn't care why it happened; she was just thankful for the relief Shane provided from the burning agony in her brain.

But couldn't figure out his end game. Why had he been going out of his way to help her? To make sure she had food, rest, or whatever she needed? She was the creative force behind one of the most popular shows on television. She could afford to hire a whole posse who waited on her hand and foot, but she didn't want to let people into her personal space. Nadine was the exception. Her sisters were also, when she saw them. They were allowed to be close.

But never a man. She'd never wanted to let one inside her personal circle.

Not that she'd never been intimate; it just had never been what she'd hoped it could be. She'd been too aware of their tension. Good moods, bad moods, smugness. She might not have let herself read their actual thoughts, but their general emotions had always seeped through. It hadn't been worth the few minutes of physical pleasure she got out of it.

Looking at Shane she couldn't help but feel it would be different with him. Even from a distance, everything about him was appealing. Not just the physical package—although

God knew he could give just about every actor here a run for his money in the looks department, with his brown hair, blue eyes, and chiseled jaw.

And his droolworthy abs. She may have been cold and tired after jumping in the lake to help him rescue the scuba diver in trouble, but she surely hadn't forgotten what his abs looked like after he stripped off his shirt. Neither had any woman on the set.

And all the physical appeal was great, but what made her wonder about Shane went way beyond just his looks.

She was willing to bet Shane would not be emoting nervousness and tension when he was intimate with a woman. If he was emoting anything at all.

He looked up from his conversation and caught her staring, pinning her with his eyes. She couldn't look away now even if she wanted to.

She shivered. Not just from his coolness washing over her mind, but from what her body was feeling too.

She wanted Shane Westman. That scared the hell out of her.

She finally looked away from those blue eyes, afraid for once that he'd be able to hear *her* thoughts, instead of the other way around.

She was careful not to catch his eye again as the cast and crew shot the last scene before the break. This was their third season, and the midseason break was always a big deal. Everybody was ready for their time off. No one had had five days in a row off for the past four months.

It was especially needed now, given everything that had been occurring on the set. How tense they'd all been.

Everyone would be leaving later tonight or maybe tomorrow. Chloe had considered going back to her house in Los Angeles but hadn't made any plans or bought any tickets. Usually she and Nadine went there and decompressed, but Nadine and Travis were going to Wilmington for a few days.

Chloe knew the real reason she hadn't made any plans was because she was waiting to see what was happening with Shane. Maybe she could invite him to LA and they could do a different type of decompression.

Or maybe that was too much. Chloe was terrible at this sort of thing. It was much easier to just live with the voices in her head than to take chances with real-life relationship stuff. This wasn't a scene that she could just rewrite if the dialogue didn't flow smoothly the first time.

The final scene wrapped, and everyone hugged one another and began preparations for their escape. Some members of the crew would stay on the set, security also of course, but everyone else was ready to go.

"Beautiful Wilmington, here I come!" Nadine snaked her arm around Chloe's shoulder, her friend's grin infectious. "This is it for Travis and me. He's been wanting to take it slow, and I appreciate him being a gentleman, but it's time for some decidedly not-gentlemanly behavior."

"You guys are going to have a great time."

Nadine's smile slipped a little. "I didn't even think about what you were going to do. I guess we always spend breaks together."

"You don't have to worry about me. I'm probably going to go back to the Malibu house and just sleep and eat. You know, what we normally do. There will be so much sleeping and eating I probably won't even know you're not there."

That wasn't true. Chloe would miss her friend, but there was no way in hell she was going to ask her to give up her romantic getaway.

Travis walked up behind Nadine. "You ready to get going? I thought we could grab a bite to eat before we hit the road."

Nadine still looked a little concerned. "I'm just making sure Chloe is okay."

"Oh, did you want to come with us?" The awkwardness in Travis's tone was almost laughable.

Chloe smiled. "No, thank you. Like I was telling Nadine, I'm planning on sleeping for the full five days."

Even though that had been an almost nonexistent concept for her the last week and a half. She hoped it wouldn't be the case over break. Hoped that Conversation Hearts would stay far from her head.

That if she wasn't getting any sleep, it was because Shane had decided to join her in her bed.

Nadine pulled her in for a hug. "Are you sure? It doesn't have to be weird; we can get a second room."

Chloe hugged her friend tighter. "I'm fine. I promise. You two go have fun."

They were off just a few minutes later.

A few others stopped to say goodbye. Noah, God bless that kid, asked if she needed anything before he left to go home. He looked as exhausted and frustrated as she felt, and he wasn't even getting paid for the hundred-hour work-weeks he put in. She made a mental note to buy him some-thing nice, since he was only being paid in college credit.

She turned to make her way back to the Pit, then stopped. She should ask Shane what he would be doing for the break.

She felt a hitch in her stomach and rubbed it. Having voices in her head that often projected violence and ugliness didn't scare her. Writing about creatures of the night and things that could snap someone like a twig didn't scare her. Going up against a board of Hollywood producers to demand whatever it was the show needed didn't either.

The thought of asking Shane out to dinner . . . had her about to vomit on the ground.

She couldn't see him now that everyone was milling

around. She would go and catch him at the security trailer before she lost her nerve.

A few more people stopped her to talk, slowing her progress, but she honestly didn't mind; she was trying to figure out exactly what she would say to him.

Hey, I know I've been cursing at you and telling you to get lost since the day I met you, but I was wondering if you wanted to go to dinner.

She rubbed her eyes tiredly. This wasn't going to go well.

Taking a deep breath, she was about to round the corner of the security trailer when she heard Shane's voice. His laugh. She wasn't sure she'd heard that before.

"New York, huh? Would've taken you for a Los Angeles girl."

"Oh, sugar, I'm both. Those of us who can successfully manage to be both a West and East Coast girl are a rare breed."

Alexandra. Shane was laughing and talking with Alexandra.

Chloe knew she should move. She should the corner to let them know she was there or back away to give them privacy. But her feet could not seem to do either.

"You should come with me. The house in the Hamptons has plenty of room." Alexandra gave a soft, sexy laugh. The kind Chloe had never managed in her entire life. "Not that we would need a lot of room."

"East Coast beach. Hmmm. Interesting," Shane said.

"So we leave in a couple hours? I have a private jet ready."

Of course he would go with Alexandra. Who in his right mind would get invited by Alexandra Adams to anywhere in the world and not go?

"Miss Jeffries, I'm so glad I caught you. I forgot I needed your signature on this form to send to the studio."

Chloe cringed as Noah shoved the paper under her nose,

knowing there was no way Alexandra and Shane hadn't heard him. She grabbed the paper and walked around the corner, trying to save face.

"Oh, hey, guys," she said as casually as she could before she signed last week's budget report and handed it back to Noah with a tight smile.

"Noah, we're all on break now," she told the younger man. "Go enjoy yourself."

"Is there anything new to report about the stalker?" Noah asked. "Studio wants an update. They are skeptical, and I can understand why, to think that there has been nothing for ten days."

"Thank God," Alexandra said. She put her hand on Shane's arm. "I'm sure that has everything to do with you."

"It's definitely a team effort." Shane turned to Noah. "But yes, you can tell them there's nothing new to report. Especially since I'm sending them daily reports anyway."

Noah took the budget paper from Chloe, said his good-byes, and left, leaving Chloe feeling like the most awkward third wheel in the history of mankind.

"Okeydokey." Oh good Lord, did she just say *okeydokey*? Chloe had to get out of here right now. "You guys enjoy the Hamptons. We'll see you after the break."

Chloe gave a little wave, trying to be friendly and nonchalant but failing miserably, and turned and walked toward the Pit, barely able to stop herself from running.

She was walking up the steps when Shane caught up to her.

"Chloe, are you all right?" he asked.

Why do you ask? Because I'm acting like a complete moron?

She turned slowly to him. "I'm fine."

Shane studied her for a moment, looking like he was going to say something else, but finally asked, "Are you going anywhere for the break?"

"Oh, I have a house in Los Angeles. Nadine and I have always gone there for the break." All of that was at least true.

"I see."

He didn't see what she really wanted him to, that was for sure. "Enjoy your time in the Hamptons."

"I've been invited to the Hamptons, but I didn't say I was going."

"What kind of person turns down five days in the Hamptons with America's sweetheart? Don't you have some friends who would kick your ass just on general principle?"

Shane smiled. "Maybe. But I've never been afraid of a good fight."

Was he really considering *not* going with Alexandra?

A blinding pain chose that moment to burn its way through her brain.

You're mine.

We are meant to be.

Forever.

"Chloe!" Shane was holding both her upper arms in a tight grip. She had no recollection of him grabbing her at all.

"What?" She focused on the button at the collar of his shirt, fighting dizziness.

"You spaced out for like two minutes in the middle of a conversation. I thought you were going to faint."

That might still happen.

"I don't faint." She breathed through her nose, trying to manage the pain without vomiting. Conversation Hearts was overwhelming her even past Shane's coolness.

"You're white as a ghost. Let's get you inside."

She grabbed the doorframe and planted her feet. "No, I'm fine. Just . . . low blood sugar or something. Listen, you should go to the Hamptons with Alexandra. I need a break from everything."

Shane stepped closer. "Maybe I don't want to go to the

Hamptons with Alexandra. Maybe I'd rather spend time with you."

Hearing those words an hour ago would've had her pulling him by his shirt and throwing him to the couch to have her way with him.

Now all she wanted to do was get him to leave. Even if she wanted to be with him, how could she explain everything going on in her head? She'd told people too many times only to have them never look at her the same way again. To think she was a freak.

And Chloe was a freak. Maybe she could explain hearing voices in her head. But standing here almost doubled over in pain because some lunatic was blasting his obsessive emotions through her mind?

She couldn't expect Shane to understand that. Hell, Chloe didn't even understand it.

He was much better off with Alexandra.

Chloe opened the door to the den trailer and stepped inside, careful to position herself so he couldn't come in after her.

"I just need to be alone. You should go with Alexandra. Trust me; you'll regret it if you don't." She shut the door between them.

Chapter 11

Chloe waited until Shane was no longer outside the Pit door, then somehow managed to drag herself over to her own trailer and into bed.

She stayed there for twenty-four hours just trying to survive.

At one point the pain inside her head became so bad she almost hoped she would die. All of Conversation Hearts' obsessive thoughts were starting to blend together. Every heartbeat the man took was consumed with this woman. He needed her with a desperation that bordered on panic, and the longer they were apart, the more manic he became.

And Chloe was suffering the consequences.

She only got out of the bed to use the bathroom. She sipped water and ate peanut butter crackers that happened to be on her bedside table.

How long could she continue to live like this? She couldn't keep hiding it. There was no way she could function, no way to think clearly, with someone so desperate inside her head.

She lay clutching a pillow to herself, trying to focus on

anything else but the screaming voice in her mind. The only thing she could think of was Shane. The only man in years who had caught and held her attention in every possible way. The man Chloe had successfully chased straight into the arms of a beautiful and charming actress.

Now a different type of pain overwhelmed Chloe.

It wasn't the sharp agony of a burning ice pick being poked into her head; it was just the dull sadness of what would never be. Shane wasn't meant to be hers.

She latched on to that ache, since it eased the agony. She pretended Shane was in bed holding her. She could almost feel his arms around her as if her body were remembering it. She drifted off to sleep in a hazy memory of his body wrapped around hers on the Pit couch.

When she woke, she felt a little better. Conversation Hearts' emotions were gone from her brain, at least for right now. Maybe he was asleep. Maybe he'd gotten his girl. Hell, maybe he was stoned, and it was taking his desperate edge off. Chloe didn't care. All she cared about was that her mind was her own. Perhaps the cast and crew wouldn't come back from the break and find her dead body in her trailer.

She looked over at the clock and saw the bright-red 10:30 glaring at her—a.m. or p.m.? A glance at the window confirmed p.m. She'd been in bed for nearly thirty hours. Chloe forced her stiff muscles to move, then shuffled into the kitchen to make coffee. She slipped on yoga pants and a sweater.

She would work, since she was going to be up all night anyway. For the past few months, every time she kicked everyone out for one of her infamous "writing alone" sessions, it had really been because she was afraid she wouldn't be able to hide what was happening to her. So she needed a real one.

She made and ate a sandwich and brought her coffee cup

to the kitchen table, listening to a thunderstorm begin to rumble in the distance. Good. Let it rain; she loved storms, especially when she wanted to write, to get lost in her creativity.

Opening her laptop, she shifted in her chair, thankful Conversation Hearts was still silent. The other voices floated in her head, but she ignored them, as she had her whole life.

They were almost like a stream rushing by, the thoughts of others, both positive and negative. She wasn't sure whose voices she heard—she'd never been—whether it was people who were close by, or just loud emotionally. Usually she didn't care.

She closed her eyes and waded into the river of voices. She needed to write a scene where Tia Day, the main character Alexandra played in *Day's End*, had to sneak through the woods to find shelter and food for the creatures she was taking care of.

The hunters were after her. Wanted to lure her out. This was what she needed the voices in her head to help give her inspiration for.

One good thing about the voices was that they rarely failed her. Too many options. She just had to pick the cleverest ones and apply them to the situation she was writing. It was her superpower. And it felt good to be back in her element, to have a little break from the crazy.

Well, *one* of the crazies. There were so many to pick from in her life.

She began to write, the scene flowing easily, other voices making themselves known to her mind as she let the words surge through her. She smiled. She could almost smell another Emmy. The thunder rolled closer, and Chloe stood to crack a window, breathing in the water-permeated air.

I will teach them to ignore me. His body will rest on the bottom of the lake the way the other should have. But this one will never be found.

It was just a normal voice, not Conversation Hearts. The thought was just one of many that ran through her mind in the river of voices. Her subconscious caught it. Held it. It didn't work for the scene she was currently on, but maybe it would another. She let it go. Focusing on just one voice in her head was exhausting, like constantly swimming upstream. She could only do it for short spurts at a time, so she tended not to try at all unless it was pretty important. She sat back down and began writing again.

The evil must be stopped. Everyone is gone. Very convenient to schedule a break now.

Chloe stopped typing. Break? Everyone gone? Evil must be stopped?

Crap. These were the thoughts of the show's stalker. Chloe closed her eyes and cast all her focus on catching that one voice in her mind.

To protect the evil is worse than the evil itself. He must die.

Chloe stood, still trying to focus on that one voice over all the others.

If this was happening right now, she had to try to stop it. She couldn't sit back and do nothing while some maniac decided to kill one of the guards in charge of protecting the empty set.

She slipped on her shoes and stumbled out the door, trying to remain locked on the thoughts of that one voice in her head.

Fitting. He saved the last one, and now he would be the one to die. He took them out of the lake, and now he would die there.

Oh my God. The guy was talking about *Shane*. But Shane wasn't here, right? Hadn't he gone with Alexandra? Chloe flew down the steps, across the field, and into the woods that surrounded three quarters of the lake. The moon provided some light in the darkness, but despite how well she knew this area after shooting here so long, she still had to struggle not to fall.

A bullet in his skull, just like something from this evil show. It's not as effective as the knives to cut out the evil, but at least a part of it will be gone.

Should she yell for Shane? Would he hear her? No, that would just cause the stalker to panic, right? To shoot?

She could feel the stalker savoring the moment. She pushed herself to run faster, limbs and branches smacking at her, leaving scratches on her face and hands. The rain was beginning to fall now, making the ground more slippery, treacherous. Chloe fell but forced herself to get back up.

For someone who was in the Special Forces, he sure is a sitting duck. Yes, stand at the edge of the water, duck.

Focusing on just the stalker was becoming more exhausting. Spots were beginning to blur her vision. She kept running, her breath sawing in and out as she pushed herself farther. She was almost there.

The thunder will hide my tracks.

She was too late. She wasn't going to make it to the water, to Shane, in time. But maybe she could make it to the shooter, stop him. She pushed herself faster.

Time to die, soldier. You should have stayed honorable and protected the country rather than whoring yourself and protecting evil.

Using every ounce of mental energy she had left, she focused on the voice, trying to picture more clearly in her mind what he was seeing.

And then she didn't have to. She saw him standing just a few yards in front of her, dressed in all black, including a hood over his face, rifle pressed up to his shoulder. She was breathing so hard she couldn't even shout to get his attention.

She just ran as fast as she could and barreled right into him.

Chloe had never tackled anyone in her life. It freaking hurt. The loud roar of the rifle going off half deafened her as she and the stalker fell into a tree beside them.

Had she been in time? Had the bullet hit Shane?

Chloe rolled over, away from the stalker, struggling to get her breath. She sucked air in and yelled at the top of her voice, "Shane!"

It wasn't nearly as loud as she wanted it to be. Even if the shot hadn't hit him, would he hear her?

She kept crawling away, trying to see through the dark and drizzle, fighting against the exhaustion that already pulled at her from concentrating on the stalker's voice in her head. A rough hand grabbed her ponytail and yanked her back.

"Bitch." The word ground out of the man's lips as he moved over her. Chloe brought her arms up to try to protect her head, but she was too late to stop his backhand catching her in the face.

Stunned by the onslaught of pain, Chloe bucked her hips, trying to get the man's weight off her. She freed one leg, brought it up, and used it to kick him as hard as she could in his ribs. She grabbed at the rifle lying beside them and tried to use it as a club to hit him.

He caught it and threw it out of reach. "I don't need a gun to kill you."

Chloe screamed as loud as she could, cursing when the thunder drowned it out. Was anyone close enough to hear her? Had the shot hit Shane? And even if it hadn't, how would he be able to find her? If anyone could, it would be him.

She bucked again, trying to get away, but this time her

attacker was ready. His laugh—full of vindictive joy—echoed in her ear.

She tried to scream again, but he was ready for that too. One hand pushed over her mouth, stopping any noise.

The other wrapped around her throat and began to squeeze.

Chapter 12

Shane hit the ground the moment he heard the gunfire. It didn't come close enough to put his life in danger, but the shot had definitely been fired in his direction. There were zero positive reasons why anyone would be out here in this weather. Even fewer why they would be with a rifle.

Shane's own weapon was out of his holster in an instant as he ran from the edge of the water into the cover of the trees. There he stopped. Breathing. Listening. Pulling that focus he was so famous for around him like a blanket.

Chloe screaming his name, barely discernible through the damn storm, almost splintered that focus entirely. What the hell was she doing here?

Chloe should be relaxing in her house in Los Angeles right now, not on this set, in a storm, screaming his damn name, for God's sake.

Particularly not when it was following a gunshot.

Shane rushed into the wooded area, safety be damned. He didn't care if someone shot at him. Getting to Chloe, protecting her, keeping her safe, was important.

His black T-shirt and jeans gave him more freedom of movement than a blazer would have. As the rain began to fall more steadily, his wet clothes would help him blend in better with the darkness.

Burying all his emotions under a wall of ice—particularly the feeling of panic that threatened to bloom at the thought of Chloe being out here in the woods with a killer—Shane stopped again and listened. Something ahead—a grunt, a branch breaking—caught his attention, and he ran once again.

Glock in hand, Shane moved silently through the trees. It didn't matter who the shooter was; Shane had no doubt in his ability to outmaneuver him in the current situation under the cover of darkness. Uncle Sam had made sure Shane could outmaneuver anyone in this situation.

Chloe, on the other hand, was relatively defenseless.

Her terrified scream, so weak it was almost drowned out by the thunder, had him sprinting again.

Where were they? Shane would find him. But could he do it before Chloe was hurt or killed?

For just a moment, the nightmare of his last mission pressed down on Shane. Chloe's life depended on his decisions now, just like his men's lives had.

They had all died.

He was not going to allow that to happen to her. Shane waited a few more seconds to see if he could get a fix on the shooter. When he couldn't, he did what he would never normally do: gave up tactical advantage.

"Chloe, where are you?"

He yelled it as loud as he could, knowing it now made him a target, letting the shooter know exactly where Shane was. It would hopefully draw the man's attention to Shane and away from Chloe.

Chloe's lack of response threatened to rip the air from

Shane's lungs. There were many reasons he could think of why Chloe wouldn't respond. None were good.

Closing his eyes, he listened for anything that would clue him in to where she was. A moment later he heard it.

A sob.

He sprinted toward the sound, Glock raised. A few seconds later he rounded a tree and found Chloe there on the ground. He looked around, but she seemed to be alone.

Keeping his weapon raised, Shane crouched beside her, relief beating in time with his heart. She was breathing. She was injured, but she was at least alive. "Chloe, are you okay, sweetheart?"

"He ran when you yelled, but he's still nearby." Her voice was cracky. Strained. "Y-you should go after him."

Damn it, Shane was tempted to. He wanted to catch this bastard. But there was no way in hell he was leaving Chloe here. She might not have any life-threatening injuries, but Chloe definitely wasn't okay.

He helped her sit up, but even then, she remained huddled against the tree. "We need to move, just to make sure we're not sitting ducks if he decides to double back."

She nodded, but he didn't like how still she was. She moved all the time. "Chloe, are you hurt, baby? You are, aren't you?"

"No." Her voice was hoarse again. "He was choking me but stopped when you yelled. Ran."

He pushed her damp hair away from her face. "No broken bones? Internal injuries?"

"No." She shook her head, but it was weak at best. "Let's move."

She was almost too shaky to go. She was in shock at least. He needed to get her somewhere safe and warm. He tucked an arm around her and led her back toward the direction of the lake. The shooter would not have gone that way if he were trying to make an escape.

By the time they were near the water, he was carrying most of Chloe's slight weight. He found a unique cluster of trees, providing shelter on three sides and a slight overhang. He tucked Chloe into the small hole the trunks made, then crouched himself in front of her, his back to her. No one was getting to her without going through him first.

He took his phone out of his pocket and called the security trailer. All the bodyguards had gone with their respective actors or actresses, but there were still half a dozen security members—all of whom Shane had vetted himself—working the safety of the set.

"Security of—"

"Kassler. It's Shane." He cut the man off. "We've got a shooter down on the east side of the lake. Send the entire team in this direction. Now. Track my location on this phone and send it to them so they know where we are. And have them be on the lookout for someone carrying a rifle. Call the sheriff and have him get an officer out here right away. Crime lab too."

"Okay."

Shane glanced over his shoulder where Chloe was leaned up against one of the trees, eyes closed. The whirlwind he knew was not one to lay huddled against anything. "And paramedics."

"No," she whispered. "I'm okay. I just need a minute. I don't have any injuries, I promise."

She didn't look injured, but she sure as hell didn't seem okay either.

"No paramedics needed. But get the team out here ASAP."

"Got it, boss."

Shane kept guard, alert and watchful, impervious to the rain except to wish he had a way to better shelter Chloe for the next few minutes until the rest of the security team arrived.

Within three minutes, the first of the guards was out there. Within ten, the whole area was surrounded. By then it was clear the shooter had left, making his getaway while Shane stayed with Chloe.

Shane didn't regret the choice.

He filled the team in on what had happened and provided info on where the shot had come from and the general vicinity of where Shane thought the bullet had probably hit. They spread out and began to look around, trying to destroy as little evidence as possible, which was difficult in the dark and rain.

When he turned back to Chloe, she was still lying against the tree. This definitely wasn't right. "Chloe, I need you to tell me what's really wrong."

"I-I just used all my energy running out here from my trailer. I'm tired." Her voice was weak. He put his fingers against her neck to take her pulse. Thready. Not the way it should be just from a sprint.

"I think you're in shock."

"I'm just tired." She looked away as she said it. God damn it, she was *still* hiding stuff from him. Of course, the whole question of why she was out here to begin with and how she'd known there was danger still had to be answered.

Would be.

Kassler came rushing over to them. "Thomas found a shell casing," he said. "From where it fell, the shooter had a pretty clear view of where you said you were standing. It's a miracle you're not dead right now."

"Chloe did something." He turned to her. "What did you do to distract him? Cause him to miss?"

She shrugged. "I tackled him."

Shane's curse was low and vile. "Let me make sure I

JANIE CROUCH

understand. There was a guy with a rifle, and you decided to just tackle him? Why didn't you warn me instead?"

She shrugged again. "You were too far away. It wasn't like I had time to sit down and make a pro and con list. I was just trying to stop the guy from killing you."

Her smartass comment made him feel a little better about her condition. "Did you get a look at him?"

"No. He was wearing a mask."

That just furthered Shane's theory that the stalker was part of the cast or crew. "Kassler, we need a list of anyone who chose to stay local during the break. *Anyone*. And this area is officially a crime scene. Attempted murder. The sheriff needs to process it as such."

Shane turned to Chloe. "Unless you plan on trying to talk him into filing this as an accident also."

He felt a little bad about harassing her when she looked so weak sitting against the tree. He felt *less* so when she stuck her middle finger up at him.

But she still didn't open her eyes.

He turned back to Kassler. "I'm taking her home. To my house in town. If you need me, call me there. Tell the sheriff we'll give a statement tomorrow. That Chloe needs to rest tonight. Try to have everyone be as careful as possible." Most of the evidence would've already been destroyed by nature or the team, but maybe not all.

Kassler began directing the other team members. Shane returned to where Chloe still sat against the tree. It was time, way beyond it, for her to tell him exactly what was going on. He crouched down beside her and gently tucked a strand of her blonde hair behind her ear. Her eyes remained closed.

"You ready to go? We need to get you out of this rain. There's nothing more either of us can do now."

"Okay. I just need a few more minutes to rest. I guess I'm

more out of shape than I thought. The running . . . you know?"

"You guess that, huh?" It was such bullshit. "You know what I guess? I guess there's something wrong with you that you've been hiding from me and damn near everyone for weeks, and probably a lot longer. I guess that you couldn't get up and walk back to your trailer right now even if your life depended on it. How am I doing so far?"

She opened her eyes long enough to turn a death glare at him before shutting them again.

"Give me the evil eye all you want. It doesn't change the fact that you don't have the strength to walk out of here. And it has nothing to do with physical injuries."

"I should've fought harder to have you fired at the very beginning," she muttered.

He chuckled. She was frustrated with her own body's limitations and angry at him for noticing. People noticed a lot of things about Chloe, but her limitations weren't one of them. "Too late to get me fired now, shortstop."

He reached an arm under her knees and another around her back. Before she could find the words to protest—and he knew she would—he had her up in his arms and was walking back toward the trailers.

"Westman, put me down," she hissed.

"It's either me or we call a paramedic and wait for a stretcher. Because I'm damn well not letting you lay out there for hours in the rain until you get enough strength to walk back to the trailers. I know you're used to bossing or charming everyone into giving you your own way, but not this time."

"Whatever. It's your hernia."

"You are no heavier than the last time I carried you."

Those whiskey eyes glared at him again. Damned if it

wasn't the sexiest thing he'd ever seen. "When have you ever carried me?"

At least their argument was putting a little color back into her cheeks. "A couple weeks ago. You fell asleep on your desk, face on top of your stapler, so I carried you to the couch."

"I don't remember that."

"That was because you had once again worked yourself into a near-coma state. But that's not it, is it? Everybody thinks it's work that keeps you exhausted, but there's something else happening, isn't there?"

She didn't respond. Didn't fight. That was almost scarier than anything that sharp little tongue could say. Instead, she just pressed her cheek closer to his shoulder. Not unlike what she'd done in her sleep when he carried her.

They traveled in silence. Shane walked all the way to the trailers and put her in his car.

He was taking her to his house and getting what he'd wanted from the first day he met her: the truth.

Chapter 13

*H*er strength was returning. She could feel it. Concentrating on the shooter had completely depleted her physically, but it hadn't damaged her the way Conversation Hearts blasting his sicko emotions into her mind did.

If Shane had just given her another hour she would've been able to walk back on her own. Of course, explaining to the rest of the security team why she was just sitting for an hour in the rain would've been difficult. So maybe she shouldn't be too pissed at him.

Not to mention he'd carried her half a mile without even breaking a sweat. Sure, she wasn't a sumo wrestler, but a hundred pounds could get heavy. Evidently not for invincible ex-Special Forces soldiers.

She watched as Shane came back out of her trailer, laptop and notebook in one hand, her overnight bag in the other. Evidently, she wouldn't be back for a few days. He didn't say anything as he put the items in the back seat, then went into the security trailer, returning quickly.

Twenty minutes later they were pulling up to a house on

the outskirts of Black Mountain. It was small with an adorable wraparound porch. The plot of land it sat on was large; no other houses were visible. She could barely make out a small barn behind it.

"You live here?"

"Grew up here, me and my grandmother. But I haven't really lived here since I left for college and then the army."

Chloe was strong enough now to make it out of the car on her own. She'd be damned if he was going to carry her over the threshold like some bride just because she was a little shaky.

He was around to her side of the car before she'd taken a few steps. "Can you make it?"

She glared at him. "Careful there, Avalanche. I write for a show where we regularly sit around thinking of how we can kill people. You don't want to get on my bad side."

He gave her a lopsided grin that did things to her girly parts she didn't even know could happen with just a look. "Get even further on your bad side, you mean."

"Yeah. That too."

He grabbed the stuff from the back seat and led her to the house, holding a hand out in case she needed help up the stairs. She didn't take it, but that didn't mean she didn't appreciate the consideration behind the offer. Or that he was offended by her determination to make it on her own.

Shane didn't feel threatened by much. Not a lot shook him. Certainly not a woman's strength or independence.

He unlocked the door and ushered her inside and straight to a couch.

"I know you're feeling better, but sit for a minute, okay? Let me warm up some soup. And I'll make coffee."

"You're being nice."

"Forcing you to eat out of a can isn't nice, but it gets calories in you. I'll have to really cook for you another time."

"You cook?"

"I've spent the past six months living in Europe, mostly Italy. So, yeah, I know some things."

"Not me. I don't cook at all. Thank God for the caterers on set. My house in LA has an entire kitchen drawer dedicated to takeout menus."

"Speaking of, weren't you supposed to be in Los Angeles?"

She tilted her head, holding his gaze. "Weren't you supposed to be in the Hamptons with Alexandra?"

"I was invited. Someone else *assumed* I'd be going before pushing me out the door to get rid of me." He left her and walked into the kitchen. She could hear him making the soup.

She'd pushed him for this very reason. Because she didn't want to be in a situation where she had to answer questions that had no believable explanations. To put him in a position where he'd have to call her either a liar or crazy.

Chloe now understood why her sister, Paige, had been so terrified to tell the man she loved that she had been drawing dead women in her sleep. That her brain was connected to the man who had attacked her.

Because it was easier to carry that weight yourself than to see someone you cared about look at you differently. The way Shane was surely going to if Chloe explained the voices in her head.

Chloe searched for ways out of this. Ways to explain . . . everything. How she'd known the shooter was out there. How she'd known to look for the scuba diver in trouble in the water before anyone else. Why her body had been shutting down for the past few weeks.

She couldn't.

Shane continued clanking around in the kitchen. Maybe she could make a run for it before he got back.

No, he would just chase her. She had to tell him. Or at least try.

He walked in holding a tray with two bowls of soup and mugs of coffee. He set it down on the coffee table and handed her a bowl.

They ate in silence for most of the simple meal.

"Honestly, I thought you might try to run away while I was making the soup."

She met his eyes. "Honestly, I thought about it. I know you're full of questions. I don't know that I have logical answers for all of them."

Shane took their soup bowls and put them on the tray, then handed her the mug of coffee.

It was full of cream and sugar just the way she liked it. The knowledge that he knew exactly how she liked it gave her the courage to continue.

"Have you ever heard of Occam's razor?" she asked, clutching her cup and taking a sip of the brew.

"I'm not very familiar with the science behind it, but it's the concept that the simplest answer is usually correct, right?"

"Yes, exactly."

"Yeah, well I've rarely found that to be true," he said.

"Good. Because my entire life is in opposition to Occam's razor."

He took a sip of his coffee. "Just answer what you can, as best you can."

"Where do you want to start?"

He studied her with those blue eyes for a long minute. She could feel him focusing. But where most people would be projecting whatever emotions they were feeling about this conversation—confusion, disgust, concern—all she could feel from him was coolness. Control.

"Let's start with how you knew someone was going to be at the lake with a gun tonight."

Well, that certainly brought them straight into the crux of the matter. As she looked into his eyes she wondered if this was the last moment he would be gazing at her without something negative tinging his perspective.

"You know how most people joke about hearing voices in their head? Well, they are real for me. I've been able to hear other people's thoughts my entire life."

≈

SHE HAD to give him credit. He listened.

Those blue eyes stayed focused on her as she told him, not everything, but enough to make anybody understand how weird her life was. No sarcastic comments, no judgments.

But questions. Definitely questions.

"The best way for me to explain it is that all the voices are like a river flowing through a narrow channel, and I just flow along with it in my head."

"Does it hurt? Bother you?"

Only when someone like Conversation Hearts blasted his emotions into her brain. But this talk was weird enough without bringing the truly Bizzaroville into it. "Not usually. It's happened for as long as I can remember, so most of the time I just ignore it, unless I want to try to use the voices for ideas for scenes or dialogue. Then it comes in pretty handy. Most of the time the stream moves along at a pretty brisk pace, but other times it trickles to something less frantic. That's always nice."

"And sometimes it floods and roars through the channel."

She nodded. "Yes, exactly. And that's not so nice."

"Is that what happened tonight? Why you were so exhausted? Because of so many in your head?"

He didn't even stare at her like she was crazy as he asked.

"No, the opposite in fact. Almost by accident I heard a voice talking about the lake, evil, and finishing what it started. So I focused on it. That's what exhausted me."

"So picking out one voice is hard?"

"Yes. It's like trying to stand still in the fast-moving river. It's always hard, exhausting. Sometimes it's downright impossible. But tonight I knew the voice was talking about the set. And killing. And then . . . you. So I did what I could, and thank goodness it was enough."

He seemed to be processing it all. Studying her, but at least not looking at her like she was some sort of freak or liar. He took the final sip of his coffee before setting the cup on the table. She'd long since finished hers. And she wished for something stronger.

"So you seem pretty calm about all this," she said. "Formulating an argument about why it can't possibly be true?"

He raised an eyebrow, making his face with the five o'clock shadow look more boyish. Playful. But it couldn't quite take away the aura of danger that lurked underneath. "Do I strike you as someone stupid enough to call you a liar?"

She couldn't stop the smile that pulled at her lips. "Maybe not with that exact word. But I'm sure you could find a way to argue your point without actually saying it."

"Is that what most people do when you tell them about this?"

She shrugged. "I don't tell people anymore. Mostly I stopped when I was a kid once I figured out I couldn't actually explain what was happening or prove it. But I tried a few years ago with a guy I thought might become important to me."

"He didn't believe you?"

"At that point, I think he figured it was better to get out regardless. Either I was a liar, delusional, or would always be able to know what he was thinking. I guess none of those seemed liked good options, so he bailed. That was before the show became big. He contacted me a couple times after I became more well known, but I wasn't interested in getting back together."

"I'll need to get his info from you. He might be someone we should look into."

Amazing how Shane could compartmentalize. Here she was, telling him what had to be some of the weirdest stuff ever, and he was still able to focus on what might be important to catch the stalker. "Okay. I do think Brandon is probably behind a lot of the rumors that got out to the gossip rags about me and my woo-wooness, but I don't think he'd actually harm anyone."

Shane nodded, but she knew he'd still follow through on making sure Brandon was investigated.

"So you haven't told anyone since him? Your creative team?"

"Nadine knows. But she and I don't talk about it a whole lot. She kind of grew up with it like I did, so it's always just been a part of our narrative."

"And the others? Travis? Justin? Alexandra?"

"Alexandra? Hell, no. Although honestly, I don't think she would care. She just wants us to create the best vehicle possible for her to shine from. If that involved sacrificing small goats in the full moon I don't think she would mind." Chloe shook her head. "The guys? No, I don't talk about it, but honestly, I think they're both around because they heard rumors and were curious. But they do their jobs well, so I don't care. I try to keep it to myself. It would make people nervous, at best. Or they'd want me to prove it."

"Want you to do parlor tricks? 'What number am I holding behind my back' sort of thing?"

"Exactly." She couldn't sit on the couch anymore, so she stood and began looking around. Shane was obviously in the process of packing his grandmother's things. "I can't do that. It's not worth the mental exhaustion of wading through the voices, and even then, I might not be able to pinpoint that person's thoughts. Then people generally just think I'm making it all up. I don't blame them. So it's been a long time since I tried to tell anyone."

"So you can't tell what I'm thinking right now."

"You?" she scoffed, turning from the bookshelf she'd been looking at. "Most people I can get some sort of general emotional state from without actually trying to catch their thoughts."

"Not me?"

"No, you're . . ." She didn't want to offend him. "You're impenetrable. Nothing gets through. Cold, for lack of a better word."

"Hmmm." He leaned back farther on the couch, crossing his arms over his chest.

"I'm not trying to offend you. For me, it's actually very refreshing. You . . . help." She didn't want to go further. "I'm sorry."

"It's funny, really. I was married for a couple years when I was younger, not long after I joined the army. It didn't work out, since she needed someone who wanted to climb the ranks, and I was more interested in active missions than being promoted."

"I can't imagine you in anything but active missions. Paperwork? Desks? I can't see that."

He shrugged. "Yeah, desks were never part of my plan. Anyway, Robin accused me of being cold. In a bar in front of just about my entire team. Said that being with me was like living in a sudden blizzard where ice just covered everything with no warning. The guys thought it was the most hilarious thing they'd ever heard."

She had to smile at that.

Shane rolled his eyes. "The next day, my locker was covered in pictures of snowstorms and ice. But the most striking photo—the one I ended up keeping—was of an avalanche in midfury. Zac Mackay, my teammate then, and soon to be my boss at Linear, said that was what I was like in combat situations. That I pulled ice around myself and got the job done, no matter what. Like the avalanche. Name stuck."

She leaned back against the wall, feigning a calmness she didn't feel. She appreciated his story and him telling her about his life. But she couldn't keep waiting for the other shoe to drop. If he was going to end up giving her *the look*, she wanted to go ahead and get it out of the way. "So, Avalanche, is it your innate coolness that's allowing you to take what I'm saying at face value?"

He stretched his long legs out in front of him onto the coffee table, crossing them at the ankles, a comfortable action that spoke of many years of doing the same thing. His grandmother's house had obviously been his home.

"What if I tell you that you're not the weirdest thing I've ever seen?"

"I guess I should be offended that you called me weird, but honestly, I'm just glad you're not already running for the hills. So you've seen some weird stuff?"

"I've seen men who have been severely injured get themselves and their teammates to a safe location miles away. In an Afghan village I saw a mother—not much bigger than you —lift a boulder twice her weight to save a child trapped underneath. I had an army captain who could always tell when we were being watched. Saved our asses multiple times."

"That's not exactly the same."

"No, it's not. But it's not exactly different either. All I'm saying is that our bodies and minds have pieces that we're not fully utilizing at any given time. Maybe your mind is doing that with a piece others don't use."

Chloe had discussed this very thing with Adrienne and Paige. "My sisters have abilities too. We call them gifts, but sometimes they don't feel that way. Paige was connected to the mind of a killer and drew his victims in her sleep. Adrienne can get a sort of reading from items that criminals handle."

Shane shrugged. "The three of you have a highly developed mental sensitivity. I think we all probably have sensitivities; it's just about how pronounced they are."

She pushed off the wall. "Like a sensitivity to light, gluten, or something?"

"Not an allergy. Something that comes naturally to you. We've all seen YouTube videos of a three-year-old piano prodigy who can play music most people wouldn't be able to even after a decade of lessons. Does that kid practice? Maybe, some. But mostly, it's a gift that was already in his brain that was somehow discovered. Your gift was the same; it just didn't need to be discovered. It announced itself from the beginning."

Could it be that simple? "But . . ." She trailed off. It made sense.

She sagged against the wall. *What Shane said made sense.*

And sort of changed how she thought about everything. A gift, rather than an aberration. Prodigy, rather than a freak.

It made Chloe realize that she'd been waiting all her adult life—and most of her childhood too—to explain to someone what happened inside her head and for them to keep talking to her as if it were nothing more than a unique part of her.

Like a birthmark shaped exactly like a cat. Or having perfect pitch. Or a photographic memory.

Someone who thought it was interesting but didn't think it warranted grabbing a pitchfork.

Sure, Chloe had her sisters who accepted her, but they had their own crazy inside their heads. And Nadine. God bless her; she loved Chloe no matter what. Had done so since Chloe protected her from the bullies when they were eight. Wouldn't care if Chloe woke with a second head.

But Shane had no reason to look at her with such calm acceptance. To gaze at her with such unflappable assurance that she was, if not normal, at least not something to be feared. Not something evil, like the stalker thought.

The sound of a little sob in the room startled Chloe. Even more so when she realized it was coming from her.

What the hell? She *never* cried.

But now she couldn't seem to stop. Huge, heaving sobs broke out. She was so tired of hiding everything. So tired of not being able to control what was inside her mind. And, oh God, she and Shane had almost been killed today.

She felt a hand on her shoulder and realized she'd sunk to the floor and Shane was crouched beside her.

"Let me hold you," he said. "You don't have to carry this alone anymore, sweetheart."

The fact that he hadn't assumed she would want him to touch her, hadn't just pulled her into his arms, meant everything to her. She all but threw herself at him, cries she didn't know how to stop ripping at the very fabric of her being.

Shane caught her and wrapped her in his arms. Didn't try to say anything that would make it better. Just held her.

Chapter 14

The strength of this tiny woman sitting in his lap was astounding.

He'd been telling her the truth when he'd said she wasn't the weirdest thing he'd ever seen. Maybe the most fascinating, but he'd encountered too many things that couldn't be logically explained to get into a tizzy because her brain picked up on frequencies other people's didn't.

Shane had no doubt that anyone else who had a constant stream of voices running through her head would've gone insane or used them for some other more nefarious reason than creating a damned entertaining television show. Someone without Chloe's mental fortitude would've crumbled long ago.

Hell, her own tears had panicked her more than anything else. And he'd been studying her—unable to stop—since her first smartass comment to him three weeks ago.

For someone with the nickname Avalanche, his feelings for this petite woman were decidedly not cold.

He knew there was more she wasn't telling him. But that

would have to wait. She'd been through enough for one night.

She wasn't crying any more, but every once in a while, an adorable blubbering hiccup would pop out of her.

"We all have gifts, Chloe. Stuff our brain does more easily than others. Mine is situational awareness. That's why Linear Tactical sent me here. I don't have any law enforcement investigation credentials, but Zac knows that not much gets by me." He gestured at her with his arm. "Take you, for example. You've never told me anything about yourself—the opposite, actually—but because of my strengths I'm able to pick up on stuff others might have missed."

"Like what?"

"Such as the fact that you've chosen to surround yourself with people who think out loud all the time. A field in which everybody is constantly talking over one another. And it never bothers you. Never causes you to lose your concentration. I thought at first it was because you were just unmindful. That you didn't pay attention, so you didn't notice all the clamor. I realize now, you've deliberately surrounded yourself with these people so it balances the noise that's inside your head."

She nodded.

"You move around so rapidly for the same reason. You're matching an internal rhythm. I'm sure as a kid you got labeled as having Attention Deficit Disorder or something."

She nodded again. "It took me a long time to be able to sit still. To ignore everything inside my head so I could focus on what was at hand."

They sat in silence for long minutes. Shane leaned against the wall. There wasn't anywhere else he'd rather be than right here holding her.

She shifted slightly in his lap. Well, maybe there was *some-where* he'd rather be with her. Definitely without so many clothes on. But he'd be damned if he would take advantage of her after the physical and emotional wringer she'd been through today.

He was trying desperately to hold on to that vow when she snuggled closer to him, inching her fingers into the hair at his nape and planting soft kisses along his neck and jaw.

His eyes closed. Icy was very definitely the last thing he was feeling right now. He moved the hand that had been stroking her back down to her hip, grasping her tightly, pulling her closer against him.

Before moving her away.

With his free hand, he found her other hip, and he picked her up off his lap—wanting to groan at the loss of her soft lips against his neck—and placed her on the floor in front of him so they were sitting face to face.

"Chloe." He struggled to find the right words, praying she wouldn't make this any harder—oh God, the pun—than it already was.

Of course, being her, she was going to, in every way. She immediately climbed back into his lap. "Are you trying to tell me you don't want this also?"

She affixed her lips to his, and he couldn't stop himself. All he wanted to do was sink into that wet, soft mouth. To trace it with his tongue, tease those lips apart and explore. A knot of need twisted in him as he pulled her closer.

What was it about this one compact bundle of energy, with voices in her head and a mouth that could cut a man to shreds, that made him lose every bit of control?

He fisted a handful of her hair to keep her anchored in place as he pulled her closer, his tongue stroking against hers. He nipped at her bottom lip as she sucked on his upper, then thrust his tongue inside her mouth, a foreshadowing of what was to come.

He breathed in her scent.

And that was what broke the spell.

Chloe had a unique scent to her, soft and gentle—so unlike her personality—like lilacs. Shane smelled it every time he handed her coffee or she buzzed by him in a whirlwind to get to wherever she was going.

That scent was drowned out now by the smell of forest and rain. It was not unpleasant, but it was a reminder that Chloe had damn near died tonight. Tomorrow she'd have bruises surrounding that slender neck, a testament of just how hard she'd been knocking on death's door.

He cupped her face with his hands. "Chloe."

She echoed his serious tone. "Shane." She rolled her eyes. "Let me use my advanced mind-reading skills, which are not even needed for this situation, to guess your next words. 'We need to stop.'"

He sighed and set her on the floor in front of him again, not sure that if she attempted a full-frontal attack with her mouth again that he'd be able to do anything but throw her down on the ground and give them what they both wanted. He closed his eyes for just a moment to pull his reserve around him. His control.

"Whoa," she whispered. "What did you just do?"

"Tried to find some damn resolve when it comes to you. Why? What did you feel?"

"Ever see those gum commercials where they bite into it, and their whole mouth gets a blast of icy fresh? That's what it felt like in my head."

He gripped her arms with his fingers. "Did it hurt?" Her face hadn't seemed pained, but maybe she was just good at hiding it.

"No. It didn't hurt. Was a little refreshing, actually. I've felt it before around you."

He stroked a finger down her cheek. "Believe me when I say I want to be with you. But you've had a pretty traumatic

123

day. Tomorrow, if this is what you still want, I will definitely not be stopping you."

"What if I know it's what I want now?"

Resisting the plea in her husky voice was the hardest thing he'd ever done. But the very huskiness, born of trauma to those delicate tissues of her throat from the stalker choking her, strengthened his resolve.

"Tomorrow." He smiled gently. "Just to make sure."

He helped them both from the floor, then walked her down to the guest bedroom, thankful it was in user-friendly condition. He set down the small bag of items he'd grabbed from her trailer and handed her some towels from the closet.

Those brown eyes followed him from where she sat on the edge of the bed. It was all he could do to keep from going over and kissing her again, sliding his fingers into that blonde hair and pulling her to him.

"Shower. Sleep." He finally got the words out, his voice sounding guttural even to his own ears. "Tomorrow."

"You promise?" she whispered. "Tomorrow?"

Everything in him screamed to take a step forward, but he took one back instead. "Yes. If that's what you want, then tomorrow." There was no way he'd be able to resist anyway. He knew better than to try.

He left before either of them could say or do anything else and went into the master bedroom, the one his grandmother always insisted be his, since it was the only room that could hold a king-size bed that would fit his frame.

His own—cold—shower did nothing to stop his mind from dwelling on the knowledge that Chloe was in a bed just a few yards down the hall. That she wanted him right now.

That pretty much made him the most stupid bastard in the history of the world.

Tomorrow. By God, if she came to him tomorrow, there

was no way he was turning her away. Plus, he'd given her his promise.

Lying in bed, staring up at the ceiling, he knew he should go to sleep. It was almost midnight. Chloe aside, there would be a number of things that needed handling tomorrow: police reports, reporting to the studio, finding out who from the cast and crew had still been on the set. Shane would also like to go over the scene in the woods himself.

So yeah, he should go to sleep. But an hour later, he was still awake when he heard the bedroom door creak open.

"Chloe? Is everything okay?"

He sat up as she continued inside. Her bare legs peeked out from the oversize T-shirt she wore. Gorgeous, toned, bare legs.

Shane forced his gaze back up to her face. Did she have a nightmare? Residual terror from what had happened?

"Are you a man of your word, Shane?"

Not the question he'd been expecting. "I try to be. It's the way my grandmother raised me. And it's part of what gave me the Avalanche nickname—I give the cold truth. Won't lie to you to save your feelings or mine."

She continued walking toward the bed. "Good."

"Why?"

"Because it's after midnight. So it's tomorrow. And I still want you."

Shane swallowed hard, then couldn't help the smile that crept up the side of his mouth. "You're too clever for your own good, you know that, right?"

She took a step closer. "I hope I'm too clever for both our own goods."

He threw his legs over the side of the bed and sat up as she made her way to stand in front of him. They were almost eye to eye. Shane couldn't remember ever wanting someone as much as he did Chloe right now. The air around them was charged with attraction. It crackled and sizzled like the storm floating away outside.

"Chloe." He had to try, once more, to make sure this was really what she wanted.

"You don't want to take advantage of me."

"Yes, exactly."

She took the final step forward, his legs parting, so she could stand between them. His hands fell to her hips of their own accord.

"Then how about if I take advantage of you?" she whispered. "Multiple times."

Her lips met his. Hot, wet, open. Shane didn't even try to resist. One hand moved from her hips to her shoulder and into her hair, gripping her head to pull her closer to him.

The kiss left them both shredded. Desperate. He licked deep into her mouth, swallowing the gasp that fell from her. Keeping a grip on the back of her head, mindful of the wounds on her face and throat, he curled his other arm the rest of the way around her hips and flipped her onto her back on his bed.

His lips never left hers. He wasn't sure he was ever going to be able to leave them again. He devoured her. He couldn't hide the effect she had on him. Didn't even try.

Avalanche was nowhere to be found.

Pleasure arced through him. He swallowed her sigh as their tongues dueled, mated. He felt her fingers gripping his hair, keeping him close.

As if he were going anywhere else.

Shane eased his weight more fully on top of her. He moaned as he felt one of her legs move up to wrap around his hips. Finally, he forced himself to let his lips release hers so he could pull her T-shirt over her head.

Now there were so many more places to kiss. She arched toward him as he made a wet and possessive line down her throat, to her chest, her perfect breasts, beyond. She was curved everywhere that drove him crazy.

That little gasp she made as he closed his mouth around her breast made him desperate to bury himself inside her so he could hear it again and again.

He peeled them out of the rest of their clothes, donning protection from his nightstand and moving back up her body with his mouth, starting with her feet and legs. He took the time to stroke, lick, and nibble as he moved up—concentrating on her most sensitive areas—until she was alternating between moaning his name and cursing it.

"You owe quite a bit of money to the jar," he whispered against her belly as he continued his way up.

"Westman, stop messing around." Her voice was a mixture between a plea and a command, her whiskey eyes hooded, lips swollen, as her fists grabbed his hair and pulled him up so he was poised over her.

Shane had never seen anything as beautiful in his life as this woman—so alive, so passionate—looking at him like she wasn't sure whether to kiss or deck him. He hooked one of her legs over the outside of his thighs and slid inside her.

Both of them cried out.

Shane couldn't stop his groan as he began to move in and out of her. He entwined his fingers with hers from where they'd grasped the sheets, and as she fell apart, his control snapped. All he knew was Chloe.

Forget ice. He was on fire. They both were. Burning to glorious ash.

Chapter 15

For the next three days, Shane gave Chloe little opportunity to hear any other voices than his, inside or out of her head. Not that she wanted to.

She'd had no idea it could be like this. Sex. A relationship. *Life*.

It wasn't that Shane quieted all the voices; it was just that, for the first time, she didn't feel like she needed to do anything about them. At all. She didn't need to listen or ignore them. She had somewhere else to turn her attention.

And it was wondrous.

She was also exhausted. Sore in places she didn't even know could get that way, much to her delight.

She'd had a few moments of self-doubt when she'd woken up draped over Shane's oh-so-lickable body. Had she been too easy? After all, they hadn't even been on a date. Had only shared one kiss.

He might have been around all the time, but they certainly hadn't had a relationship.

As she lay on his chest, stroking the muscle of his bicep as he slept, she'd realized it had felt like they did have one. Like he'd been *courting* her for the past couple of weeks, for Pete's sake. With bringing her coffee, making sure she ate, and pushing a chair under her when she was about to collapse. Plus, carrying her to the couch when she'd fallen asleep on a stapler.

He'd infused himself in her life, and she hadn't even noticed.

But for the last couple of weeks, he'd been the first person she'd looked for each morning and the last face in her mind as she fell asleep. The only person whose nearness caused less chaos in her mind rather than more.

He had begun trailing his hand up and down her spine, and she knew he was awake.

"You're a sneaky little bastard, you know that?"

His chuckle was deep, full of sleep. "So I've been told. Are you referring to something in particular?"

"You snuck into my life."

"I'm pretty sure I was hired into it."

"Not that. All the stuff you've been doing lately. Getting through my defenses without me even realizing." She pinched him lightly on the arm, and he chuckled again. "You know what I'm talking about. The coffee. Food."

"When I was in Special Forces, one of my specialties was enemy infiltration. Getting on the inside before they even knew I was there."

"Good to know you have a skill set that can be applied other places." She knew she sounded sulky but couldn't help it.

He rolled her so she was completely on top of his chest and he could wrap his arms securely around her. "Looking for weaknesses and using those to accomplish my goal were my specialty. Same with you, for example."

She brought her arms up on his chest. "Yes? What was your goal with me?"

He gave her a devilish grin that made her want to forget this entire conversation and just slide her body a little lower on his. "Getting you naked in my bed, of course."

She sulked again. "I guess I wasn't too difficult."

"Are you kidding? You were more mentally and emotionally fortified than most highly guarded enemy compounds I've ever tried to infiltrate."

"What?"

Shane rolled his eyes. "Half-pint, if I had asked you out, you would've said no outright. Made some excuse about how you didn't date people attached with the show, or were too busy, or didn't like men in khakis or something."

"You do iron your khakis to within an inch of their life," she muttered.

He ignored that. "Once I knew I wanted you, which was about eighty-seven seconds after I met you, I knew a direct approach wouldn't work. So I had to work my way inside your perimeter without you realizing I was doing it."

"Like I said, sneaky bastard."

He'd kissed her then and proceeded to work his way inside a much more pleasurable perimeter.

They'd eaten every meal together. He could cook as well as he'd bragged. Italian cuisine. French. Even some German. Chloe had just watched in awe of his skills. Evidently, a lot of his time in the army had been spent on bases in Europe.

The man was good with his hands. As if she weren't already well aware of that.

And so far they'd only lost one meal because Chloe had distracted Shane in the kitchen. How was she to know that mentioning she was dressed only in his shirt and nothing underneath would cause him to stop what he was doing and attack her right then?

The rigatoni had been unsalvageable by the time they were finished. But cheap Chinese takeout had been just fine, given the circumstances.

She worked all three days, when they weren't in bed or arguing about the best movies of all time. He had worked too, mostly involving adding more security to the set and coordinating with the sheriff's office.

A Deputy Hammell had come out to take their statements about the shooting. Neither she nor Shane had mentioned any voices in Chloe's head. As far as official law enforcement reports went, Chloe stumbled onto the shooter while she was walking and had saved Shane's life. He'd done the same for her by barreling up into the trees and scaring the attempted murderer away.

Sheriff Linenberger was on his way over now. Shane had files he wanted to go over with him.

"I'd like for you to be part of the conversation too," Shane said.

Chloe was pounding away at her computer, right in the middle of a scene. Since Conversation Hearts hadn't been around in a few days—she was hoping he'd convinced his lady friend to be his one and only and was gone for good—Chloe had been trying to make up the work she'd missed the past few weeks. These blessed, quiet hours had to be used to regain what she'd lost.

Or to give in to Shane when he'd distracted her. Fortunately, he'd had his own work to do too.

"I'm working. You and Sheriff Linenberger can handle it. I trust you."

He hitched a hip on the kitchen table next to her computer. Shane all casual in jeans was hard to resist. She liked soldier Shane, but casual Shane did all sorts of funny things to her insides. Her girlie parts *and* heart. Which was a little scary.

He dipped a finger under her chin, and she found herself looking into blue eyes. "Linenberger is coming over for us to discuss who of the cast and crew were still here locally during the break. Anyone we know who was gone will be off our suspect list."

"Wait, you think the stalker is a member of the cast or crew?"

He nodded. "I've already talked to Nadine and Travis about this, but they didn't want to mention it to you if we didn't have to. The stalker, the shooter, he's almost definitely someone in the cast or crew. Someone who has access to the set. Who could come and go unnoticed."

Chloe stood, unable to process this. "But I thought we were focusing on people connected to Alexandra? She's had stalkers before, a couple who weren't caught. Isn't it more likely that it's someone related to her past?"

"We looked into that and still are. But I don't think Alexandra is the target. I think the show as a whole is."

He moved closer to her but didn't try to touch her as she paced back and forth. "I can't stand that thought, Shane. These people are . . ." She shrugged.

"They're like a second family to you. I understand. I felt the same way about the men in my unit. Thinking of one of them as a traitor sucks."

She stopped pacing and walked to him, putting her forehead against his chest. Now he put his arms around her, now that she was ready—God, observation really was his superpower—and she leaned closer to him.

"We'll eliminate a lot of people by their location over the break. Obviously, if they weren't in the state, then they weren't the one shooting at me or attempting to strangle you."

She did not want to think about the stalker, the would-be killer, being someone she knew. Part of the team.

Someone whose face she looked at every day. Who would do that?

She snuggled closer to Shane, breathing in his scent. She wasn't great with defining smells, probably a byproduct of having her other senses overwhelmed all the time, but she loved the way Shane smelled. It was clean, strong. A hint of something she couldn't really define but reminded her of rich cinnamon.

She wanted to lick him. Partially to not have to think about someone she knew trying to destroy what meant so much to her, but mostly just because she just wanted to. And knew he would lick her back.

Sheriff Linenberger would love to walk in on that.

"Get your brain out of the gutter, Jeffries."

"Now who's reading minds?"

"Your mind has nothing to do with how you're rubbing against me. The sheriff will be here in just a minute."

"The sheriff is already here and can hear you through the open window." A voice rang out from the porch.

Chloe smiled as Shane cursed under his breath and then released her to go open the door.

The two men obviously knew each other, which in a town the size of Black Mountain wasn't surprising.

"I didn't realize when you came to see me the other day that the questions had a personal nature to them," Sheriff Linenberger said.

Shane shrugged and let the man into the living room. "The *personal nature* is a more recent development."

The sheriff turned to Chloe. "I hope you give him hell. It will only serve him right after all he gave us growing up."

Chloe's eyes widened. "Mr. Ironed-khakis raised hell? I'm pretty much going to need to hear every story there is."

Shane groaned as Linenberger chuckled. "It will be my pleasure. You know he is Betty Cordell's grandson, right?"

Chloe's eyes flew to Shane. "Miss Betty was your grandmother?"

Shane looked as surprised as her. "Did you know her?"

"Are you kidding me? She was a fantastic lady. All of us knew and loved her. She came to visit us all the time on the set. Even made us muffins."

And so much more than that, but Shane needed to see it without Chloe spoiling it. The sheriff was biting his tongue too. "She was a real fan of the show. Have you watched it? The last season especially. You'd probably get a kick out of seeing places you know."

Shane looked a little sheepish. "I haven't watched it at all. As a matter of fact, until this job I hadn't even really heard of it, except for what my grandmother told me. She did leave me a DVD set of the first three seasons, with the command to watch them."

Chloe met the sheriff's eyes, and they both grinned. "Well, I definitely think your grandmother would want you to watch it."

And Chloe hoped to be there when he did. When he saw his beloved grandmother on camera in full zombie gear. They'd offered her a chance to be whatever type of extra she wanted: vampire, faerie, shapeshifter, even human.

Miss Betty had chosen zombie. And she'd kicked ass in the small role she'd had on the show for one episode. Chloe couldn't wait for Shane to watch it.

She walked over to where Shane was setting up files on the dining room table and kissed him on the cheek. "I'm sorry for your loss. Your grandmother was a remarkable woman. Her visits were highlights on the set for everyone, but me especially. She and I became pretty close. She mentioned a grandson, but I didn't know it was you."

Shane nodded. "Grammi was amazing. Everyone thought so."

Chloe touched one of her small ruby stud earrings. "The last time she visited, she gave me these. I had mentioned before how striking they were. I didn't mean for her to give them to me, but she said she wanted me to have them, since she didn't have a daughter or granddaughter to give them to. But you can have them back if you want. I would totally understand."

He reached up and touched the earring before trailing his hand down her back and hooking it around her waist. "No, you keep them. I'm glad she knew you. Glad she was able to come hang out on the set and get into trouble with you."

He kissed her, then began working with the sheriff.

Chloe half listened to the guys as they went over files as she typed on her computer in the living room. She appreciated, as she knew Shane did, that the sheriff himself was helping sort through this. Buncombe County might not be very big, but that didn't mean that Linenberger didn't have other things to do.

They were discussing not only people, but access points to the set and the most difficult areas to guard. Chloe had no idea there were such nuances involved with security. She'd never even thought about it before.

They'd been at it for a couple of hours, Chloe's attention going back and forth between them and her work, when Shane called her over.

She stood next to him at the dining room table as he looped an arm loosely around her hips and gestured to the files in front of him.

"Here's who we've cleared. Hopefully this sets your mind at ease somewhat that those closest to you are not responsible."

Nadine and Travis had both been in Wilmington for the past four days. Not that Chloe had suspected them anyway. Justin had gone back home to Portland, so that cleared him.

Most of the other main actresses and actors were cleared, including Alexandra.

Although she was glad to know no one in her creative team had betrayed them in this way, there were still dozens of people—extras, crew—who we were still unaccounted for.

"It's a start," Shane said. "Knowing who we don't have to watch gives us more eyes on who we need to. And at least it's not your core team. I'll be honest, I had some concerns about Justin."

Chloe nodded. "I know he's not easy to work with or talk to. And gets sickly quite a bit. But he's brilliant when it comes to scenarios and dialogue."

"Well, being in Portland pretty much eliminates him from being the shooter."

There were still faces looking back at her from the files that Chloe couldn't believe would be behind this. Adam Woods, the stunt coordinator. Kendal Mitchell, one of the main set designers.

"Kendal is gay, you know."

Shane just shrugged. "Doesn't eliminate him from being the stalker. As a matter of fact, I know you think it's a man, but I've left some of the taller women in the suspect group also. I learned the hard way on a mission in Afghanistan that a woman can look very much like a man, or vice versa, and that both can kill just as easily."

The voice she'd heard in her head hadn't been female. But was that Chloe projecting her own assumptions onto it or had she really heard a man's voice? Chloe couldn't be positive.

"Based on your struggle with the shooter," Sheriff Linenberger said, "we think he or she is at least five foot ten. There are some women who fit that bill."

"Thank God Nadine was in Wilmington so we don't have to include her." Not that Chloe would've done that anyway.

She picked up Noah's file. "Poor kid. We run him ragged and he doesn't even get paid. If I was him, I'd be tempted to shoot everyone on the set just on principle."

Shane chuckled. "I'm sure he'll be eliminated as a suspect soon. He's local, but has been at his parents' house. So hopefully someone can verify his whereabouts."

They went over a few others before Sheriff Linenberger was preparing to leave and Shane was packing the files.

"I'm going with John back over to the set," Shane said to her. "We want to try to get everything as air-tight as possible before everyone returns tomorrow."

Chloe nodded. "I'm sure by now the studio has sent even more security. Joy."

Shane kissed her on the forehead. "More means catching this person faster. I'll be back later and we can try the rigatoni again."

She smiled. "I can't make any promises that the same thing won't happen."

His lips caught hers. "Then it will be Chinese takeout again."

The sheriff cleared his throat. Shane smiled and they walked out the door. Chloe sat down with her laptop to get to work. And did so for hours.

She had one episode almost completely written, and was outlining another when the pain hit her.

Having gone so many days without it, the agony crashed over her like a wave. She fell from her chair at the table onto the floor. Could see blood dripping from her nose onto the hardwood at a rapid pace.

Complete me.
Make me whole.
No one else.
Only you.
Mine.

Mine.

Mine.

Chloe sobbed as the agony burned through her. She curled up on the floor, grabbed her head, and just tried to survive.

Chapter 16

Shane stopped by the grocery store on his way home to pick up what was needed for the rigatoni. Not that he would mind if they ended up eating Chinese again.

He and the sheriff had met with the new members of the security force, as well as the private bodyguards that were making their way back onto the set. Everyone was debriefed and notified that they were now looking to catch an attempted murderer, not just a stalker. Shane knew Chloe wouldn't like having this many new strangers in khakis—and damned if he wasn't going to think of her and her smart little mouth every single time he ironed his pants for the rest of his life—but at least she agreed it was necessary.

Shane wanted to catch this person, not only because he didn't want to do personal security for the rest of his life, but he wanted to make sure Chloe was safe.

Shane didn't kid himself into downplaying how right it felt to have Chloe in his home. How having her there somehow made it his again, not just Grammi's. And knowing that the two women had known each other—liked one another—somehow made it all even more perfect. He'd talked to Chloe about how he'd snuck in under her defenses, but the truth was, she'd done the exact same thing to him without even trying. Just by being her half-crazy self.

He had no idea what any of this meant, just knew he wanted to get home to her as soon as possible. Home to her. Not something he'd ever expected to be saying again.

And yet somehow it didn't freak him out.

He was still smiling when he pulled into his driveway. He shifted the grocery bags so he could open his front door.

"Honey, I'm home!" He smiled knowing Chloe would roll her eyes as soon as she heard the words, and waited for her smartass response.

It didn't come.

Terror shot through Shane as he saw Chloe's legs on the floor half out of the dining room where she'd been working last. The grocery bags fell unheeded as Shane drew his weapon and ran toward her.

She was lying on her side, face pale as death. The only color was the blood dripping from her nose. Her eyes were open but staring blankly in front of her.

"Jesus. Chloe?" He reholstered his weapon so he could take her pulse, glancing down at her body to see if she had any noticeable injuries.

Some of the terror shifted off his chest when he finally found her pulse. He kept one hand on her neck and used the other to probe up and down her body to see if she had some injury he had missed. He couldn't find anything.

"Chloe? Talk to me, baby. What happened?" He used his shirt sleeve to wipe the blood dripping from her nose. "Did someone break in? Did they hurt you?"

He hadn't noticed any signs of forced entry when he'd come in, but an intruder could've used another door.

"Mine," Chloe whispered without moving. "Mine. Mine."

This was something inside her head, Shane realized. Was the final piece of whatever she hadn't been telling him. But regardless, it was still taking a toll on her body. Shane pulled his phone from his pocket and dialed 911, giving the dispatcher info about the situation and the address. He then asked to be transferred to the sheriff's office.

"Sheriff Linenberger."

"John, it's Shane. I'm back at my house and something has happened to Chloe. She's had some sort of collapse. I've called 911, but I wanted to fill you in."

"Are you sure it's not the stalker? Could he have found her at your house?"

"No, I don't think so. I think this is something she's been dealing with for a while but hasn't been telling anyone. Her friend, Nadine, is scheduled to get back today. Can you send someone to get her and bring her to the hospital?"

"Sure. Keep me updated if anything changes."

Shane disconnected the call and turned all his focus back to Chloe. Her arms were wrapped tightly around her head, so Shane slipped his hands under them, to rub her temples and maybe help ease some of her pain.

"Only you. Only you. Only you."

Shane never would've heard or made out the words if he hadn't been so close to her face. Her lips were barely moving, the sound not carrying more than a few inches from her mouth.

"It's okay, baby," he murmured. "We're going to get you help. Just hang on."

He felt the tiniest bit better when he wrapped his hand around one of hers and felt a small squeeze. It was the first response he'd had from her that suggested Chloe was still in there.

And she was, he knew it. Something was trying to take over her mind, but she would fight it.

Blood dripped from her nose again. She was fighting, but could she win?

"Hang in there, sweetheart. Keep fighting. I'm right here."

The paramedics seemed to take forever to arrive and then didn't want to let Shane ride in the ambulance with them. He explained in no uncertain terms that he did not care about their usual policy. He would not be leaving Chloe's side.

They either decided it wasn't worth the effort or weren't going to win the argument, or maybe they were afraid he was going to pull his weapon on them—not an impossibility—but they allowed Shane to ride with her.

The sight of Chloe so pale, an oxygen mask on her face, blood pressure cuff and pulse monitor on her arm, looking so opposite from her normal fireball self, wrecked something inside Shane.

This was too similar to the men he lost. The team under his leadership who hadn't come home. He forced the ice around himself. It was the only way he could function.

Chloe's arm without all the medical equipment reached up to pull away the oxygen mask. "Shane?"

"I'm here." He crouched closer to her so she could see him. "You collapsed or something. We are on our way to the hospital."

"I'm feeling better."

He put a hand on top of her head. "I'm glad, sweetheart. But we're still going."

"They can't do anything. It's Conversation Hearts. He's inside my head."

The EMT looked over at Shane who just shrugged. He had no idea what Chloe was talking about either. He moved the oxygen mask back over her face.

"Just rest. Let the doctors check you over to make sure."

Her eyes shut and Shane tried to move away from her but found he couldn't force himself to do it. His mind might want to ice itself over but his body wasn't letting her go.

She was looking much better when they got to the hospital and the staff took her back. Since Shane wasn't family, he was relegated to the waiting room.

He hadn't been there even ten minutes when a harried looking nurse came out. "You've got to be Shane Westman." The lady rolled her eyes. "She said just look for the hottest guy in the room."

"What? Who did? Chloe?"

The nurse nodded. "She categorically refused to cooperate until I came out here and told you not to contact her sisters. That they would just worry, and it's nothing."

It sure as hell hadn't looked like nothing when he found her in a comatose state on the floor less than an hour ago.

But he would use this to his advantage. "Tell her fine, but I'll be making multiple phone calls if she doesn't tell me what's going on."

The nurse rolled her eyes again. "Are you sure you don't want me to pass a note back to her? I like you. Do you like me? Check yes or no."

Shane supposed it was all sorts of juvenile, but couldn't find it in him to care. "Please just tell her. And make sure she's all right. Something was very wrong."

The nurse softened. "We'll take care of your girl. But Lordy, does she have a mouth on her."

The tension inside Shane eased slightly. If Chloe was filling up the swear jar fund, then she was feeling better. He'd take a cursing Chloe over a traumatized one any day.

A couple of hours later Shane was allowed back to Chloe's room. She was asleep.

"I'm Dr. Marsh." The doctor shook Shane's hand. "You're Shane Westman?"

JANIE CROUCH

Shane nodded.

The doctor chuckled. "Miss Jeffries said she would probably regret it, but that you were allowed in her room and I was given permission to provide her medical updates to you."

"How is she?"

"I'll be honest, we did complete bloodwork and a CT scan and the answer is both good and bad. Basically, we found nothing. No blood clots, no aneurysms, no cancer."

"So, good in that it's not something life-threatening, but bad because you have no idea what's going on."

The doctor nodded. "Exactly. Miss Jeffries doesn't strike me as a hypochondriac."

That Shane was sure of. "She's not."

"Yeah, our hypochondriacs generally don't start asking to be released fifteen minutes after they're admitted. Miss Jeffries was obviously in a lot of pain. Her blood pressure was very low, she was sluggish, and her response times were slow in the beginning. The bloodwork didn't show any signs of anemia and she isn't pregnant, so our two biggest usual culprits are out."

"Did you give her something to make her sleep?"

The doctor chuckled. "I offered. Let's just say her negative response was probably a little overkill. She definitely did not want any drugs in her system. Honestly, there's not even any reason for us to keep her overnight. I would like to, but again that suggestion was met with quite a few inappropriate foul words on her part."

"Maybe we should donate her curse jar fund to you. She has to put in a dollar every time she curses."

The doctor's laugh was genuine. "Oh no, please, use the millions of dollars you're going to have to support a needy country." Dr. Marsh got serious. "I know who Miss Jeffries is, of course. I would imagine she's under a lot of stress.

144

Collapsing and nosebleeds might be a sign that she needs a break, an extended one."

Shane smirked. "Why don't you try telling her that, and I'll cover you with my weapon from behind the chair?"

The doctor laughed again. "Obviously, I'm not that stupid, or I would've never made it through medical school. But the truth is, our bodies can only take what they can take. Chloe seems otherwise healthy, but something is obviously going on."

Shane knew there was, but also that it wasn't something that would show up in a blood test or CT scan.

"Believe me, I will be keeping a much closer eye on her."

Dr. Marsh slapped Shane on the shoulder. "Good luck with that. You're going to have your hands full. See if you can talk her in to staying overnight. Either way, if this happens again do exactly what you did: call 911 and get her here."

"I will." But by then he would have a lot more answers.

"Because I value my own life, I've already signed her discharge papers. It's up to her when she wants to leave."

The doctor hadn't been gone very long before Nadine came rushing in, Travis on her tail.

"Shane, what happened? A deputy picked us up at the airport. He said Chloe was here, that she collapsed. That she'd been shot at and choked. Why wasn't she in Los Angeles?"

Nadine's voice was getting faster, higher pitched, and louder as her questions continued. Shane motioned with his head for them to step out in the hallway so they didn't wake Chloe.

Shane filled them in on what had happened while they had been gone. He included the parts about the shooter and how Chloe had stopped him. He left out the parts about how she'd spent the rest of the break at his house, most of it in his bed. Chloe could tell that part to her friends if she wanted to.

"Why wasn't she at her Malibu house?" Nadine asked.

"Honestly, I don't know why she decided not to go. But I do know I would've been dead if she had."

Nadine glared at him. "Why didn't anyone call me immediately?"

Shane shook his head. "I'm sure Chloe just wanted you to enjoy your break. Both of you. She's been . . . busy."

"The stalker is getting out of control, Westman," Travis said. "Something needs to be done."

Travis's angry tone was an exact reflection of Shane's own feelings. "Believe me, no one agrees with you more than I do. We know it's one of the cast or crew, and we know it's someone who wasn't away on the break. We are running down that info right now."

"Is this collapse from what happened with the shooter?" Nadine asked. "Was Chloe hurt and didn't tell anyone?"

Shane looked at Chloe's friend with hard eyes. "No. I'm pretty sure this is whatever's been eating at her for the last few weeks or months. The thing neither of you will talk about, but both of you know what I'm referring to."

Travis turned to Nadine. "What is he talking about? Is something wrong with Chloe?"

"There are things you don't know," the woman said softly. "Things I'm not at liberty to talk about."

"Like what?" Travis asked.

Shane ignored the man and put his hand on Nadine's shoulder. "I know some of it. She told me."

"Told you what? What is going on?" Travis continued.

Nadine glanced between the two of them. "I'm sorry, but I'm not at liberty to talk about it with either of you. This is something deeply personal for Chloe, and my rule has been to never discuss it."

Shane glanced at Travis and saw fury cover the man's

features before he masked it. Shane himself was frustrated but understood Nadine's loyalty.

The door opened to the hospital room. Chloe stood there in her gown glaring at them.

"Quit picking on Nadine. I'm the only one who's going to give you the answers you want."

Chapter 17

Chloe banished Shane and Travis to the hallway as she talked alone with Nadine inside. A couple of minutes later when Nadine's happy squeal came through the door, Shane couldn't help but smile.

Looked like his and Chloe's relationship was out in the open now.

"Did you guys have a good time?" Shane asked Travis from where they stood in the hallway, staring at the door. "You went to Wilmington, right?"

"Yes. It was nice to get away from the routine." Travis gestured stiffly with his hand toward the door. "What do you think they're talking about in there?"

Shane definitely wasn't jumping on that slippery slope, and especially not with Travis, who wasn't looking too thrilled at this whole situation. "Who knows? Girl stuff."

"Are you guys a couple now?" Travis's fists were clenching. "Do you think they're talking about us?"

Shane slapped him on the shoulder. "A couple?" Yes. Definitely. For as long as he could talk Chloe into it. But again, not something he was comfortable getting into with Travis.

"I don't know that I would call us a couple. And I'm sure they're not talking about us. They're probably talking about Chloe's health issue."

Nadine squealed again and giggled. Travis rolled his eyes. "Yeah, health issues."

A few minutes later the women allowed them back in. Chloe was dressed in the clothes she'd arrived in. Nadine and Travis left and Chloe took care of the paperwork to get herself released. She had every intention of being back on set tomorrow when everyone returned.

Which was fine, Shane wouldn't try to stop her. He knew how important it was for her to be there, for both her sake and for the stability of the set. But he'd be damned if he was going back into the situation blind.

He never wanted to find her on the floor in that state ever again. He couldn't protect her if she didn't give him the tools he needed to do so.

They got home, and even though it was the middle of the night, he fixed them a meal and then made the coffee he knew she would want.

"Everything," he said, sitting on the coffee table directly in front of her as she sat on the couch. "It's time for you to tell me every damn thing."

Those endless brown eyes looked back at him over her coffee mug. "Even if I don't understand it myself? Even if it's weird?"

"I think we've already established that I'm pretty good with weird."

She took a deep breath, then spewed it all out. "It's a voice in my head. A particular one. It comes through louder than the rest. Much, much louder. Doesn't give me the option of ignoring it."

Shane nodded and leaned his forearms on his knees. "Violent? Angry?"

"He's not violent, at least not in my head. The best word for it is obsessed. I call him Conversation Hearts."

Shane raised an eyebrow. "Like the valentine candy?"

"Yeah. Because all I ever hear are these crazy individual extreme thoughts that he has for some woman. You are mine. We'll be together. You complete me. Mine. Only you. Like a really bad love card."

When Shane had found her on the floor, she'd been saying that over and over. Only you. Mine. She'd been echoing the thoughts in her mind.

"Is he thinking these things about you?" Shane straightened. "Could the stalker and your Conversation Hearts guy be the same person?"

"I don't think he's thinking about me, nor that the stalker would've tried to kill me if he had these sorts of intense feelings for me. Conversation Hearts is obsessed with his woman. It literally overwhelms his brain, this need to be with her. I don't think he wants to kill her."

That made sense, but Shane still wouldn't rule out the possibility they were dealing with the same person.

"How long has it been happening?"

"It started six months ago. But it's been escalating more recently. Like he's getting more desperate. His need for this woman to give him . . . whatever it is he's hoping for. Honestly, I wish I could get a picture of the woman's face and try to warn her. Because this level of emotional absorption cannot be good."

"If you do get a picture or name, we'll do what we can to find and warn her. I promise." He could see that the thought of some unnamed woman being harmed because Chloe couldn't figure out who she was weighed on her.

"It's like he goes on mental rampages. He'll be out of my head for days or longer and then will slam back in." She took a sip of her coffee in fortification. "The pain, Shane. Have you ever had a brain freeze? It's like that, but with fire. It's impossible for me to function when he's in there, screaming about his obsession and need for this woman."

"That's what was wrong with you the night the hot tub exploded. I thought you were drunk or something the way you were stumbling around when I first saw you. But it was him, wasn't it?"

"Yeah, that night was one of the worst. My body was so cold, and my brain was on fire, and I thought the hot tub would help. But it was you who ended up helping. Usually when I'm around you, all I can feel is the cold."

Shane couldn't help himself; he grimaced. "My ex-wife pretty much said the same thing as she handed me divorce papers."

Chloe leaned forward, put her coffee cup on the table, and grabbed his knees. "For me, it's the opposite. Trust me, when you're burning in the agonizing flow of a madman's thoughts, cold is good. Cold is exactly what I need."

At least his emotional distance was finally helping something.

"Plus, you're definitely not cold when it counts." She wagged her eyebrows at him.

He shook his head and grabbed her hands that had been sliding up his legs. "Focus."

She pouted, possibly the most adorable thing he'd ever seen. The temptation to throw her down on the couch and finish this conversation later—much later—was overwhelming. But he knew there was still something she wasn't telling him.

"Give me the rest, Chloe. I can't form a plan of action without all the information."

"That's it; I promise. I hear voices in my head on a regular basis, and one in particular that pretty much takes over my entire mind and body."

"And?"

She stared at him for a long moment. "Okay, fine. And Conversation Hearts' rampages are getting worse, more frequent. They'll stop for a while, of course. The guy has to sleep, or he's distracted with other things. But then they come back."

Her voice dropped to a whisper. "And it's going to kill me; I know it in my bones. Right now, your avalanche superpowers are enough to keep it at bay, but I don't think they will forever. He's escalating. He's going to lose it. His control. I don't know what he's going to do to the woman if she rejects him. Maybe then he will kill her. And it will kill me too. And there's not a damn thing you or I or anybody can do about it." She sat back against the couch. "Is that what you wanted to hear?"

It was what he was afraid she was going to say, but it very definitely wasn't what he'd wanted to hear. He reached over and hauled her into his lap.

"We're not going to let that happen."

He loved the way she snuggled into him. "I'm not sure we have any say in the matter."

"Maybe he's close by. Maybe that's why you're picking up on his frequency so much stronger than everyone else's."

She shrugged. "Maybe. I'll admit if I'm trying to concentrate on one particular voice, that person being nearby is helpful. But not a necessity."

"If you wanted to pick up on your sisters, could you do it? Could you find them?"

"Probably. They are easier because we're connected."

He tucked her into him more closely. "Okay, someone else then. Nadine. Could you focus in on her thoughts if it was necessary?"

"Maybe, but it would be exhausting. And I would only know it was her because I know her so well. I can't just pick out someone across the country and listen to their thoughts. It's too hard to figure out which voice is theirs." She shrugged. "Not to mention I've spent my entire life deliberately trying to not hear people's thoughts. Nobody wants someone else in their head. I know that for a fact."

So she couldn't track Conversation Hearts with her mind. Shane took another track. "So this happened for the first time six months ago? You know that for sure?"

"Yes. April 5."

Shane stiffened as soon as he heard the date.

"I know," she continued, "because that was your grandmother's funeral. I thought maybe I was having some sort of stress reaction to grief or something. I'm not good with emotions in case you haven't figured that out." She paused. "Were you at the funeral? I don't remember seeing you. I don't think I would've forgotten that."

Shane slid her off his lap so he could stand. "No, I wasn't there."

"Oh, I see." A glance at her told him she didn't at all. "I thought you and your grandmother had a good relationship. She talked very highly of you, although she always referred to you as the troublemaker."

"We did. I loved her very much." God, he didn't want to talk about this. Didn't even want to think about it. "There was a mission. An important one that I thought might put a lot of people in danger if I backed out at the last second."

"I'm sure Betty would've understood. She knew what you did was important."

Shane gave a bitter laugh. "The irony of it was that every man on my team died that day because of decisions I made. If I had left, gone to the funeral, maybe things would've been different."

"Decisions you made because of grief? Because you weren't thinking clearly?"

He shook his head, then turned around to look at the knickknacks that still sat on the mantel. Grammi's stuff. "No. It wasn't because of grief. I know it sounds cold—no surprise —but I had buried that so I could function. It was a lot of things that went wrong on that mission. All things I could've done something about, looking back on it now, but at the time I just didn't have all the information."

He felt her small hand on his back. "Did they blame you?"

"Officially, I was cleared of all blame. Not a blemish on my record. But that didn't stop the fact that seven men went on that mission with me and none of them returned. I got out of the service after that, wasn't sure if I could trust myself. My choices. Had lost my feel for it all."

"I'm sorry," she whispered. "I know that doesn't mean much. And it definitely doesn't change anything."

Shane turned and slid his arms around her. "The individual words may not matter, but I very much appreciate the sentiment behind them. When the shooter had you, and I didn't know where, I had to choose. Yell and give up where I was hidden or stay silent and try to find you on my own."

"You yelled."

He nodded. "My training said to keep quiet, but my gut said to yell."

"He was choking me. Would've killed me. I don't think you could've gotten to me in time. If you hadn't called out when you did, I would've died."

"Trusting our instincts isn't always the easiest, but it's usually the best plan. I've just got to relearn that fact."

"Why don't you take me to bed and see where your instincts lead us?" She tilted back so that they could see each other's faces.

God, that impish grin. She'd only been in his bed for three days, and he wasn't sure he was ever going to let her out of it.

"You know we have to be back on the set early tomorrow,

right?" Even as he asked the question, he bent his knees and dropped his arms under her hips and then stood, lifting her up. She laughed and hooked her legs around his waist.

He turned and pinned her against the wall. "We're going to figure out a way to stop this. Get that lunatic out of your head. If it means I've got to stay close until we figure out how to do it,"—he thrust his hips against hers—"then I guess we'll both just have to learn to live with that."

She pulled him in closer with her legs. "I guess we'll find a way to suffer through it."

Chapter 18

"*A*re you just going to stay on top of me for the rest of your life?"

It had been over a week since the break. The set was all but crawling with security and bodyguards. Even a couple of the local police force were around a lot of the time. It was enough to drive Chloe crazy.

She wanted peace. Wanted to be able to create the show she loved in the environment they'd always had before. One of artistic freedom and willingness to take risks to provide a story that people ran to their televisions to watch every week. The show they'd been able to create in the past.

Instead, the mood was cautious at best. Closer to suspicious. Everyone looking at everyone else and wondering if he or she was the stalker. Knowing someone was a traitor was causing just about everything to break down.

True to his word Shane had stayed by her side almost every minute of every day since she'd gone to the hospital. Not that she had minded. The opposite in fact.

They fit together.

For lack of a better word that wouldn't have her owe

money to the jar, it scared the be-hoohoo out of her how well he fit into her life. How well both of them seemed to fit with each other considering they were pretty much loners. Neither of them wanted clingers or someone who made undue demands on their time. Yet both of them found the other's presence comforting.

It had nothing to do with Shane the security expert and everything to do with Shane the man. His presence . . . soothed something in her. Something Chloe hadn't even been aware was so ragged until it rubbed against him and became smoother.

Had it been anyone else so close she would've gone bat-shit crazy, for sure. And even though she liked being with him, she knew this situation couldn't work long-term.

Although it was just fine this very second, as he was kissing her senseless on the couch in the Pit. "Are you going to stay on top of me for the rest of your life?" she asked again when his lips lifted from hers.

He raised an eyebrow. "Well, actually I don't mind being under you or a number of other positions."

She shook her head. "I need you gone." Her actions completely belied her words as she began kissing his neck, pulling him closer.

"Now you're just hurting my feelings," he said. "You're going to have to make it up to me." He pulled her leg over his hip and shifted his weight down on her, causing them both to groan. They knew they couldn't do this. Not now, not here. Not when there were a number of people who might walk in at any moment, including one of the five million new security guards.

Chloe sat up, reluctantly pulling away from Shane. He did too, but he kept an arm around her on the couch, stretching his long legs—back in the pressed khakis—out in front of him.

"The team and I need to get the season finale written."

"I thought you weren't filming that for a few weeks yet?"

"We're not, but we've got to get the details worked out. Topping last year's conclusion is going to be tough enough creatively. Plus, given that no one is fully focused on just the show, we're already running at a deficit." She rolled her shoulders. "The creative team and I want to give them the very best story we can. They're going to need it."

"I don't want to risk your health."

There hadn't been a Conversation Hearts attack all week. She hadn't heard anything from him at all. "Maybe he already got his girl. Maybe he's done. We don't have any proof that you are actually blocking him from my mind."

"That's true."

"Plus, like I said, you can't stay on top of me forever. You've got other things to do. A life to live."

He picked her up and shifted her so she was across his lap. "Right now, let's worry about catching the stalker and getting Conversation Hearts out of your head. This is my job, but moreover there isn't anywhere else I want to be."

The words did something to her heart. Something that made her feel all feminine and gooey.

And hot. Very, very hot.

"Me too. But I also want to get the show where it needs to be."

"On top."

She shrugged. "Honestly, it being popular doesn't mean much to me except that it allows it to keep going. I wouldn't know what to do with myself if I couldn't create these stories. This world. Tia's world." She kissed him and stood. "Even if Alexandra has been giving me the eye of death all week."

Chloe turned away so he couldn't see how happy her own words made her. Alexandra wasn't a bad person, and as actresses went, wasn't even that finicky. But the woman definitely hadn't been very excited that she and Shane were a couple now.

Alexandra couldn't fathom how anyone would choose Chloe over her. Chloe had a little bit of a difficult time processing it also.

"Okay, so you need to do work, and my awesomeness distracts you."

She flung a dishtowel at him, which he caught easily, and moved to the coffee pot, brewing it strong and dark like they both preferred. "The team can't get the magic going with others around. Especially others who happen to distract me."

He kissed her on the way to the coffeemaker, pressing her against the counter. "Turnabout is fair play, since you distract me just by breathing."

"While I'm glad the feeling is mutual, it doesn't help me get these scenes written. You've got to go, Westman. I need forty-eight hours. The creative team and I will have a lock-in. Get written what we need to."

Shane reached behind her and grabbed a coffee mug from the rack. "No problem. I'll just go hang out with Alexandra."

Chloe snatched the cup out of his hand. "No coffee for you, you stinking traitor."

He smiled and reached down to nip her lip with his teeth. "I'll stay out. Give you the room you need to work. But the deal is, if you start to get any Conversation Hearts vibes, then you call me as soon as possible, and we'll see if I can help you ice it out. Don't wait until you're comatose on the floor."

"Deal."

"And I promise to keep away from Alexandra."

She handed him the coffee cup. "Okay, I guess you're allowed to have coffee. Maybe."

FORTY-EIGHT HOURS TURNED to over seventy-two. It wasn't the longest time the creative team had spent locked away. But it seemed like it for Chloe.

The first twenty hours went by fairly quickly. Ideas were flowing; the teammates, trapped in the Pit, were working well off one another. Noah brought them food when they needed it and anything else they asked for. Chloe hardly noticed that Shane wasn't around and was thankful that Conversation Hearts was quiet also.

The next day, things took a turn for the worse. Justin got sick with a fever and sore throat and slept most of the day. Finally, he decided to leave and go see a doctor. That broke the flow they had. Words and ideas seemed to dry up, even though Justin wasn't the driving force behind many of those they were working on.

"All he wants to concentrate on is the psychics angle anyway," Travis muttered after Justin left.

Nadine moved behind Travis's chair to rub his shoulders. "Yeah. That's going to have to wait until next season if we get it in at all. He's obsessed with this serial killer targeting psychics story."

Chloe scrubbed her hand across her face. "Yeah, he mentioned it again after the break. Evidently there's been another killing?" Honestly, Chloe hadn't been paying much attention. She had enough of her own worries without having to borrow someone else's.

Travis and Nadine both nodded. "Yeah. Another in South Carolina and one here while we were on the break. Evidently the guy finds them online, goes in for a reading, and kills them," Nadine said.

Chloe shook her head. "Maybe Justin's right. Maybe we should get a psychic plot thread going now while there's some buzz."

"I don't think we should jump on a bandwagon just

because it's got some media attention," Travis said. "It doesn't fit into the overall concept organically."

Chloe nodded. "That's true. If it's not going to flow, we don't want it in, no matter how much buzz is on it right now." She sat back at the table. "Was it just me, or is Justin getting even more difficult to be around?"

Nadine rolled her eyes. "He's always been that way. Brilliant but difficult."

"We've got to go on without him. We're not even halfway done." The two-hour finale cliffhanger required the unraveling of so many strings that had been knotted together over the season. Plus, adding some sort of unexpected element that would have viewers biting their fingernails until the new season began.

The next two days dragged by at a snail's pace. They wrote, bounced ideas off one another, took turns sleeping, and made inches of progress at a time. More ideas were scrapped than were suggested.

Chloe invited some of the more fledgling members of the creative team to join them to try to get more energy in the room. She was tempted to bring in some of the security team she knew had to be hovering around outside. Anything had to be better than this.

And she missed having Shane around. They'd successfully proven that either he did not need to be in her general proximity to block Conversation Hearts from her head, or he didn't block the other man at all. But evidently, she didn't need Shane around as a mental bodyguard.

Which made Chloe happy. They couldn't live their entire future attached at the hip. Not that they'd talked about an attached one in any sort of way.

Shane was probably glad to have the freedom—and honestly, she'd expected to have felt more relieved herself—during these three days apart. She was not the clingy type.

Not the kind to depend unduly on others. She was always going to get wrapped up in her writing and forget everything else existed. Hell, she'd been known to go for days without brushing her hair or eating a full meal when she was in the middle of one of her creative sprees.

But this time Shane had always been in the back of her mind. Just sort of there, like a talisman that protected her.

And she missed him. Maybe it was being trapped with Nadine and Travis, who seemed so happy together.

But either way Chloe didn't like it. Didn't want to feel like she couldn't get by on her own. Because otherwise, how would she cope when he finally left? She should probably start easing back now.

When they finally released themselves from the Pit early the next morning, agreeing that the creative fire they needed couldn't be found in the current circumstances, Nadine and Travis headed in their own direction together, probably to Nadine's trailer. Chloe stood there in the residential section of the set, trying to figure out where she should go. Her own trailer, right? That's where she should go to sleep in her own bed. And yet her steps began to take her toward the security offices.

Toward Shane. And she couldn't seem to stop herself.

The voice behind her ear stopped her. "I hope you got all your writing done, because that might have been the longest three days of my entire life."

She tried to wipe the huge smile off her face before turning around to face Shane but couldn't manage it. "It was utter shit."

"The writing or being away from each other?" His arms slid around her.

Her tension eased at his touch. So much for pulling back. She wouldn't know how to even if she could find the strength to do it.

She eased into his strength, smelled the scent of his body pressed against hers.

"Both."

"In that case, I won't tell Nadine you owe another dollar for the curse jar."

Chloe shook her head against his chest, winding her arms tighter around his waist. "After the last three days, I owe her so much money for that damned jar I'm going to have to get a second mortgage for my house."

"That bad, huh?"

"Yes. Justin got sick, so we lost him, and then progress slowed to a crawl. It happens that way sometimes, but it doesn't mean I have to like it."

His hand reached up to stroke her hair. Chloe was afraid she was going to start purring like a cat. "Any problems with Conversation Hearts?"

She shook her head. "Nothing. So I'm not sure what that means. Maybe he's gone for good. Who knows?"

He pulled her closer. "Are you needed here on the set?"

"Only if the stunt department is looking for someone who can be used to beat the sh . . . crap out of something. I could definitely use the tension release."

"How about"—his fingers slid to the nape of her neck—"if we head back to my house for a few hours and work on that tension release?"

"You want me to beat the crap out of you instead? That's pretty kinky, Westman."

Shane chuckled. "How about you let me have my best shot at loosening your tension, and if I can't manage, then you can beat the crap out of me? Which I still think is a curse word, by the way."

"If it is, it's only worth a quarter," she muttered.

Shane's hands moved around to cup her face. "You up for a little tension release?" He nipped at her lips.

There were so many reasons why she should say no. Slow this down. Keep her heart guarded.

Damned if she could think of a single one of them.

They began walking toward his car. "Well, I guess if you insist—"

Chloe broke off as a woman's petrified scream echoed just a few yards away from them.

Chapter 19

Shane thrust Chloe behind his back to keep her out of the path of any danger and had his weapon raised at the scream.

Three seconds later Alexandra Adams was running at him and throwing herself bodily into his arms.

"Oh my God, my trailer!" the woman sobbed, wrapping her arms around him.

Markus, Alexandra's head of security, was the first to make it to them. Other security team members weren't far behind.

"Miss Adams, what happened?"

"My trailer, Markus!" Alexandra continued to sob and kept herself tightly wrapped around Shane, even as he was trying to disengage.

Shane gripped her arms, pulling her away from him. "Alexandra, what happened? Are you hurt?"

"N—no." She looked up at him through those green eyes that had made her a household name across the nation. "But I'm so scared."

If she wasn't hurt, he needed to check out the trailer. He

reached down to where her arms were clamped around his waist and pulled her away. While she was still sobbing, he handed Alexandra off to one of her personal bodyguards. He turned and glanced at Chloe, who looked like she was trying to process what was happening over Alexandra's sobs.

"You okay?"

She nodded, and Shane turned back to Markus. "Let's check out the trailer."

Weapons raised, they entered the building, covering each other as they searched room by room. Only after they were assured no one was hidden anywhere did they reholster their guns.

Someone had completely ransacked Alexandra's trailer, particularly her bedroom. Had destroyed it from top to bottom, knocking over furniture, ripping through the mattress and pillows, shredding every piece of clothing anywhere in the room.

And a dozen knives had been thrust into the mattress, a note in the middle of them.

Evil actresses must die.

Shane and Markus looked around, touching as little as possible.

"I have to be honest," Markus murmured. "I thought we were going to find a dead body in here."

Shane nodded. "Yeah, that had occurred to me given all the hysterical sobbing."

"Alexandra is an actress. And those knives are pretty jarring."

"Yeah. Especially walking in on her own."

They backed slowly out of the room. "You better believe I'll have one of my personal team checking any buildings she's going into from now on," Markus said.

"We have some cameras set up too that I've been careful not to mention. I don't think any are pointed exactly at this trailer, but maybe we can pick out someone who doesn't belong in this area."

"Shane?" Chloe called from the doorway. "What is it? Alexandra's still pretty shook up. Is someone . . . ?"

"No, no dead body. That's what Markus and I were afraid of also."

"Okay, okay good." Relief was evident in her voice. "What happened?"

"Someone wrecked her bedroom. Destroyed everything. It's better if you don't come in, helps keep the crime scene cleaner."

"Okay."

Shane and Markus exited, touching as little as possible. The three of them stepped outside. Markus left to report back to Alexandra, who was still crying, surrounded by her assistants and some of the other actors, but at least wasn't hysterical any longer.

"There are probably a dozen knives stabbed into her mattress," Shane told Chloe. "It's not hard to see why she was so upset. Especially since tension has run so high recently anyway."

Chloe rubbed a hand across her face. "The studio is going to want to add another hundred security guards. *If* we can even convince Alexandra to stay."

Shane looked over at the other woman and then back to Chloe. "Maybe I was wrong, and she really is the target. Maybe it's someone from her past who has a grudge against her. We'll look more closely."

Chloe nodded, and Shane touched her arm. There was nothing he wanted more than to slip away with her like they'd been talking about just a few minutes before. Show her exactly how much he'd been missing her while she'd been holed away writing. He pulled her just the slightest bit toward him, aware there were eyes on them and that Chloe may not be big on PDA.

But she stepped closer. "You've got work," she murmured.

"I'd rather have you. In my bed. Right now."

Her smile was gorgeous. "We've got time. Neither of us can slip away now, and we both know it."

Watchers be damned, Shane trailed a finger down her cheek. She didn't pull away. "I don't like it."

"I don't either. Later. Promise."

He had every intention of making her keep that promise. But Alexandra started wailing again, and Chloe hurried to see if she could help. Shane called Sheriff Linenberger to let him know what had happened and to send a crime scene team.

Shane spent the entire rest of the afternoon coordinating the efforts to try to find out who had access to Alexandra's trailer. The CSI processed the scene and would run everything, hopefully providing them with a set of fingerprints to work with. Although Shane wasn't holding his breath.

Two members of the security team had been tasked with watching the closed-circuit television footage from the security cameras they had set up. The problem was, going through forty-eight hours of footage, looking for someone who was probably around all the time wasn't very conducive to finding the stalker. Unless someone did something overtly suspicious, there wouldn't be much to see.

And Shane was already kicking himself for not having a camera directly pointed at Alexandra's trailer. But he'd truly believed that she wasn't the target.

Alexandra herself constantly demanded his attention. For the first few hours, he cut her some slack; anyone would be a little traumatized by finding their possessions in that state, not to mention a bed full of knives. But after having her next to him every moment, constantly asking him to explain what was going on and what they would do to make sure she was safe, Shane knew he had to find a way to get rid of her.

If his Special Forces buddies could hear that. Shane trying to find a way to put physical distance between him and Alexandra Adams. Any of them would pay a great deal of money to be in his place.

And he'd let them be here for free.

It was the exact reasons why Shane tended to avoid any sort of serious relationships. He couldn't tolerate someone constantly demanding his attention.

He glanced over at Chloe, who had been quietly working all day, even though she'd spent the last seventy-two hours doing so. Given the fact that she wrote one of the most creative shows on television, Chloe was surprisingly low drama and maintenance. Able to take care of herself and her own problems. Not needing constant attention from anyone.

Forget America's sweetheart; Shane would take Chloe over Alexandra any day. For so many reasons.

She looked up from where she was sitting at a desk across the room, on the phone with some executives in Los Angeles, and smiled softly at him.

That was just one of the reasons.

The three days without her hadn't been enjoyable. Hadn't been the breath of fresh air he'd been expecting. As a matter of fact, it had shifted his thinking about a lot of things.

Like staying permanently in Black Mountain.

He could work for Linear Tactical for East Coast–based jobs, instead of going to Wyoming.

Shane wasn't one to make knee-jerk decisions. He liked to study the options and know his best tactical advantage. But the thought of going anywhere without Chloe just wasn't acceptable to him.

He had no idea how she'd come to mean so much to him in such a short period of time, but he wasn't going to fight it.

Instead of freezing someone out, Avalanche was going to let himself thaw.

~

THE NEXT MORNING, they had another all-hands security meeting. Most of the security team had a pretty sleepless night, either on high alert or on the detail trying to figure out how the stalker had gotten into Alexandra's trailer.

Nothing.

Shane had finally crawled into bed with Chloe around five a.m. She hadn't said anything, just pulled him to her and held him as they got whatever sleep they could in the few hours left of the night.

Chloe was sitting next to him now, her silence and calm a direct opposite to Alexandra's mania and hysteria.

"Chloe, I cannot work like this." Alexandra's words were punctuated by a slap to the table with each syllable. "It's not just my physical safety I'm talking about, but my creative synapses are being flattened by the fear. I'm being targeted."

Chloe leaned from her chair and put her arms on the conference table. "I understand, Alexandra, and your safety is of primary importance to everyone. We all take that very seriously."

Alexandra nodded and then turned to Shane. "I'm not trying to be a bitch, but I'm scared. What if I had been in the trailer when the stalker came in? Would I have a dozen knives in me rather than in my bed?" She shuddered and huddled back in her chair.

Shane felt for her. Everyone did. It was impossible to look at Alexandra Adams, any woman, huddled in that chair and not want to break the person who was making her feel so helpless and scared. Even if Shane wasn't interested in her romantically, it didn't mean he didn't want to stop whoever was behind this.

"Nobody thinks you're a bitch or being unreasonable," he said. "But we are going to keep you safe. We will make that happen."

"Our only other option is to shut down production or move it to an enclosed set," Chloe said. "Moving would cause a lot of continuity problems and, of course, wouldn't have the same feel. And shutting down . . ."

Chloe didn't finish; she just shrugged. Shane wasn't well versed enough in the television filming business practices to know what shutting down meant exactly, but he knew it couldn't be good.

Tears rolled slowly down both Alexandra's cheeks. "I don't want us to shut down production. I know the schedule is nearly impossible as it is," she whispered.

Chloe rubbed her fingers over her eyes. "No matter what, it's not worth someone's life."

Markus took a step closer to Alexandra. "We will keep someone with you at all times."

More tears leaked out of those huge green eyes that had made her famous. "No offense, but that's just not enough. Not anymore. Every third person is security around here, and it's still not enough."

"What would be, Alexandra? What would make you feel secure?" Chloe asked.

Alexandra blinked her tears away. "Shane. I want Shane."

You could hear a grasshopper karate chop a fly.

"Excuse me?" Chloe finally asked.

Alexandra unhuddled herself and sat up straighter in her chair. "No offense to Markus or anybody else in my personal protection entourage, but Shane was a real soldier. Knows what true danger looks like and can protect me."

Shane shot a glance a Markus, whose face was like stone.

Shane knew Markus had military experience in his back-ground too, if Alexandra had bothered to check.

"Your security team is more than capable of keeping you safe," Shane responded. "You don't need me."

Surprisingly, Alexandra looked at Chloe, as if Chloe were the one who needed to be convinced. Which actually was pretty damn smart, since there was no way in hell he was going to do it without Chloe giving her blessing. And may not even if she gave it.

Every eye in the room turned to look at Chloe.

"This isn't a good idea," Shane said softly, aware everyone could still hear them. Chloe shrugged as if she honestly didn't know what to do.

Shane turned back to the group. "First of all, I doubt there's anything I would catch that Markus wouldn't. He's more aware of your normal behaviors and patterns and can anticipate your moves."

"No offense to Markus," Alexandra snapped back. "But that can also make him miss things that fresh eyes might see."

"I'm not here to be personal security. You have the best money can buy, Alexandra," Shane said. "I'm here to coordi-nate. Try to gain tactical advantage."

Alexandra looked at Chloe again. "I just can't do my job if I don't feel safe. It won't be my best work, and I refuse to give anything less than that. I would rather pause the shooting of the show."

"And having Shane would make you feel better? Safer?" Chloe was studying Alexandra.

"Something has to." Fear pulled at Alexandra's features again. "All those knives, Chloe . . ." A shudder shook her deli-cate frame.

Chloe put her hand on Shane's arm. "I know you weren't hired to be anyone's bodyguard, but Alexandra is right. She needs to be able to concentrate on her work, not on the stalker. If you would be willing to be part of her team, that might be the best thing."

Shane could understand the point, but the last thing he really wanted was to spend all his time around Alexandra.

"It's not my preference. I might be needed for other things." Like if Chloe had another Conversation Hearts attack.

Other people in the room began talking softly to one another to give Shane and Chloe a semblance of privacy. But Shane also knew everyone was listening to what they were saying to each other.

Chloe scooted closer to him in her chair. "This is not my preference either. Trust me, sending you to stay with one of America's most gorgeous women twenty-four seven is not what I want to do. But there's nothing more important to me than the show."

"Not even your own health? What if you need me?"

"You won't be far. We just have to make sure of it."

Shane gave a curt nod.

Chloe turned to Alexandra. "Okay, Shane will help out with your security detail until we have more information about the stalker." She turned to everyone else in the room. "We need to get these last weeks of shooting finished. Everyone needs to stay focused on what we're here to do: continue to make *Day's End* the best show on television. Let your security team do their job, and we'll do ours."

Shane went over the plan, where they would be focusing their attention, and the meeting was ended. He slid a hand to Chloe's back as they walked toward the door.

"Shane, I'll see you in my new trailer in a few minutes?" Alexandra called out. Shane felt Chloe stiffen under his fingers.

"Yeah, in a few, Alexandra."

"Lexi, sugar. If you're going to be this close, call me Lexi."

Chapter 20

The next three days were great in terms of production. Obviously having Shane around to protect her gave Alexandra the confidence she needed to truly focus on her work. And honestly, it was some of the best acting Chloe had seen out of her the whole season.

Tia Day, the show's main character, was dear to Chloe's heart. The woman's struggles, strength, and perseverance against overwhelming odds made her remarkable.. Her survival instinct that made her one of the most beloved characters on television.

Watching Alexandra embrace the strength of Tia Day, to reach deep and utilize the same grit Tia would, went a long way in helping Chloe not be upset that Alexandra had wanted Shane with her twenty-four hours a day.

Definitely not all the way, but part of the way. Because although things were going much better production-wise, personally, Chloe could admit that it just sucked. Alexandra's light and flirtatious banter never went over any lines, but it didn't seem quite innocent either. Watching Shane around Alexandra hurt something in Chloe.

She missed having him around. Not just the sex, although heaven knew she missed that too, but just talking to him. Being around him. Getting each other's coffee. He'd been such a huge part of her life the last three weeks that now his absence was noticeable.

That certainly did not bode well for when he eventually left. Because they were either going to catch this stalker, or the studio would change their filming locations. Regardless, she knew what she had with Shane was temporary. She couldn't very well see herself moving to Wyoming. And couldn't see him staying on the set for the rest of his life.

She pushed the thought out of her head. At least the writing was finally going well. Justin was back from whatever flu he'd had, and even though he was still in just as bad of a mood as always, they were able to get the season finale written. And written well.

"If Shane's presence is going to cause her to act this well, maybe we should talk the studio into hiring him as her full-time personal entourage," Nadine said about Alexandra as they watched a particularly emotional scene where she had to choose between saving one friend or another.

"Yeah, don't remind me," Chloe said. She looked over at Shane standing near where Alexandra would be returning to sit between scenes. Admittedly, he wasn't watching Alexandra; he was constantly observing other people, looking for potential threats.

Especially since another had come in the form of a letter yesterday. Chloe hadn't seen it, hadn't wanted to, but heard it had arrived in the mail and had targeted Alexandra specifically. Violently.

Alexandra Adams must die.

Typed just like the other notes from the stalker. Blood dripped on the paper for good measure.

So Shane was watching diligently for any signs of danger.

That was always the case. Chloe had never once seen him looking at Alexandra with anything other than complete professionalism. Alexandra was a job to Shane. Chloe knew that. Knew he was an honorable man.

That still didn't mean that she liked having one of the most gorgeous women in the world fawning all over him.

"Are we still up to go see that cliff area and the cabin Noah found tomorrow?" Nadine asked.

"Yeah. How about if it's just you and me? We'll leave Travis behind. And Shane will be working anyway. We could use a little time just the two of us." Chloe slipped her arm through Nadine's. "I can't remember an instance when both of us had . . . boyfriends at the same time."

Boyfriend. Was that what Shane was? He seemed like so much more. Although in reality it wasn't even that, since they'd never spoken about it.

Nadine got that gooey smile. "Yeah, I think Travis really might be the one. For both of us to be writers? He understands me. Understands deadlines. Understands the importance of the show. I don't want to jinx it, but I like him so much, Chlo. Our time in Wilmington was fantastic. He even showed me his sailboat."

Chloe smiled at her friend. "Good. You deserve someone who understands and appreciates you. That he loves the show so much is just a bonus."

"I know." Nadine beamed.

"Okay, so we are on for tomorrow. They might make us take security, but that's fine. It'll be nice to get out of here for a few hours."

The scene in front of them wrapped. There was some applause at Alexandra's performance, and she gave a slight curtsy before flouncing over to her chair. And Shane.

Alexandra's hand immediately flew to Shane's arm as she reached up on her tiptoes to tell him something. Shane nodded, keeping his arms crossed over his chest. It was all professional, but Chloe still didn't like it. She ground her teeth as she turned away to walk back toward her trailer.

"I'll catch you later. I'm grabbing lunch with Travis." Nadine's goofy love smile was still plastered all over her face. Chloe gave her a smile back. It wasn't Nadine's fault that Alexandra's hand seemed to be permanently attached to Shane's bicep.

Nadine went off in her own direction as Chloe walked toward the trailer. This was not the direction she wanted to go. She wanted to go to Shane. Just wanted to touch him. Say hello.

Oh hell, who was she kidding? She wanted to march over there, plant a huge kiss on his lips, and stake her claim.

Would that embarrass Shane? Would he even allow her close enough to do it?

Would Alexandra see it as a challenge and just decide to work even harder to get Shane's attention? Because the woman was definitely taking advantage of his physical proximity.

Chloe kept walking in the other direction. She grimaced as tightness gathered in her head again.

Conversation Hearts.

She was thankful that he'd stopped blasting his emotions through her mind lately. She hadn't had any more blinding headaches or nosebleeds. Something had changed. He was still there, more obvious than everyone else, except now his thoughts were quiet.

Now his silence screamed through her mind. It wasn't nearly as painful, but it was scary as hell.

He was waiting. He had a plan; she knew it. Chloe couldn't help but feel sorry for the poor girl he had set his attention on. She knew he definitely didn't have her yet;

there was no satisfaction in his emotions. But he knew he would have her soon.

Feeling Conversation Hearts butting up so heavily against the insides of her mind had made sleep difficult. Or maybe it was not having Shane around.

Chloe shuddered. Was it too much to ask to want to get rid of both the stalker on the set, the one in her mind, and get her boyfriend out of the clutches of a gorgeous actress?

Chloe forced herself all afternoon to stay away from anywhere Alexandra, and thus Shane, might be. She had calls to make, reports to file, and budgets to create for next season. A number of things that she needed to do. That she *tried* to do. But really all she could do was think about Shane.

She just needed to see him. Touch him just for a second. How pathetic was that?

She wanted to feel the coolness of his emotions inside her mind coupled with the heat his touch brought her body.

Chloe knew she could find him near where catering was providing dinner. Knew the cast and crew were doing another scene tonight so Alexandra would still be on set.

And damn it, she was going to see him.

Chloe all but marched to the catering hall. As she stepped in the doorway she saw Alexandra first. The other woman's eyes met hers from across the room where she was grabbing a cup of coffee, then kept Chloe's gaze as she walked slowly back to the table and sat down next to Shane, who was texting someone on his phone.

Alexandra motioned for Shane to move in closer so she could tell him something. Something that made Shane smile before nodding.

It was only after Shane's gaze was fixed on her that Alexandra moved her eyes from Chloe's.

Chloe wasn't sure what to do. Wasn't sure what Shane would even say if she came closer. He was still leaning toward Alexandra. True, Alexandra was known for being friendly with her touches. But Shane didn't look very interested in pulling away. Not that Chloe could blame him.

She had done this. She'd given him permission, even encouraged him to become Alexandra's personal bodyguard.

What sort of idiot was she?

Chloe wasn't an unsure person. She learned at an early age to be independent. Self-sufficient. But hell if she knew what to do now. To stay or go.

Shane was just doing his job. There were more important things at stake than the casual hookup between the two of them. Then why did it feel like this moment was the tipping point for everything?

Chloe turned. She should go.

"Stay."

She'd been so wrapped up in her own thoughts, she hadn't felt the coolness surround her mind, but now it was unmistakable. Shane was right there behind her, but she found it impossible to turn.

"There's nowhere I would rather be, no other person I'd rather be with, than you." His hands spun her around so he was standing directly in front of her, so close she could smell the scent of him. Fresh. Male. Shane.

"I know you have a job to do," she murmured. "I just didn't think this would be so hard. You being with her all the time, especially knowing she wants you."

"I don't give a rat's ass what Alexandra Adams wants. She can't have me. I want you."

If possible, he stepped even closer. They were touching now from shoulder to knee. She finally looked up at him, her gaze immediately caught by those blue eyes. He moved his hands to her hips.

"You did catch me texting on the job though." He pulled

her flush against him. "Telling Markus to get his ass over here because I needed to see you tonight."

Chloe glanced for a second over his shoulder and saw Alexandra studying them through narrowed eyes.

"Alexandra's not going to like that."

"Perhaps you didn't hear the part about the rat's ass."

"You owe the curse jar a few dollars."

Shane's lips moved till they were just inches from hers. She could almost feel herself breathing him in. Them breathing each other in. She wanted to resist, to hang on to her independence. She fought it.

"The curse jar will have to bill me. I need you." He set his forehead against hers. "I need you, Chloe."

The last of her resistance fled. "You can have me."

Shane's phone beeped, and he grabbed it from his pocket to look at it. "Thank God. Markus is here."

He turned to look back through the catering hall and gave a nod. Then he grabbed her hand and pulled Chloe out the door. She could hear Alexandra screeching behind them, but Shane didn't even so much as slow down.

Chloe was nearly having to run to keep up with him. "Shane, slow down. I—"

He paused and backed her against the side of the security office trailer. The air left her lungs in a rush as he slammed his mouth down on top of hers. There was no finesse in this kiss, just need and hunger. Chloe didn't care, wasn't interested in stopping it. She was already coming apart inside. When he pulled back, they were both breathing hard.

"I'm going to need you to walk faster, peanut. Because if you don't, the boys in the security room watching the CCTV feed are going to get much more of an eyeful than I think either of us want. Not to mention anyone walking by."

He began walking again, and this time Chloe was right beside him.

The second the door was closed on her private trailer, Shane had her against the wall again, his lips back on hers.

"This is as far as I can make it."

It was far enough.

He stopped for a second to remove the waist holster and set his gun on the counter, and then he was back on her. Chloe peeled his jacket off his shoulders as he untucked her shirt from her jeans and pulled it over her head. The rest of their clothes were soon scattered on the floor as he grabbed protection.

"Your khakis are going to get wrinkled," she said against his mouth.

He laughed. "This is worth wrinkled khakis." He moved his lips down to her throat and bit at the place where her neck and shoulder joined. Chloe felt like her body was on fire, every part of her alive with excitement. She clutched his shoulders, pulling him closer, as he grabbed the nape of her neck and held her in place for his mouth to go wherever it wanted.

They both moaned.

"I can't wait," he said against her shoulder, kissing back up her jaw.

"I don't want you to." She hooked a leg over his thigh, pulling his naked body closer to hers, then let out a sigh as he reached down and hoisted her legs around his hips. They both stopped breathing, only able to feel, as he slid inside her.

She felt only Shane. Heard only Shane. Knew only Shane.

And it was all she'd ever wanted.

Chapter 21

The next morning, Shane's phone was beeping nonstop. He checked the messages but didn't respond.

"I'm assuming Alexandra isn't happy," Chloe said from where she was tucked next to him in the bed.

"Alexandra will get over it. She's safe; she has all the security she needs. She's fine." He tightened his arm around her, pulled her closer, and kissed her forehead. "Good morning."

"We did say that you could be assigned to her."

"And I'm still willing to be. But that doesn't mean that I'm by her side twenty-four hours a day, seven days a week. Everybody gets time off."

"For good behavior?" She grinned at him. "Because I think some of yours last night actually qualifies as very naughty."

He loved to see her so relaxed. Even if he knew they both had to get back to the real world soon, right now it was just the two of them.

"I don't recall you complaining last night." He felt her slide her foot up and down his calf.

"No, no complaints whatsoever. The opposite in fact." He felt her lips against his shoulder. "I guess you've got to go back to her today. I sort of feel like the other woman."

Shane reached his arm around her hips and rolled her on top of him so she was lying on his chest. "You are very definitely not the other woman. You are the *only* woman."

"That's easier to believe right now when we're both in this bed, but it's a little bit more difficult when you have one of the most gorgeous women on the planet hanging all over you, like she does after every scene."

Shane gripped her hair gently to force her eyes up to his. "Temporary," he said simply. "We're going to catch the stalker, and this will all be over."

She shifted her eyes away again. "Exactly. This will *all* be over."

She was talking about *them,* he realized. "Is that what you want, for us to be over too once the stalker is gone?"

"Is it what you want?"

"You know I have a job waiting for me out in Wyoming. We—"

His phone rang this time, cutting him off, and he let out a curse under his breath, grabbing it. "Damn it, it's Sheriff Linenberger. I've got to take this."

"Of course," Chloe whispered, slipping off him and walking toward the bathroom.

"Chloe—"

"It's okay, we'll talk later," she said, still not looking at him.

Shane cursed again and hit the button on his phone. "Westman."

"Shane, it's John."

"What's going on, Sheriff?"

"I had some of my boys doing follow-up on where the

cast and crew were during the break. Came up with a discrepancy."

"What sort?"

"Seems that one of the crew had bought a ticket to Portland but ended up at a cabin just outside of Charlotte."

Shane sat up. "Who?"

"Guy by the name of Justin Poll."

Shane's expletive definitely would've cost him a dollar.

"I'm assuming you know the guy? I don't recollect ever talking to him."

"Yeah, he's part of the writing team. Not very sociable, so I'm not surprised that you haven't had much contact with him in town."

"Writing team? As in, works with Chloe on a regular basis?"

"Yep. As in, every day."

Now it was the sheriff's turn to curse. John knew as much as Shane how much Chloe didn't want the stalker to be someone they worked closely with.

"I think we need to bring him in for questioning," the sheriff said. "I can't let you do it, but I can let you observe. Maybe he has an alibi for the cabin, and we won't even need to let Chloe know about this."

"That sounds good. Send someone to pick him up quietly. I'll get to the station as soon as I can."

Shane hung up with the sheriff and made a call to Markus, explaining the situation. Alexandra would have to wait even longer before she had her pet bodyguard back.

Chloe was coming out of the bathroom, obviously having taken a very quick shower. She'd already dressed in jeans and a T-shirt.

"Everything okay?" She was pulling her long blonde hair back in a ponytail.

"Yeah, I just need to go to town and check out a few

things. Leads the sheriff might have. I'll let you know if it comes to anything."

"This afternoon Nadine and I are going to check out a set location Noah found. It's a cabin on a cliff an hour or so from here. It might be perfect for what we have envisioned for the season finale."

Having Chloe out of the way while they checked out Justin was probably a good idea.

"Not just the two of you, right? You're taking somebody from the security team?"

She damn well would be. Shane wished he could go himself.

Chloe nodded. "Kassler."

"Okay, good. Kassler is good."

They stood there, staring at each other awkwardly. Shane wanted to bring back up the subject they were discussing before, mainly to get her opinion about him sticking around rather than going to Wyoming, but the moment had passed. It would have to wait.

"Um, I'm going to head out and let you take a shower. I know we both have stuff to do," she said, moving farther away.

"Chloe, we need to talk."

At his words, her features shuttered more. "A big talk isn't necessary. This was always temporary, right? We both knew that. No need for either of us to get caught up in emotions or anything."

Shane's shoulders straightened. He guessed he had his answer: she definitely wasn't interested in him staying once they caught the stalker. "Right. No need to get caught up. Exactly."

She nodded. "I guess I'll catch you later. Or maybe even tomorrow. Nadine and I need to see the new set possibility at twilight, so I'm not sure when I'll be back."

"Yeah, I'll be with Alexandra, so I probably won't be available. She, at least, wants me around." He knew it was a low blow even as he said it. Her flinch confirmed that. Damn it. "Chloe . . ." He reached for her, but she slid by him, and he couldn't go after her in his current state of undress.

"Catch you later, Avalanche."

He watched her walk out the door.

～

JUSTIN POLL WAS a pasty bastard with dark eyes that constantly darted around and uptight posture that screamed surly. Shane hadn't talked to him much—hell, nobody seemed to talk to him much, the guy was so prickly. Chloe had mentioned how Justin didn't get along with others. But evidently, he was a damn good writer, so she kept him around.

But given how pale and stiff the guy was, Shane was certain he did not get out and enjoy the North Carolina mountains around him.

Shane and Sheriff Linenberger stood watching Deputy Hammell, the same deputy who had taken Shane and Chloe's statements after the attempted shooting on the set, through the two-way mirror in the small interrogation room of the county sheriff's office. Just like they had been for the past two and a half hours.

"He's hiding something, that's for sure," Shane said. "And it's damn suspicious to be in town both during the break *and* to have gotten 'sick' on the same night Alexandra's trailer was destroyed."

"You think he's the guy?" the sheriff asked.

"I want him to be our guy." Wanted to have this stalker put away behind bars. Wanted to put all this behind him as soon as possible so he could make up for the dumbass stuff he'd said to Chloe this morning.

"If Justin lawyers up, we'll have to let him go," the sheriff said, arms crossed over his chest. "Except for the fact that he was in the general vicinity, there's absolutely nothing to tie him to any crime. An attorney would have him out in under five minutes. And even if he doesn't get a lawyer, we can only hold him for twenty-four hours without some sort of charge."

Justin had been notified that he could have counsel with him but had declined. That either made him stupid, conceited, or innocent of wrongdoing. Shane knew he wasn't stupid. And he knew he *was* conceited. He just didn't know if Justin was innocent or not.

The man could certainly talk in circles. For every question Hammell asked, Justin had three of his own plus suggestions for investigative elements that law enforcement might have missed. Some of them weren't half bad.

The guy really was brilliant, which didn't surprise Shane at all. Chloe wouldn't hire someone who wasn't.

"Mr. Poll, explain to me again why you were holed up in a cabin outside of Charlotte over the break rather than going back to Portland like you'd planned," Hammell asked again. He hadn't gotten a straight answer the first two times he'd asked.

Justin shrugged, then sighed out loud. "I decided it wasn't worth the trek across the country. I just wanted to be alone, and I could do that just as easily here."

"Why did you want to be alone, Mr. Poll?"

Justin's eyes narrowed. "Look, what is this all about? I haven't heard anything about you pulling anyone else in for questioning. Yes, I wanted to be alone. I like to be alone. Anyone could tell you that."

"Damn it, we're going to lose him," Sheriff Linenberger said. "He's going to lawyer up."

"Let me go in there and talk to him, John. I know I'm not law enforcement, but maybe he'd be more willing to talk to me."

"You know you'd have no authority in there, right? You couldn't compel him to answer anything. You'd just be friends talking. He could leave at any time."

Shane inclined his head. "It looks like he's close to that anyway."

The sheriff nodded, then walked with him into the interrogation room, allowing Hammell to go on a break.

"Westman." Justin threw his arms up in the air. "What the hell is going on? Are they questioning you also?"

Shane took the seat directly across from Justin. The sheriff leaned against a side wall, out of Justin's line of sight.

Shane decided a straight approach would be better with this man. He was too hard to deal with to waste time on pleasantries.

"We've got a problem, Justin. How about if you stop talking circles around everyone just because you can, and we try to solve that problem together rather than waste time butting heads with each other?"

Justin sat back in his chair, crossing his arms over his chest. "Do you expect me to just come out and admit I'm the stalker? Full confession, right now, just because Mr. Navy SEAL comes in and starts putting pressure on me?"

So he wasn't going to stop talking in circles. But that didn't necessarily mean he was guilty. It just meant the man liked to play.

"One, trust me when I say Rangers get offended when you refer to them as Squids, but I'll let that slide, because, once again, you're back to talking in circles. Do you like your job, Justin?"

His eyes narrowed. "Yessss." He drew the sound out.

"Your records say you got fired from your last job for taking too much personal time. That you're sort of sickly."

"So?"

"So it's pretty interesting that those 'sickliness' periods—when you happen to be alone—coincide with when the stalker was known to be on the *Day's End* set. If we were to look into the days you took off at your other job due to being *sick*, would we find some suspicious behavior there also? Maybe another stalker that just hasn't been linked to this one yet?"

Now Justin sat up straighter. "No, you wouldn't. I was not a stalker then. I am not the stalker now." There was a long silence. "I love my job on *Day's End*."

Justin didn't say anything else, but Shane could hear the "but" as loudly as if the man had yelled it.

"Tell me, Justin." Shane put his elbows on the table and leaned toward him. "Whatever it is, just tell me."

But he didn't. It was a stare down in silence between the two of them. For once, Justin wasn't talking.

And as much as Shane wanted this surly jackass to be the stalker, Shane didn't think he was. It came back to not calling a lawyer. It would've been the first thing he'd done if he were guilty.

Finally, Shane stood. It didn't do anybody any good for Shane to stay if they weren't going to get any further info from Justin.

"I'll leave you to him, Sheriff, to charge or release as you see fit." Shane turned to Justin. "Every minute I waste on false leads is a minute I'm not protecting the show. Not protecting the job you claim to love so much."

Shane turned to leave.

"Westman." Shane stopped but didn't look back. "I'm not the stalker."

Now he turned. "So you said. But I also know two things, Justin. One, you are in fact, smart enough to be the stalker and two, you are keeping secrets."

Justin sighed and looked over at the sheriff. "Do you have a pen and piece of paper?"

Sheriff gave him both, and Justin scribbled something on the sheet, then slid it across the table. Sheriff Linenberger picked it up.

"Two names and numbers," he said to Shane. "Who are these people?" he asked Justin.

Justin remained focused on Shane. "I'm telling you this because I've been writing suspense long enough to know when the final scene is coming. When something big is about to go down. So you're right, Westman, every minute you waste on false leads is a minute longer the show is left unprotected. Something's coming. Something bad."

Shane took a step toward him. "You're not the stalker."

"I'm not the stalker. But I am an alcoholic. It's why I got fired from my last show. And it's where I was both over the break and when I got 'sick' during the writing lock-in. Those numbers won't give you exact alibis, but the people will attest I wasn't in any shape to do anything as meticulous as trying to shoot at someone or breaking into a trailer unnoticed. They were partying with me for most of the time."

Shane looked at John, who nodded. "We'll run them. Make sure he's telling the truth."

Shane didn't have much doubt Justin was.

An hour later they had their confirmation. The contacts Justin provided could confirm that he'd been with them, and inebriated, for the times in question.

Shane left the sheriff to wrap things up with Justin and headed back to the set. He was glad Justin wasn't the stalker —having a member of her inner team be the one trying to destroy the show would've devastated Chloe. It was going to hurt her enough when Justin eventually came clean about his alcohol problem.

And Chloe didn't need to be hurt again, especially not today. She'd already been hurt enough with Shane's careless statement about Alexandra. He didn't know why he'd implied that he was going to allow something to happen between him and the actress. It didn't matter if his relationship with Chloe was over or not; Shane was never going to get involved with Alexandra.

She just didn't compare to Chloe in any way that mattered to him.

He'd itched to tell Chloe that all morning through the mess with Justin. Itched to tell her that as he drove back to the set with no more answers than he'd had when he left. He headed straight to her trailer, only to find that he'd missed her by about fifteen minutes, as she'd left with Nadine.

Now he'd have to wait until she got back to apologize. To get their conversation back on track.

Shane knew Chloe's past. Knew how hard it was for her to open up, to make the first move, to trust. He couldn't let his own natural tendencies to pull away ruin the chance he had with someone he was so interested in. He needed to explain that he'd like to see what was happening between them, even once they caught the stalker. Shane was going to need to talk to Zac and see what the options were with Linear Tactical. Because it didn't look like Wyoming was in his near future.

But first they had to catch this damn stalker.

Because Justin was right. Something bad was coming. And it was coming soon.

Chapter 22

By lunch Shane was back on Alexandra detail. He half expected Alexandra to be hysterical after his absence last night and this morning. Walking over to where they were filming on an interior set, Shane found Markus standing watchfully at the door.

"Anything happen while I was gone? I expect she threw a fit."

The older man shook his head. "She wasn't happy but surprisingly kept it together. I hear you have a possible suspect in custody? Nobody knew who it was."

"Justin Poll, part of the creative team. He's got problems, but he's not the stalker. He's been cleared."

"You going to be on Alexandra duty this evening? She wants to get off the set, go to her house."

The last thing Shane wanted to do was go to Alexandra's house with her. Even though they wouldn't be alone, he had no interest in it, especially not after what he'd said to Chloe. But Markus also needed a break.

"Yeah, I appreciate the break last night. I can take the shift tonight." Chloe would be gone most of the evening anyway.

He would find her in the morning, and they would hash this out. "I want to look back over the files. The pictures from the stalker's attacks before I got here and the more recent ones. All the letters. I feel like we're missing something."

Shane was convinced of it. Call it his own psychic senses, but something was wrong. Maybe another attack was about to happen; Shane didn't know. But he damn well wasn't going to let anyone get to Alexandra. He didn't have to like her to be able to protect her.

"Something bad's coming, Markus. I can feel it."

The older man studied Shane. "I've been in this business too long to ignore when someone like you gets a gut feeling. We'll both stay at Alexandra's house and grab a couple other men. I can have a night off later."

Shane nodded. "Why don't you take a break now, then? I'll watch until she's done."

Markus agreed and left, and Shane went inside to watch the recording. Alexandra was a talented actress for sure, but he was too busy watching the other people. Someone here, maybe even in this room, was a liar and would-be killer.

"She's really good." Noah, the intern, stepped up next to Shane, holding two cups of coffee. "Talented. But the show doesn't depend on any one actor or actress. Miss Jeffries is the only one whose loss would cause the show to collapse. Even if Alexandra quit, the show would still go on."

"But she's the title character."

Noah shrugged. "*Day* is the title. If Alexandra quit, Miss Jeffries would just write another character named Day—a sister, brother, somebody. It would still be *Day's End.*"

"I guess that's true. The show must go on, right? Do you think Alexandra knows it?"

"I think Alexandra is playing a dangerous game." Noah's eyes were narrowed as he looked at the woman getting her makeup retouched for the final scene she'd be filming today.

"Dangerous?"

Noah gave a self-depreciating smile. "Dangerous isn't the right word. *Risky* is better. With her career, you know. If she demands too much, they might decide she's not worth it."

"Fire Alexandra Adams?" Shane shook his head. "I don't think they'll do that if they have any other choice."

"But like you said, the show would go on without her. It wouldn't stop. Wouldn't change anything." Noah held up a cup of coffee. "I've learned to carry an extra one when I'm sent to get coffee. Would you like it?"

Shane took it. "Sure, thanks."

"Got to get this over before they dock my non-existent pay." Noah gave a little salute and walked the coffee cup over to the director. The older man said something to him, then Noah slipped out the other door. Chloe was right; that kid never stopped working.

An hour later they were finished shooting. Shane and Markus waited until Alexandra was ready, and then they escorted her to the car. Markus drove, and Shane sat in back, keeping an even-more-careful-than-usual eye out for possible trouble.

"So you're back with me tonight?" Alexandra asked.

"I'm back on your security detail. And yes, I'll be staying at your house tonight, along with Markus and four other members of the team."

"Okay." Shane didn't know why Alexandra was so calm when he'd just told her they'd doubled the security at her house, but he wasn't going to question his good fortune. Nobody needed or wanted a hysterical Alexandra.

The other team members had completely swept Alexandra's two-story cabin by the time they arrived. After a brief meeting, they agreed three men would be inside, two outside, and one on break. They had a couple of hours before it got dark.

Shane couldn't shake his bad feeling.

Catering had made sandwiches and salads to bring with them, which they'd be eating in shifts, always making sure someone had a close eye on the house.

"I'm going to eat first," he told Markus. "We'll give the newer guys their break during graveyard hours." Markus agreed and headed outside. The late-night watch shifts were hard for everyone, particularly to younger guards with less experience. Shane and Markus would take those.

Those shifts were also when someone was most likely to try to attack the house.

Shane got his food and sat down at Alexandra's kitchen table. He also wanted to look over the files again. Couldn't shake the feeling that he was missing something.

"Mind if I join you?" Alexandra had showered and changed into yoga pants and a black sweater. She had no makeup on, and her hair hung damp on her shoulders. It was the best Shane had ever seen her look.

And she still didn't hold a candle to Chloe.

"I'm going over some of the files. Trying to figure out what I'm missing. I'm here to work, Alexandra. That's all."

"I really do wish you would call me Lexi. So few people do. And I obviously know you're with Chloe now. There could be no doubt of that after yesterday's scene at the catering hall."

Shane looked at the woman, so much more human-looking now, makeup free, no fancy clothes, no entourage. She was still beautiful, but studying her closer he could see tension pulling at her eyes, bracketing her mouth. Alexandra Adams wasn't as calm as she appeared to be. Frightened, probably.

"Lexi, then, and you're welcome to sit with me. But yes, Chloe and I are together." He hoped for the long haul. He just had to convince Chloe of that. But first, he would be concentrating on keeping Alexandra safe through the night.

Shane got out the case files and laid them on the table as Alexandra went into the kitchen warming herself up something in the oven.

He looked at all the early photos of what the stalker had left. It started with letters.

Day's End *is evil. The evil must be eliminated.*

Day's End *is evil. Evil must burn.*

The evil of Day's End *will be brought down.*

All basically the same theme, printed in the same plain block font. Nothing unusual about the paper or ink used for the notes.

Next, he'd escalated to notes attached to weapons. Knives. Hunting knives of different sizes. That was when everyone started taking it all a little bit more seriously. It was one thing to get a letter left on the set. Quite another to get one attached to a deadly weapon.

But still the theme had remained the same. The evil of *Day's End*. How it needed to be eradicated.

When the next knife had been covered in blood, that's when Shane had been brought in.

Then the stalker had really upped his game, but in a much subtler form:

The scuba diving and hydraulics accident.

The hot tub building blowing up.

The shooter who had almost killed him and Chloe both.

After that, the sheer amount of security had to make it difficult for the stalker. Everyone was watching everyone else. Hell, there were so many hidden cameras around the set, Shane couldn't even remember exactly where they all were.

So, what? The stalker had taken a step back? De-escalated? Because both the attack on Alexandra's trailer and the letter she'd received the next day seemed to be a step backward, or at least sideways, for this stalker.

That didn't feel right.

Finding a dead body in the trailer, like Shane had half expected when he heard Alexandra's scream, *that* would've been a logical next step for this maniac.

Shane sat back in his chair. As morbid as it sounded, that was what was bugging him about the last few days.

Someone should be dead. Killing was the next step for the *Day's End* stalker. It was what he'd been moving toward from the beginning. It should've been a race to see if they could catch him before he killed someone. The security had made it damn difficult to do so, especially if he hadn't wanted to get caught.

But then he'd turned his focus on Alexandra. Almost taken a step backward. And announced that she was his intended victim.

It didn't make sense. Not from the stalker's tactical standpoint.

"How's it going?" Even though there were a number of seats around the table, Alexandra brought her plate and sat down in the chair right next to Shane.

"I'm just trying to figure this guy out. Make sense of these latest moves."

"Figuring him out, that's important, right? That's how you stop him?"

"Yes. Unless he messes something up; then we'll have to try to figure out who he is from all this." He gestured to the files on the table.

She ate in silence for a while as he studied the pictures, trying to pinpoint what he was missing.

"I feel better having you here," Alexandra finally said after he spent a while studying the information around him.

Shane glanced at her, and she gave him one of her megawatt smiles. He had to hand it to her; she didn't give up.

"Actually, I'm taking my turn inside right now, but I'll be outside most of the night."

Her smile faded. "And if I asked you to stay inside with me? That it makes me feel safer to know that you're next to me?"

"Alexandra." Shane let out a breath, struggling for patience. "Lexi. Your safety is a priority for me. I'll keep you that way by being the one outside during nighttime hours. I have the most experience; it makes the most tactical sense."

"Look, like I said, I know you and Chloe have something going on. But if it's not exclusive . . ." Her hand rested on his arm lightly, her fingers moving in gentle circles. "Or if it needs to be just our little secret . . . I know you take my safety seriously, but I'd like for you to protect me in the house tonight. In my bedroom."

It wasn't even a question for Shane. "No."

Surprise flashed across her features. Alexandra Adams probably wasn't turned down so abruptly by many men.

"*No?* That's it? Just *no?*"

"First of all, I wouldn't do it even if I wasn't involved with someone. I'm on a job. It would be completely unprofessional. But yes, I am involved with Chloe. And it is exclusive. And she is important to me."

More important than he let himself, and especially Chloe, realize. Something he planned to rectify next time he saw her.

Alexandra stood, grabbing her plate. "I can't believe I went to so much trouble to—" She cut herself off.

Shane's eyes narrowed. "What trouble? You went to a lot of trouble to do what?" Shane had no idea what she was talking about. Some sort of seduction scene? Alexandra now looked sad rather than angry. Like she was in pain.

"Never mind. It doesn't matter. If I had seen you and Chloe together in the catering hall before . . ." She trailed off again. "Never mind."

She stalked into the kitchen, and he heard her placing her dishes in the sink. A few minutes later, Alexandra walked by him without a word, went into her bedroom, and shut the door.

"Stay away from the windows. We already know he's good with a rifle," he called out to her.

Alexandra's absence didn't bother Shane in the least. If she confined herself to one room, that would make it even easier for them to protect her.

He looked down at the pictures again. The newest ones from Alexandra's trailer.

Evil actresses must die. That was the one found on her bed with all the knives.

Alexandra Adams must die. The one sent in the mail.

Definitely targeting her. The notes had become more specific. Shane looked at the pictures of them more closely. The notes themselves had changed too. They'd been so busy looking at the content that they hadn't noticed the slight change of font used. It was almost the same, boxy, plain lettering, but it was slightly different.

Both the one found in Alexandra's trailer and the letter that had been received in the mail the day after.

Shane wasn't sure what that meant, if anything. He was a soldier, not a crime scene analyst for crying out loud. Did it mean the stalker was escalating? Changing? Becoming careless? Becoming impatient?

Shane looked at the knives that had been stabbed into Alexandra's mattress. Both the pictures of them in the mattress and ones taken later by the CSI team showing them stacked side-by-side. They were all the same type. Large, formidable-looking kitchen knives.

Kitchen knives.

Shane looked back at the early reports. All the original knives left by the stalker had been *hunting* knives, not kitchen. The same black handle, and even similar in appearance, but different in purpose.

Oh shit.

His phone rang. It was Hobbes from the security trailer.

"Hobbes, what's going on?"

"Shane, where are you? Are you at Alexandra's house?"

"Yes. Why? Did something happen?" Shane couldn't swallow the dread pooling in his throat.

"No. A breakthrough, actually. But you're not going to like it. Nobody's going to."

Shane stood. "Tell me."

"I know we had no good angles covering Alexandra's trailer, but earlier this afternoon I caught a reflection of the trailer on a different feed. So Tony and I have spent hours enhancing the footage from the time leading up to when we found Alexandra's trailer destroyed. We got an ID."

"Who?"

"You're not going to believe me."

Shane rubbed his fingers over his eyes and looked at the closed bedroom door across the hall.

"Alexandra herself," he said.

"Yes. How did you know?"

"I just figured out that the destroyed trailer and the letter the next day were both slightly different. That it probably wasn't from the same person as the other threats."

Hobbes's tone was incredulous. "Why would Alexandra send threats to herself? That doesn't make any sense."

Because she'd wanted Shane nearby. Because she'd wanted the focus on herself. "It doesn't matter. What does is that we've still got a stalker out there, and he's not necessarily after Alexandra. Have you heard from Kassler?"

"Yeah, he's right here, why?"

"Did they have any problems while scouting out the site today?" It would've been a perfect time for an attack. Their focus had been so consumed with Alexandra, assuming the stalker was after her, that everyone else had been basically unprotected.

Shane heard Hobbes talking to Kassler in the background.

"Um, Shane, Kassler didn't go with them. Chloe convinced him he was needed more here, since we all thought Alexandra was the one in danger."

Shane felt like all the oxygen had been sucked out of the room. He took a second and focused.

"Where was the location? Does anyone know?"

"Noah, that intern kid, found it. I'll find him and ask."

Noah. All the pieces were starting to come together for Shane now.

"I want to know right away and send a team out there."

Shane hung up the phone and called Chloe. He cursed when it went straight to voicemail. He tried a text but received no response.

He covered his panic with ice and told Markus to bring the team back into the house. They weren't needed here. Once the men were in, Shane explained what was going on. A few minutes later, Hobbes called him back.

"Shane, we can't find or get in touch with Noah. And none of us of have been successful getting a call through to Chloe or Nadine. I got a bad feeling about this."

The same one Shane had had all day. They had focused their efforts on Alexandra and left the true target unprotected.

Chloe.

And then put her straight into the arms of a maniac. One who looked like the most helpful person on the set: Noah.

The only person whose loss would cause this show to collapse is Chloe.

Noah had announced it to Shane earlier today, but Shane hadn't realized what the younger man was saying.

He looked up and saw Alexandra studying the chaos in her living room, her arms wrapped around herself.

"Why did you do it?" he asked her.

She didn't even pretend like she didn't know what he was talking about.

"I just wanted someone to look at me the way you look at her. Willing to give your life for her. To give her whatever she needs to make her whole." Alexandra took a step forward, but at Shane's sharp look, she moved back. "I just wanted someone to focus on me in that way. I never dreamed it would turn into this."

Shane couldn't even look at her anymore. "Someone stay with her. The sheriff will be by to arrest her soon. I'm going to find Chloe."

Chapter 23

"So I think this is going to work perfectly. We've definitely got to figure out how to give Noah a raise. I don't know how he found this place, but it's breathtaking. We would've never discovered it on our own."

Chloe and Nadine were standing together, looking over a steep mountain drop-off as the sun began to set. To call it gorgeous was an understatement.

"Can you see it?" Chloe asked Nadine. "Can't you just see Tia looking out here, trying to come to terms with the choices she made? The people she had to leave behind?"

"It's definitely perfect." Nadine nodded. "Seriously, I want to come live here."

They'd known it was the right spot for the finale the moment they'd arrived but had stuck around, had dinner, and talked so they could see the lighting as the sun started to go down.

It had been worth the wait.

They watched in silence a few more minutes before heading back to the car in the deepening twilight.

"Shane is going to be pretty mad that we didn't bring Kassler with us," Nadine said.

Chloe just shrugged. They had successfully avoided talking about men all day. It hurt to think about Shane. Hurt to think that it might already be over, that he might have decided that Alexandra was whom he really wanted if she was still making the offer.

Chloe kept her hands on the wheel as she answered, since there were ditches on either side of the road. "I think the stalker has made it abundantly clear that Alexandra is the target. Plus, I just needed to get away from everything. Everybody."

"That's not what I heard about how you and Shane were acting in the catering hall last night. I was told he couldn't keep his hands off you." Nadine shifted her weight so she could lean against the passenger side door and study Chloe.

"Yeah, well, that was last night. And it was good. But this morning . . . I just don't know."

"Was he distant? Did he say something that made you mad?"

"Well, it started when he was about to give me the talk regarding how things aren't permanent. Will never be permanent."

"Are you serious? What a bastard. I can't believe he said that."

Chloe grimaced.

"Wait a minute." Nadine smacked her on the arm. "I know that look. Did he *actually* say those things?"

"No. But he would've. They were coming."

"So let me guess, you said something to shut it down before he could even speak."

"Hey. You weren't there. I was."

Nadine rolled her eyes. "And we both know that you're the best judge when it comes to emotional intimacy. Because you're always willing to give people a shot. You're always willing to be the first to open up to encourage others to do the same."

Everything Nadine was saying was the truth, but Chloe didn't want to hear it. Didn't want to think about the fact that her own defensive nature was what had driven a wedge between her and Shane.

"I can still fire you, you know," she muttered.

Nadine wasn't worried. "You can fire me as part of your creative team but not as your friend. And that's not going to stop me from trying to talk some sense into you."

"He told me he would be with Alexandra when I got back tonight." That had hurt.

"*'With Alexandra'* as in, naked doing the horizontal tango, or as in his job to provide security for her, which you approved?" Nadine asked with one eyebrow raised.

He'd meant his job. She knew it. He knew it. But they both also knew he meant that if Chloe wasn't interested, someone else was.

Someone else who happened to be gorgeous, friendly, and flirty. Not prickly and difficult.

"Let's talk about something else. Like you and Travis. I haven't even had a chance to get the details about how your break went in Wilmington."

"You know Travis; he's a little moody. All creative types tend to be. And I sometimes feel like he's off in another world. But again, that comes with the territory."

"So you guys had fun?"

"Yes. He showed me his sailboat. It was docked in the harbor, and he told me he was going to take me on it someday soon." Nadine grinned. "Which almost made up for the fact that he had to take care of some research alone during our trip."

"What research? And why wouldn't he take you?"

"Who knows? He said he didn't want to talk about it until he was sure it would pan out. I didn't want to fight with him, so I just went along with it."

"Probably smart. He'll share when he's ready. And . . . romance-wise, how were things?"

Nadine's smile faltered just a little. "It was just okay. I think I had built the lovemaking up in my mind to the degree that reality couldn't possibly live up to it. I was tense. He was tense. So it was all just tense. I never really felt like he was truly into it."

Chloe reached out and grabbed her hand. "Oh sweetie, I'm sorry. I'm sure he was into you. It's just a lot of pressure the first time."

"I know. And it wasn't bad; it just wasn't great. And we were both a little anxious to get back to work since that final scene hadn't been started. And then once that psychic was killed nearby, I just wanted to get Travis out of there. You know how he and Justin fight about the topic all the time."

"That's for sure. I'm assuming since Travis is so violently opposed to having psychics in the show that you haven't said anything about me or my voices."

Nadine shrugged. "He's heard rumors, of course. He's asked me about it."

"Shane says it's me using a part of my brain that most people don't. So it's like a child prodigy on a piano or something."

"That's good and probably not untrue. And see, Shane didn't freak out. Another reason to give him a chance."

As if Chloe needed more reasons.

"What about Conversation Hearts?" Nadine asked. "You've looked much better the last few days. I haven't seen any nosebleeds."

Chloe shifted in the driver's seat. "There's been a change.

He's still there, I can feel him, but it's different. I don't know. Maybe he got his girl and he's done. I hope so."

Because right now it was worse than it had been all week. There was no burning pain, but the pressure was building. He was about to do something. Something important. She could feel it, the pressure, like someone was sitting on her chest. It was going down soon.

What Chloe didn't know was if he was going to take her down with him. Maybe this would sever the bond between them, especially since Chloe had no idea why they were attached to begin with.

But maybe it would fry her brain for good. And this time even Shane's coolness wouldn't be able to help. Especially since it didn't look like he'd be close enough to be any sort of shield anyway.

"Well, I say you just need to talk to Sha—"

Both women screamed as a car hit them from behind, almost causing them to go into the ditch.

"What the hell?" Chloe yelled.

Nadine spun around to try and see what was happening. "Do you think the driver is drunk? Should we stop?"

They had their answer a moment later when the vehicle behind them sped up and hit them again. Chloe was barely able to keep their car on the road.

All of a sudden being way out in the middle of nowhere with no members of the security team didn't seem like a good idea, even if this had nothing to do with the stalker.

Chloe hit the gas. The vehicle behind them obviously was bigger and better equipped for some *Mad Max* type ramming. But maybe they could outrun them. Or maybe if this was some sick game he or she would get bored.

But just a few seconds later Chloe realized this was no game. This had been carefully orchestrated. The road became more narrow and treacherous, the ditches on either side of them more steep.

And then Chloe heard the voice in her head.

To stop the evil, the heart of the evil must die.

"Oh my God, hang on Nadine, it's him. The stalker. He's going to hit us again."

"How do you know?"

Chloe just glanced over at her friend, her best friend since she was eight. Nadine understood.

Chloe could hear him.

Chloe tried to slow the car down, knowing she was going too fast for the curves. But as soon as she did, the vehicle behind them—it had to be a truck or Hummer from the height of the headlights—slammed into them again.

Chloe fought to keep the car under control, but she couldn't. The left wheels were already over the side, and they were sliding down the ditch. One last hit from the truck flipped them over.

The airbags deployed, and Chloe clutched the steering wheel as the car slid and flipped, her head cracking against the window. Nadine screamed, trying to brace herself on the door and roof of the car as they flipped again, finally coming to rest at the bottom of the small ravine.

It took Chloe a minute to gather her senses. To take a mental stock. She could move her toes, her fingers, her neck.

"Nadine? Nadine, are you all right?"

She couldn't see anything in the darkness and dust from the airbags. She heard Nadine cough. Chloe wrestled with her seatbelt to unbuckle it. The car had landed upside down, and all her weight was dragging on the belt.

"Nadine, talk to me."

Nadine moaned again. "I'm okay. I think I'm okay."

Chloe finally got her seatbelt to release, and she dropped

onto the ceiling of the car. She reached over to help Nadine do the same.

"We've got to get out of here," Chloe said, kicking at her door to get it open. "The stalker, he's here and wants to kill us. Kill me."

The door gave way, and Chloe eased herself out then turned to help Nadine.

"Do you have your phone?" Hers had been resting in the cup holder, and now she had no idea where it was.

"Yes," Nadine said as Chloe helped them both stand. She tapped the screen. "No service. We're too far out."

"We've got to run."

They began moving away from the car.

"But which way?" Nadine asked.

Chloe tried to think through the fear and pain in her head from where she'd hit the window. She had no idea where the nearest town was. Paralleling the road was probably their best bet.

"Let's just move," Chloe whispered. She could feel him out there. Stalking for real. Hunting. "We need to go."

Chloe and Nadine grasped hands and moved their way around the car. They hadn't gotten very far when someone stepped in front of them, shining a light.

Nadine screamed and then gave a tiny laugh. "Noah! Thank God. Somebody ran us off the road. You've got to get us out of here."

Chloe could feel Noah's eyes on her the entire time Nadine was talking.

Nadine didn't understand, but Chloe did. *Noah* was the one who wanted to kill them.

"You are evil, and you must be destroyed. Burned," Noah said in a voice that sounded nothing like the one they were used to. Nothing like the helpful intern who'd worked with them every day for months.

Nadine was beginning to understand. "Noah?"

Before either of them could react, he pulled out a gun. Chloe heard it make an odd sort of noise as he first shot Nadine, dropping her to the ground, then turned the weapon toward her. Chloe didn't even have time to react to her friend's fallen form before he shot her.

Her hand came up to the sting in her shoulder. A dart. He'd tranquilized them.

It was her last thought before the world faded to black.

Chapter 24

Chloe's head was pounding when she came to. She was handcuffed to a chair inside the same cabin she and Nadine had looked at earlier.

Noah had set this all up from the beginning.

Nadine was sitting in a chair across from Chloe, also beginning to wake up.

Chloe could hear Noah slamming around in the other room, muttering to himself. She was afraid he was trying to work himself up to something pretty horrific.

"Are you okay?" She whispered to Nadine as soon as the woman's eyes were open.

"Yes. You?"

Chloe just nodded.

"Noah is the stalker?" Nadine asked, as if she couldn't process the idea at all.

Chloe was having difficulty grasping it herself. He'd always seem so friendly. Helpful.

And now he had every intention of killing them, given the smell of gasoline throughout the room, by burning them.

"Does anyone know where we are?" Chloe asked.

"I gave the information to the security team. I also sent an email—" Nadine stopped midsentence.

"What?"

Nadine grimaced. "*I* didn't do either of those things. I asked *Noah* to give the security team our location and asked *Noah* to send out the email and pictures to the rest of the creative team."

"And we can bet he didn't do that. Or gave them a different location altogether. Did you tell Travis where we were going?"

Nadine shook her head. "Only vaguely. I told him the details were in the email."

"So we're on our own."

On their own. Tied up. And wanted dead by a madman who had fooled everyone for months.

"Chloe, I can do that thing with my wrist. Remember? Back from when David Thompson broke it?"

Nadine's wrist hadn't healed correctly, and she could pop it out of joint. It would allow her to get out of the handcuffs, but it would hurt.

"Nadine . . ."

"Anything is better than burning to death in a stupid cabin in the middle of nowhere. I can take it."

Chloe wished she could hug her friend. Nadine had always said that Chloe was the tough one, the strong one. But not right now. Right now, Nadine was the tough one.

Noah stormed back into the room, his fists clenching and unclenching.

"Noah, why don't you tell us what this is all about?" Chloe asked. She needed to distract Noah and give Nadine a chance to get out of her cuffs. "You've worked with us for months. If something is wrong, I want to try to make it right."

"Noah is dead," the man said softly. Chloe would prefer the yelling.

"Dead?"

"My daddy said the evil killed him. The evil came in the form of a cancer and killed him."

A grown man referring to his father as daddy was creepy enough without all the other crazy. Chloe had no idea what Noah was talking about.

"You're not Noah?" Maybe he had multiple personality disorder or something.

"I'm giving Noah a second chance to fight the evil. He's fighting through me."

Chloe concentrated and tried to find Noah's thoughts in her head. To see if he was thinking something different than what he was saying out loud. But she couldn't find anything. She stopped trying. All it would do was exhaust her.

And the pressure in her head was already immense. But that was from Conversation Hearts, not Noah. Conversation Hearts had finally decided to make his critical move.

Noah might have to get in line to kill Chloe. The freight train of pressure in her head could beat him to it. She could feel it growing.

"Why are you bleeding?" Noah asked, his pitch rising. "That's a sign of the evil. I didn't want to believe it, but you have the evil in you."

"Or . . ." Chloe raised her voice as he glanced over at Nadine to get his attention back on her. "I was just in a car accident and am being held by a maniac who says he wants to kill me. So maybe it's not *the evil*. Maybe it's a reaction to stress."

She didn't need to be psychic to know the punch was coming. But that was what she wanted. To give Nadine as much time as possible. Chloe's head flew to the side with the force of Noah's blow.

At least now she didn't need to worry about bleeding because of Conversation Hearts.

"You are evil." By the time Chloe dragged her head back up, Noah was just inches from her face. "I didn't want to believe it. I thought it was just the show itself that contained the evil."

"Like Alexandra? Is that why you went after her?"

Noah smirked. "Alexandra Adams is selfish and needy, but she is not evil."

"Not according to the letters you sent her."

"I didn't send those. She sent them to herself."

Noah laughed at the look on Chloe's face and rocked back on his heels. "That's right; she was using them to get your boyfriend close to her. Looks like it worked."

Chloe just stared at him. Was he telling the truth? What reason did he have to lie at this point? Alexandra had made all that up just to get Shane *closer*?

And they'd all fallen for it. Why wouldn't they? Why would anyone think Alexandra would resort to such measures? Chloe felt despair threaten to swamp her, as the last of her hope that Shane might burst through the door any minute died. Shane was back on the set guarding someone who wasn't in any danger. He had no idea Chloe was in trouble.

They truly were on their own.

"I was going to kill her, just like her letters to herself suggested," Noah continued. "To teach her a lesson. If you play with fire, then you get burned. Crying wolf and all that."

Noah began to pace back and forth. "But then I realized I had to stay the course. To complete my goal."

"And what is that?" Chloe asked.

"To eliminate the evil of *Day's End*. To remove those creatures of Satan you put on the screen each week to infest viewers. I have a responsibility to save America from itself. To stop the mindless viewing of a show that is evil incarnate."

Noah's words were becoming more calm and purposeful as he talked. It was evident he believed everything he said. Chloe couldn't even think of a way to reason with him.

How do you reason with someone who believed so completely that he was correct?

"I realized, even if I killed Alexandra Adams, although it might feel good and cause a temporary delay in filming, the evil program would not end. The evil would continue to infect all the viewers. Alexandra Adams is not the key to *Day's End*."

Noah took a step closer and trailed a finger gently down the cheek he had punched a few moments before. Chloe preferred the violence.

"You are the key. Killing you is the only way to stop the evil of the program. I've spent months trying to figure out another way. To scare you into shutting down without hurting anyone. But nobody would listen. You wouldn't take me seriously, so I knew I had to do something more."

Chloe hoped Nadine would be able to get out of the cuffs soon, because they were running out of time. Noah's thoughts were becoming clearer in her mind.

Not that she needed to hear his murderous reflections to know what he had planned. They were written all over his face.

"I knew someone had to die." He stopped pacing to study Chloe again. "It was going to be Mr. Westman. I didn't like that, since he'd been a soldier in our army. Honorable. But he'd obviously lost that honor."

Behind him, Nadine gave her arm a sharp jerk. Her face blanched, and she couldn't stop the moan of pain that escaped her as she succeeded in dislocating her wrist. Noah turned toward her.

"How had he lost his honor, Noah?"

His eyes spun back to Chloe. "I told you, Noah is dead."

Chloe had to give Nadine just a little more time. She'd done the worst part.

"How did Shane lose his honor?"

"By whoring himself out to the evil. To protect the evil is just as bad as being the evil itself."

"That's what you were thinking the night in the woods when you were going to shoot Shane. The night you tried to strangle me."

That was the wrong thing to say. Chloe knew it immediately.

"So it's true." Noah's face tightened, his skin stretching into a snarl. "You can read minds."

Chloe shook her head, trying to explain rationally, hoping it would help. "No. Sometimes I pick up on voices like a frequency on a radio. I just hear things others can't."

"Because you're *evil.*" He spat the word out.

"No. There's no power to it. No evil. It's just how my brain works. Like how you're always able to remember so many different coffee orders, exactly the way everyone likes it. I would never be able to do that, because my brain doesn't work the same way as yours. But there's no magic to it."

Noah frowned and bit his lip, considering Chloe's words. Nadine had worked her arm free and was shifting around on her chair. She couldn't just attack Noah without some sort of weapon, not with her hurt wrist.

Chloe needed to distract him further.

"Come closer and look at me," she said, careful not to use the name that seemed to trigger him. "Look me in the eye. You'll see it's not evil. It's just how my brain works. You would know evil if you saw it up close, right? So come look."

Chloe forced herself not to cringe as he did what she asked. Noah's breath was hot on her face.

She opened her eyes as wide as she could, his face only inches from hers. "Do you see? I'm not evil."

Behind him Nadine stood, making no sound. She was looking around for a weapon.

"It's just me. We've worked together for months. Laughed. Cried, even. It's just me, Noah."

Chloe winced at her mistake, hoping he wouldn't notice her calling him by name, but he did. His eyes became hard, and Chloe knew she'd lost any progress she'd made.

Nadine wasn't ready. She was grabbing a gas canister behind him, but it wouldn't be enough. Chloe slammed her head forward into Noah's, both of them crying out in pain as they connected. Nadine took the opportunity to slam the plastic gas canister against him, but Noah turned at the last second, and it caught his arm rather than his head. Chloe watched helplessly as Noah roared with rage and slammed his fist into Nadine's face. She crumpled to the ground, and Noah began to kick her. Nadine screamed, then nothing.

"Noah! Noah!" Chloe squirmed around in her chair, slamming the legs against the ground loudly. She had to get his attention back on her. "I'm the evil, not her."

Noah looked back and forth between her and Nadine, but at least he stopped kicking her.

"It doesn't matter where the evil started. It will end here. You both will burn."

He picked up the gasoline container and began pouring it over everything.

"Not Nadine. She's not evil," Chloe pleaded. "She doesn't need to die."

Noah wasn't interested in listening. "She made her choice. She has always supported you. And now she has to pay for that choice."

Noah walked into the other room, and a few minutes later Chloe could smell smoke. She pulled against the handcuffs hoping for any sort of give, but there was none.

"Nadine," she whispered. "Nadine, wake up!"

217

JANIE CROUCH

Her friend didn't move. Had Noah gotten in a well-aimed kick to the head? Chloe bit back a sob. Nadine wasn't tied to anything. If she could just wake up, maybe she could save herself.

"Nadine!" Chloe said it louder now; she didn't care if Noah heard her. "Wake up!"

Nadine shifted just the slightest bit but didn't move.

Noah came back in the room.

"Don't do this," Chloe said again.

Resolve carved his features in stone. Noah was deaf to any pleas. "Now the evil will burn. The show will end. I have saved millions of souls with this one action."

Smoke from the kitchen was beginning to fill the room. Chloe's head felt like it was about to explode, and she wasn't sure if it was from fear or from breathing in the smoke. She could feel her nose bleeding again.

All of which didn't matter, since she was about to die a fiery death.

Noah trailed a gentle finger down her cheek one last time. "I hope the evil will leave you in death."

The pain in Chloe's head ripped through her. A burning agony. Unable to help herself, she began to scream.

Noah took a step back, staring at her, but Chloe couldn't do anything but try to survive this agony. It was so much worse than it had ever been.

She saw Noah turn toward the front door and speak. "You. How did you find us?"

Was it Shane? Had he found them? Chloe tried to look over to the door, but her vision was too blurry, the pain too intense.

If the voice from the door answered, Chloe couldn't hear it. But she very clearly heard the three shots ring out. Noah fell to the floor, right next to her chair, blood spurting from his chest, his eyes open in death.

Noah wouldn't be killing any evil today.

Agony still bled through her head, causing Chloe to whimper and squint at the figure in the doorway. "Shane?"

"No, not Shane." Travis moved farther in the room.

"Travis, thank God. Get Nadine out." She panted the words. "Noah kicked her, and she's unconscious."

More smoke was barreling into the room.

Travis ignored Chloe's comment as he pulled on her hands and saw they were cuffed. He then moved to Noah's body, searching his pockets. When he found the key, Travis returned to Chloe.

"Travis." Chloe pushed him toward Nadine. "Get her. I'm fine."

He didn't move, just stood, staring at Chloe. Chloe was trying to think around the residual pain in her head that was at least easing a little now. Was he in shock at having killed Noah?

The smoke was barreling into their room. They had to get out of here. "Travis, get your girlfriend. Deal with the guilt or whatever later."

But he was still staring at her. Finally, he smiled. One full of profound joy and peace. At any other time, Chloe would've enjoyed such a keen state of happiness on a friend.

But given the circumstances, it was the spookiest thing she had ever seen.

"You complete me, Chloe. You're mine. We are meant to be."

At first his words didn't register. And then they did.

No.

She began backing away. "No. You can't be. No . . ."

Travis took a step closer. "We will be together forever."

Chloe tried to suck in air, but all she could breathe in was smoke and her own terror. She felt the world begin to spin around her. "No . . ."

She held out a hand to stop him, catch herself, or something. But Travis caught her fingers and linked them with hers.

"Forever."

The world once again faded to black.

Chapter 25

Shane pulled the ice around himself as they sped from Chloe's car to the burning building they could see a couple of miles away. They had found Chloe's car because of a tracker Shane had placed, but when they reached it, it had been crashed and emptied. Rolled into a ditch. Blood on the windows but no one around.

And then they'd seen the flames.

The letters from the stalker—from *Noah*—kept coming back to Shane's mind: *The evil must burn.*

He pulled the ice around him more tightly. There was no room for panic. No room for emotion. Chloe didn't need Shane right now; she needed Avalanche. And Avalanche wouldn't stop until she was safe, wouldn't let feelings get in the way of logic.

He took a curve much faster than was safe, and moments later was pulling up in front of a burning cabin. The entire building was awash in flames.

Someone was on the floor of the porch, obviously wounded, trying to get away from the fire. Both he and Kassler jumped out of the car and ran to the porch.

Nadine.

But she was the only one.

"Nadine." Shane crouched beside her. "Where is Chloe? Is she inside?"

He and Kassler both grabbed her, lifting her and pulling her farther away from the burning building. She cried out as soon as they touched her, obviously injured in multiple places. Shane stared into the fire. There was no way anyone could still be alive inside.

"I don't know," Nadine croaked. "I don't think so. I didn't see her when I crawled out."

"Are you sure?"

"Yes," she whispered before falling against Kassler.

Shane nodded at the man, and he carried Nadine over to the car. They needed more answers, but Nadine was obviously in bad shape.

And while Shane was more than happy that she wasn't in the burning building, where the hell was Chloe? He studied the flames a few more moments before turning back to the car.

"I'll call for fire and ambulance; you see if you can find anything." Kassler already had his phone in his hand and one arm still around Nadine, who had begun crying softly.

Shane quickly walked around the perimeter, calling for Chloe. If she had gotten out of the cabin, would she have gone into the woods? Only if she were hurt and confused. Did Noah take her somewhere else?

It didn't take him long to realize there was no one around. He ran back to the car.

"Emergency is on the way," Kassler said. "Sheriff is about five minutes out."

Shane kneeled in front of Nadine. She was holding her wrist that had obviously been broken. Her face was badly bruised, and her nose and possibly her cheek were broken also. Her legs were burned, and he knew she had to be in immense pain.

He touched her gently on the side of her head, stroking a piece of hair.

"It was Noah," she whispered.

Shane nodded. "Did he take her and leave you here?"

"I have this thing I could do with my wrist. I was able to get out of the handcuffs and try to fight him so we could get away." She started crying again. "He was too strong. He hit me. He kicked me."

Shane stroked her hair again. "You survived. That's all that matters."

"I passed out after he kicked me in the face. I think I heard gunshots, but I don't know. I'm not sure. When I came to, everything was burning. I looked for Chloe, but she wasn't in her chair. So I crawled out."

"You did the right thing."

"I didn't see her in her chair, but what if she was somewhere else? What if she was still in that building?"

"She wasn't. You know Chloe; she wasn't in that building when it burned. She wouldn't give up the fight like that."

He prayed to God that he was telling her the truth. Nadine seemed to latch onto his words, tears spilling down her cheeks. Shane reached over and kissed her gently on the forehead. "We'll find her."

Kassler look at her reassuringly. "I'll get someone on the team to find Travis and have him meet you at the hospital."

Within thirty minutes the entire area was chaos. The fire department arrived and quickly got the blaze under control. Once it had burned through the accelerants, it didn't have much left to burn. Nadine was taken away in the ambulance immediately, the pain beginning to truly overwhelm her.

Shane was glad she wasn't there when a firefighter

radioed out from inside the building that they'd found a body.

Sheriff Linenberger met Shane's eyes. Shane pulled his ice more tightly around him. That damn well was not Chloe's body in there.

But the next few minutes were the longest of his entire life. When the firefighter finally radioed out that the body was male, Shane finally felt like he could breathe again.

Once the building was safe to access, Sheriff Linenberger and Shane entered the cabin to see if they could ID the body. The face wasn't completely burned, and it didn't take Shane long to realize it was indeed Noah.

"Look at this." The sheriff pointed to Noah's chest. "Three rounds. He didn't die in this fire. Someone shot him."

"What the hell?" Noah had been shot? Shane stood and looked around. "Okay, let's say there was a struggle and Chloe was able to get the gun from Noah and shoot him."

"Then where is she?" the sheriff finished for him.

"Exactly. Because there's no way in hell she would've left Nadine in a burning building."

"So could Noah have had a partner?"

"Sheriff, we've got gun casings over here by the door," one of the firefighters said.

Shane looked at the sheriff. "So Noah was shot by someone entering the cabin. That doesn't sound like a partner."

The sheriff stood. "No, it sure doesn't."

Shane looked around. "But if it's not a partner, then what does that mean? A second stalker? Random maniac who just happened to be at the right place at the right time?" Shane shook his head. "If Noah was the stalker who has been writing these notes and causing all the problems on the set, yet Noah is dead, then who has Chloe?"

And why the hell did Shane feel like Chloe was in more

danger now, even though the stalker was lying dead at his feet?

"I'm going to get some dogs up here, see if they can catch her scent. We'll also get a search party going. Maybe she's injured and confused, wandering in the woods."

Shane hoped so. "Yeah, good idea."

"There's a lot of people around here who know Chloe and like her. They'll want to help. If she's out here, we'll find her."

Shane nodded and walked from the cabin into the darkness outside. Things were settling down; the firetruck was packing its gear. Shane turned slowly in a full circle. There was nothing around here but trees and wilderness. Chloe would've had to be pretty severely injured to have left the cabin on her own, particularly leaving Nadine behind.

She wouldn't have done that. Not if she had any other choice.

The sheriff could set up his search-and-rescue team. Shane was glad that so many people wanted to help. But that didn't change what his gut told him. Chloe wasn't wandering around lost and injured in the woods.

She was in danger of the worst possible kind.

~

"I'm sorry, Shane, I just don't remember anything else."

Shane smiled encouragingly at Nadine. Given what she had been through just a few hours ago—a dislocated wrist to get out of handcuffs, two cracked ribs and a broken nose from kicks, and second-degree burns down her legs—it was amazing she was up for talking at all.

"I was unconscious, I guess, when the second person arrived. I don't remember anyone getting shot or Chloe leaving."

"That's completely understandable. Sheriff Linenberger

has people out in the woods right now searching for her, in case she was hurt and wandered off, or something like that."

"I just want them to find her," Nadine whispered. "If I had just been able to knock Noah out, none of this would've happened."

Shane touched Nadine's shoulder from where he sat in the chair by her hospital bed. "Noah had the tactical advantage. He was bigger, stronger, hadn't been in an accident, and wasn't confused. Taking him even without a dislocated wrist would've been difficult. Your injury made it just about impossible."

"You've got to find her, Shane. I know you guys had a fight, and she's not very good at sharing her feelings, but . . ."

Shane squeezed her shoulder lightly. "I *will* find her; don't doubt that. Or think I'm scared away by her. I'm not scared by anything about her."

Except losing her.

Tears filled Nadine's eyes. "She acts so tough. Always moves so fast. But it's because she's afraid of standing still. Because deep inside she just wants someone, someone who's not me or her sisters, to love her for who she is. To not be afraid."

Shane stood. "I can keep up with Chloe Jeffries. I cool her down, and she heats me up—pretty damn perfect, if you ask me."

"Good." Nadine's eyes were already drooping closed.

"Is Travis on his way?"

Her eyes opened back up. "No. I lost my phone, and all my contact info was inside it." She gave a sad laugh. "Pretty pathetic when you don't even know your boyfriend's number, just have it programmed in your phone."

Shane smiled. "I'll make sure one of the security team finds him and sends him over."

Nadine nodded. "Also, inside my desk is an old-fashioned

address book. The contact info for Chloe's sisters—Adrienne and Paige—is in there. Somebody needs to call them. They'll want to be here. Adrienne may even be able to help, if it's needed. She has abilities also."

"I've heard about those. I'll call her sisters myself."

Shane left to let Nadine sleep. A call to the sheriff on his way back to the set only confirmed what Shane had already suspected: there was no sign of Chloe out in the woods.

There were signs of multiple vehicles coming to and from the cabin, but given all the fire and rescue personnel who had been around, there was no way to know who or when.

A dead end.

Frustration and fear were scratching at Shane. Hanging on to the ice was becoming more and more difficult.

He drove back to the studio and parked by the creative team's trailer. Chloe's face floated in front of his mind, and all he could picture was her pinched, hurt look yesterday morning as they fought. As he'd implied that he would be spending his time with Alexandra willingly.

Shane slammed his hands against the steering wheel.

"Ah, the Avalanche thaweth. Looks like Zac was right, and we're going to have to open a Linear Tactical satellite office in North Carolina."

Shane turned to the familiar voice speaking to him through the window and felt his first glimpse of hope since they'd found Nadine at the burning building.

Wyatt Highfield.

Wyatt stepped back so Shane could get out of the car.

"What are you doing here?" Wyatt should be in Cheyenne working with Zac and the others at Linear Tactical.

"Zac sent me as soon as we got the report about Chloe. Perks of having a company jet on standby."

Shane reached out to shake the other man's hand—a man he'd fought with side by side in battle, who had unparalleled abilities when it came to combat and tactical awareness—then pulled him in for a back-slapping hug.

"I'm glad you're here. The security team is good, but . . ."

"But it's not the same."

Shane nodded. He didn't have to explain any more to Wyatt. The other man understood the relief that came with having someone at your back whom you *knew*. A brother. There were very few people Shane would want there more than Wyatt.

"So you lost your girl. Are you sure she didn't just decide to find someone with a better personality?"

Shane cringed. After their conversation yesterday, Shane couldn't blame Chloe if she had.

Wyatt chuckled. "I meant it as a joke."

"The last things we said to each other, Wyatt." Shane scrubbed his hand across his face. "Not exactly ugly, but cold."

Wyatt slapped him on the back. "So we get her back so you can be sure to make up for your idiocy."

Shane led the other man into the trailer. He would gladly spend the next few weeks groveling—although he was sure Chloe wouldn't want it—if it meant she was back safely.

"It looks like someone else has Chloe," Shane explained to Wyatt. "Killed the original stalker and took Chloe. But hell if I know who."

"Was this Noah guy working with a partner? Maybe someone who wants money? Chloe's got to be worth quite a bit. Maybe a ransom demand is coming."

It had been over six hours since they'd found Nadine in the burning building. Receiving a ransom demand wasn't out of the realm of possibilities.

Shane rubbed his eyes again. "I guess taking Chloe for money is better than a nutcase having her in his clutches for no other reason than to do her harm. Although neither are good options."

"A kidnapper with a ransom demand just wants to get paid. Even if this unknown guy has nothing to do with the stalker, and just took her as a crime of opportunity, he'll still want money."

Shane looked around the Pit. This was Chloe's sacred creative space. He could almost feel her presence here. "If money will get her back, I will find a way to pay it."

"If this becomes a K-and-R case, Linear is equipped to help handle that. Zac will get the entire team out here. You know that. He won't hesitate with a Kidnap and Rescue."

Shane nodded. Yes, he did know that. Because these men were his brothers in every way except blood.

"I've got to call Chloe's sisters."

"Already done. Zac called Adrienne as soon as he heard what was going on. I'm sure she and Paige are already on their way. Adrienne might be a big help, the way she is able to read stuff." Wyatt looked sideways at Shane. "You did know about the weird stuff, right? All three of the Jeffries sisters?"

"Yeah, I know. And yes, it's weird. And yes, I'm okay with it. Like I told Chloe, I've seen weird stuff all over the world. I'm not going to start second-guessing the human body's true capabilities now."

"I hear that."

"I've got to find Nadine's boyfriend's number. Travis Oakley. She needs him at the hospital with her." Shane pointed to Nadine's desk, which Wyatt was standing next to. "Look in those drawers and see if you can find an address book. She lost his number when she lost her phone."

Wyatt begin to look.

Shane walked over to Travis's desk. Where was he? Surely he would not be helping with the sheriff's search-and-rescue

229

team without checking in with Nadine first. The desk was in perfect order, unlike Chloe's, which tended to be a cluttered mess. Just like the woman.

Shane didn't see a note or anything that suggested where the man might be.

"Travis Oakley. Got it, complete with a little heart next to his name where she wrote it. Adorbs."

Wyatt read out the number to Shane, and Shane typed it into his phone.

"Adorbs?" he asked as he waited for it to ring.

His friend, six foot three and two hundred pounds of muscle, just shrugged. "Adorable. All the cool kids say it."

Shane just shook his head as the phone began to ring, frowning as he heard a buzzing sound coming from inside Travis's desk drawer. His phone was in his desk?

Shane opened the drawer and saw that the phone was there, and it was his own number calling. He disconnected the call.

"Now it seems to me that that can't be good," Wyatt said. "Most people don't go off without their cell phone. Specifically, they don't place it in a drawer."

Had the kidnapper taken Travis also? Shane was racking his brain trying to figure out exactly what this new development meant when he saw the paper. A very benign-looking piece of printer paper that nobody else would even think twice about. The words and sentences written on it were neat and nonthreatening.

Mine.

We'll be together.

You will make me whole.

Shane couldn't say anything; he just stood, staring at the paper.

"Westman, what is it?" Wyatt moved to stand next to

Shane to see what he was staring at so hard. "Besides being some pretty corny one-liners, what is this?"

Corny... just like a *conversation heart.*

Oh shit.

"Travis Oakley is the one who has Chloe. And there won't be a ransom notice. He's been in her head all along, and he plans to keep her for himself. Forever."

Chapter 26

Shane and Wyatt were running out the door toward the car almost before Shane finished the sentence. Travis had a house just outside town, and Wyatt called and got the address from the security team while Shane called Sheriff Linenberger to let him know what they had discovered, thankful that Linenberger believed him without him having to go into too much detail. Shane was the first to admit the story was weird.

The sheriff was going to meet them at Travis's house, but hell if Shane would wait for him to get there before he stormed in. They could arrest him for breaking and entering later. Not to mention a bunch of cop cars squealing up might cause Travis to do something reckless. Shane wasn't going to risk Chloe's life.

He parked just outside the line of sight of Travis's small craftsman-style house, and he and Wyatt got out and were on the move.

"Guy is Caucasian, thirty-five years old, sandy-blond hair, medium height and build. Weird scars from a lightning strike on his arms."

Wyatt nodded. "I'll knock on the front door. He doesn't know me. That will at least let us know if he's there."

Shane nodded. "I'll go around to the back. But if there's a way in, I'm taking it. If, for some reason, I got this completely wrong, I'll beg for forgiveness later."

Weapons drawn, they separated, Wyatt heading for the front door, Shane sneaking around to the back. Shane took a moment to look through the side window of Travis's small house. He saw no sign of anyone inside.

Shane made his way around to the back door, checking those windows also. Still nothing. He tried the door knob, and it was locked. Shane didn't even hesitate to put his shoulder heavily into the door, the older wood of the framing giving way easily. He kept his weapon drawn as he quickly searched through the house, Wyatt doing his part by knocking on the door the entire time.

It didn't take Shane long to confirm no one was there. He moved to the front door and let Wyatt in.

"Anything?" Wyatt asked.

"Nothing. Nobody's here." Shane could feel frustration pulling at him again. If Travis didn't have her here, the possibilities of where he could've taken her were endless.

And did he even have her at all? Hell, maybe Chloe had told Travis about the Conversation Hearts voice in her mind. Maybe he had just written it down for some much less nefarious purpose.

But if he wasn't involved at all, where was he?

"No car in the garage either," Wyatt said. "Maybe he didn't bring her here."

Shane holstered his weapon. "Let's see if we can find anything that points us in any sort of direction."

Sheriff Linenberger arrived a few minutes later.

"Westman, I know you have not broken into this house after we discussed you waiting for me."

Shane couldn't respond to that without incriminating himself and putting the sheriff in a hard position.

Wyatt intervened.

"Sheriff, I'm Wyatt Highfield. I work with Linear Tactical. I'm afraid this entire situation is my fault. I saw the door was open, thought there might be a problem, and just waltzed on in."

The sheriff took Wyatt's outstretched hand. "Is that so?"

"Yes, sir. Just wanting to be a Good Samaritan, you know."

Obviously, they weren't fooling anyone, least of all Sheriff Linenberger, but he went along with it.

"Any sign of trouble? Any sign of Chloe?"

"Nothing at first glance. We are just starting to look around."

The sheriff gave them a hard look. "I'm going to leave here right now. I need to get a cup of coffee and wait for a warrant to come in. Because otherwise anything that may or may not be found in this house could not be used in a court of law."

Shane was about to protest, to argue that he couldn't afford—*Chloe* couldn't afford—for them to wait for anything. But the sheriff held out his hand to stop him.

"I know you are colleagues with Travis Oakley. And, since you're not law enforcement, I guess your friend won't mind if you're hanging out at his house until he gets home, given all the panic around the *Day's End* set over the past few hours."

Without another word the sheriff turned and walked out. Shane didn't hesitate to return to his search. Although what exactly he was searching for he didn't know.

They found it almost by accident.

Wyatt and Shane had done a cursory search of the closets to make sure no one was hiding in them, but they hadn't studied them in great detail. Wyatt was actually the one who saw the cutout in the wall peeking out from behind a box.

When they pulled out what was hidden in there, Shane no longer had any doubt Travis was the one who had Chloe.

He was also the person who had been killing the psychics up and down the East Coast. He had kept memorabilia from each of them in a lockbox. Newspaper clippings, pictures of the victims, even some personal items.

Wyatt whistled through his teeth. "Damn."

"He's been following Chloe for months," Shane muttered, "trying to figure out if she was real or not. A real psychic."

"And is she?" Wyatt asked.

"She hears voices, yes. But not in the way you think of getting your fortune told at a fair. She can't do parlor tricks."

"It looks like this guy Travis hates psychics. Wants to kill them."

Shane shook his head. "He doesn't want to kill them. He wants to find one who's *real*. These were all fake."

Wyatt was already on the phone with the sheriff, telling him to hurry and get his warrant, because they thought they'd heard something in the closet, and they ended up stumbling upon something much worse.

Shane backed away from the box and began looking around some more. Knowing Travis was a killer didn't tell them where he would take Chloe. Shane searched the bedroom and found nothing, then walked into the bathroom to make sure nothing was there.

He saw the ruby earring on the bathroom vanity and recognized it immediately. The one his grandmother had given Chloe.

"Wyatt, Oakley definitely has her. She was here." Wyatt rushed into the bathroom, and Shane showed him the earring, explaining its relevance.

"Don't touch it," Wyatt said. "Just in case."

"We've got to figure out where he took her." Shane knew what he had to do, but he didn't like it. They needed to talk to Nadine. She was closest to Travis and might have some idea.

~

AN HOUR LATER, Shane felt like a bastard of the worst kind. The woman in the hospital bed had already been shattered physically; now she was shattered emotionally as well.

She didn't sob, didn't scream, didn't rage at the news that her boyfriend had not only kidnapped her best friend, but had also left Nadine for dead in a burning building. She just lay in the bed with one of the emptiest looks Shane had ever seen.

"Are you sure, Shane?"

Shane held her hand and nodded. It wasn't the first time she'd asked the question.

Even Wyatt's charm, second only to Zac MacKay when it came to having women eating out of his hand, hadn't made a dent in Nadine's despair.

"Nadine, sweetheart, I'm not trying to make this more difficult. I know it already must be terrible. But I know Chloe was at Travis's house. She left an earring—the earrings my grandmother gave her—on the vanity. He's the Conversation Hearts voice."

Now Nadine began to cry very softly. Shane glanced at Wyatt, who possibly had the hardest look that Shane had ever seen on the man's face, even when they had stared down some of the most horrific enemies in grievous situations.

"I told him about her," Nadine whispered, turning to the side to look at no one. "He'd asked me about Chloe and the rumors before, and I didn't respond. But, finally, over the break, I told him that she really does hear voices."

"Is there anywhere you can think of that he might have taken her? Does he have a second house or any places he would like to travel? It couldn't be too far. He can't get her on any sort of public transportation like an airplane."

Nadine let out a shuddery breath, obviously wanting to help her friend but struggling to keep it together. Shane knew her emotions were cracking, and it wouldn't take long before she completely lost it.

"No, he never talked about any other houses or a place in particular he liked to visit. I know his family is from Michigan,"—she gave a bitter laugh—"if that's even true. Honestly, I guess I really don't know anything about him at all."

Shane nodded. "We'll get as much background info as we can."

"The only place he took me to . . . oh my God." Nadine took a deep breath, then looked at Shane in horror. "He has a boat. A really nice sailboat. He took me there when we had the break. He said he was getting it ready to take the perfect woman in his life on a special cruise soon . . ." Her voice trailed off for a moment. "I thought he meant *me*. It's docked in the main harbor of Wilmington."

Nadine turned her head to the side, obviously trying to process all this. She was done talking.

A boat. That would be perfect. Travis could keep Chloe isolated without much danger of running into anyone.

Shane reached over and touched Nadine gently on the cheek. "We're going to catch him. And we'll get Chloe back."

Nadine didn't respond.

Shane looked at Wyatt and cocked his head toward the door. They left quietly.

"If I didn't want to kill that bastard before, I sure do now," Wyatt said.

"Wilmington is about five hours from here driving.

They've got a much bigger head start. By the time we get there, Travis will have left with Chloe, if he hasn't already."

Wyatt grabbed Shane's arm and started walking him toward the exit. "We're not driving. Linear's jet is still at the local airfield. It's ready to take us wherever we need to go. We'll call Wilmington local police on the way."

"If they rush in there, he'll kill her, Wyatt. I know it. She's told me about his thoughts, how obsessed he was. She thought it was with another woman, but it's her . . ." Shane didn't let himself think about what Travis might have already done. Things he could do to her while she was alive that would make her wish she was dead. "He'll kill her before he lets someone take her away from him. Those cops can't go barreling in."

"We won't let them. We'll get there and handle him ourselves."

They ran down the hall toward the exit and car. Shane pushed away every thought except getting to Chloe and stopping Travis.

He pulled the ice around him until it was impenetrable. He couldn't allow his feelings for her to cloud any part of what was going to happen next.

Shane was gone. Avalanche was here.

Chapter 27

Travis was Conversation Hearts.

Chloe had woken up in his car wrapped in a blanket like she was some sort of treasure.

The first time he'd slowed the car to go around a curve, she'd opened the door and thrown herself out of the vehicle.

Even knowing how dangerous it was, she didn't care. Even the bone-rattling impact as she hit the dirt on the side of the road was not enough to make her sorry that she'd gotten out. There was no way she was staying with Travis. The thought of being anywhere near him made her sick on multiple levels.

He'd left Nadine to die. Chloe had no idea if her friend had made it out or not. He'd lied to everyone for months.

And most importantly, Chloe now knew that all those thoughts that had caused her so much agony were about *her*. And most importantly, Chloe now knew that the hours of manic obsessive thoughts flowing through her mind had been about *her*. When Chloe thought she needed to be worried for some poort woman far away, she should've been worried for her own life.

So throwing herself out of a moving vehicle hadn't seemed like such a hardship.

But Travis had stopped the car, caught her, and zip-tied her hands. He'd dragged her back to the car and then connected her to the door handle. So if she'd jumped again, he would just drag her along the road, tied to the vehicle.

Regardless, the thought still held some appeal.

She avoided talking to him as he took her to his house on the outskirts of Black Mountain, then carried her inside and tied her to a kitchen chair. Now he was actually *smiling* at her like he'd done so many times over the last months they'd worked together. Like they were still colleagues, friends.

He sat down across from her at the table, leaning on his elbows, putting his chin in his hands, like they were having a coffee date. "This all seems a little crazy, I'm sure."

She jerked away as he reached over to touch her hair.

"Don't touch me, Travis. You left Nadine—your *girlfriend*, the woman who thinks she's in love with you—to *die* in a burning building."

Chloe couldn't let herself focus on Nadine. If she did, she would completely fall apart. Chloe could only pray that somehow her friend had regained consciousness and made it to safety. How she would've done that with the flames already barreling up so high, Chloe had no idea. She choked back a sob.

Travis nodded. "I didn't desire Nadine's death. But getting you away was a necessity. Noah was going to kill you. The bastard was actually going to let you burn."

Chloe fought for calm. "And you, Travis? What are you going to do with me?"

Travis sat up straighter, obviously excited to share his plan. She'd seen him do the same thing when he'd had a good idea for a plot point.

"Before I came to work for you, I was a manager at a

bank. Did you know that?"

Chloe nodded. She didn't really, but she remembered Nadine had thought it was interesting how he'd changed careers so completely.

"I got struck by lightning a year ago." He reached out his arms to show her the Lichtenberg figures that covered them. "I was different after that. Something changed. I began to hear things, see things from . . ."—his voice lowered to a whisper—"the *beyond*. You're going to help me develop that."

"How am I going to do that exactly?"

He shook his head, clucking his tongue. "You don't have to hide the truth from me, Chloe. I know what you can do. I know the rumors are true. You're connected to the beyond also."

She barely refrained from rolling her eyes. First Noah, now Travis. What was it with people thinking she was connected to some sort of power source?

"Travis, yes, I'll admit I hear some voices. But not because I'm connected to some higher power or the *beyond*. My brain just sort of works at a different frequency than other people. I hear things others can't. But I don't have any magic I can rub off onto another person."

His eyes narrowed as he looked at her. "Don't be selfish, Chloe. You need to share your power. Help me develop my own more fully. You have no idea how long I've been waiting for this."

You have no idea how long I've been waiting for this.

The words echoed through her mind, just after he said them.

"You and I are meant to be together."

You and I are meant to be together.

She winced as pricks of fire burned through her thoughts even as he was saying the words. That hadn't been true a few minutes ago. Chloe realized Travis was getting worked up, that the part of his mind—the one she'd labeled *Conversation Hearts*—was taking over. The logical Travis part of his thoughts, the part she had worked with every day and had never bothered her, didn't burn her mind, but the other did.

"You're mine, Chloe."

Mine.

Chloe closed her eyes as her head felt like it was being ripped apart. She could feel her nose begin to bleed again.

"Travis, stop." She didn't know how to explain it, how to make him understand which thoughts burned her and which didn't.

"What's happening? Your nose is bleeding."

And just like that, the pain stopped. He was back to logical. She opened her eyes. Travis was staring at her with something akin to wonder.

"You could feel me, couldn't you? I knew it. You are the one, Chloe."

The burn flickered again.

"Travis, those thoughts you have. The ones you think are . . ."—Possessive. Controlling. Needy. Obsessed.—*"different*; do you know which ones I mean?"

He nodded gravely. "Yes. Those I push to you."

She stared at him. *Pushed to her.* No wonder she hadn't been able to escape them. He had been deliberately attacking her with his thoughts. The only time she'd been able to block them was when Shane was around.

Shane.

Was he still at Alexandra's house, waiting for an attack that wasn't ever going to happen? How long would it take until he even figured out Chloe was gone? He might not even realize it for a couple of days. And by then it would be too late.

She had to find a way out of this on her own.

"You can feel me, can't you, Chloe? I knew you were the

real thing. Not like the others." Travis's excitement was evident.

"What others?"

His eyes narrowed. "The fakes. I spoke with them first. I went to see these so-called psychics. Talked to them, tried to see if I could learn from them. I wanted their power." He shook his head. "But time after time they would prove they had no real abilities. They were all fakes."

Realization dawned. "You killed them. You're the serial killer who's been murdering the psychics."

"Don't look at me like that, Chloe. They were *fakes*. Not real, like you. I was ridding the world of liars and cheats who took people for their money. None of them had any genuine abilities. They couldn't complete me, help me, empower me like you can. So I did the world a favor and got rid of them."

"I don't have any power either, damn it! You've worked with me for months, and have you ever seen me be able to do anything special? For all I know, I just have an overwrought imagination that projects voices in my head."

"No, Chloe, you're special." Travis stood and walked over to crouch beside her. "I knew you were even before I was completely sure the rumors were true. That's why I got so close to Nadine. I didn't want to eliminate you if I didn't have to. After all, you weren't trying to steal from people, weren't trying to convince anyone to believe you. So I wanted to see if the rumors were true."

"Nadine."

Chloe could barely keep herself from blanching as Travis trailed a finger down her cheek. "I didn't want to sleep with her, to be honest, but what could I do? I needed the information. I needed her to tell me everything about you. But I didn't want her to get suspicious and clam up. I hope you can forgive me. I thought of you the whole time."

He moved closer. "It's always been you. You're mine."

You're mine.

"Forever, Chloe. We'll be together forever. You will be mine, forever."

Mine forever.

She winced, gritting her teeth. Travis smiled. He liked that he could affect her. He grabbed a piece of her hair and rubbed it between his fingers.

"I'll never be yours, Travis." Even as the words came out of her mouth she knew she shouldn't say them, knew she should play along. Do something to lead him on. But she couldn't. "Never. I won't help you. Won't teach you. And I damn well will never want you."

His fingers slipped down to her throat and began to squeeze. "Oh, you will, because I will be the only thing you know. It will be only us." He cut her air off completely. "And because if you don't give me what I want, if you don't share your power, teach me how to develop mine, then I will have no use for you."

Chloe struggled in her chair to get away from his grip as her lungs began to burn, but she couldn't escape.

"You are mine."

Mine. Mine. Mine. Mine.

Her brain burned from his mental attack as he released her throat and she could get air. Finally, he stopped the barrage of thoughts, and she sank back into the chair.

"And I don't even have to lay a finger on you to hurt you, do I?"

Mine!

She screamed as the agony blazed through her brain, sliding to the ground, covering her head with her hands as best she could with her wrists still attached to the arms of the chair,.

"See, neither of us want you to experience that all the time, do we?" He stood and took a paper towel from the counter and held it to her nose, which was bleeding again. "It can't be good for you. So we'll work together to make sure it doesn't. And since it will only be the two of us for a long, long time, I'm sure we'll be able to meet both our needs."

Chloe just remained collapsed on the floor, her face slumped against the seat.

"I'm not unreasonable, Chloe. I don't expect you to just fall in love with me immediately. That will take time and patience on both our parts. Trust has to be earned. If you won't hold Nadine against me, I won't hold your infidelity with Westman against you. We'll both move past it."

Chloe could feel tears squeezing out of her eyes. Travis was truly insane. But more importantly, he was right. How could she fight someone who could debilitate her without even touching her?

"Where are you going to take me?"

"I've been working on this plan for a while. My boat. It's equipped for two people to sail for six weeks without having to come back into port."

It was in Wilmington, where he'd taken Nadine over the break. Chloe couldn't even think of anything to say.

"We need to get going. I can't take a chance that they'll come here looking for either of us. I know Westman won't stop searching for you. Plus, the sooner we're on the boat, the sooner we can put this all behind us and start our new life together."

Chloe felt like she might vomit. "I need to go to the bathroom," she whispered.

He nodded, then walked over and got her a bottle of water out of the fridge. He cut the zip tie at her wrists, then led her to a small bathroom in the middle of the house.

There was no window.

"I'll find a change of clothes for you so you don't have to wear those smelling of such smoke. I have plenty of your size

245

on the boat, all you could ever need, but it would've been suspicious to have them here."

Chloe was afraid Travis was going to follow her into the bathroom, but thankfully, he gave her a clean T-shirt and sweatpants and left, closing the door behind him.

She opened the bottle of water he'd given her and drank it down, completely parched. Using a washcloth, she scrubbed the soot off her face and body as best she could, then changed out of her bloody, ruined clothes and into the shirt and pants he'd given her.

She stared at her reflection in the mirror. What was she going to do? She had to make a break from Travis before he got her on the boat, because once he did, there wouldn't be any escape.

But how could she escape him now when he could knock her unconscious with well-aimed thoughts?

She would have to do it in the car. Maybe convince him to stop, pretend like she was going to vomit—which wouldn't be hard. Just make a run for it. All she would have to do was stay conscious long enough to make someone else aware that she was in trouble.

If only she could get a message to Shane. At what point would they figure out she and Travis had both disappeared at the same time? Days from now? Longer?

She startled at the knock on the door. "It's time to go."

"Okay," she croaked.

She looked in the mirror again and realized one of the earrings Shane's grandmother had given her had gone missing in all the chaos. But the other wasn't. She took it out of her ear and set it on the bathroom counter.

If Shane saw it, he would know what it was. He would know she'd been there. That Travis had her.

He would find her. She had to believe that, because if she didn't, she was going to lose it right now.

Travis knocked on the door again, and she opened it. He immediately zip-tied her wrists once more and led her to a chair by his bedroom door, attaching her wrists to the arm again.

"You don't have to tie me; I'm not going to run away." Complete lies, but she didn't care. "I don't want you to hurt me."

He smiled at her. "I don't want to hurt you either. But, like I said, I know trust takes time. On both sides. And right now, I don't trust you at all."

Travis might be crazy, but he wasn't stupid.

She watched as he finished packing a suitcase, moving quickly and efficiently. Ironically, it was one of the things she'd always liked about Travis.

The thought made her want to giggle. Which was very wrong. There was nothing about this situation worth laughter. She felt herself slump over to the side and couldn't figure out how to sit up straight.

Soon the whole room was spinning.

"What did you do?" she asked, her words slurred. The water. He must have drugged it. She'd been so thirsty she hadn't even noticed it had a funny taste.

"Like I said, trust takes time. Once we're alone, we'll be able to work out all our differences. But I've got to get you there first. I know how smart you are." His face began to blur. "This is the best way, for both of us."

She fought as hard as she could against the blackness. If she gave in now, she would never see Shane again. Her sisters. Anyone.

"Chloe, stop," Travis whispered. "You can't fight what's happening. Just accept it. All of it."

The blackness pooled over her in waves, sucking her under.

You're mine now, Chloe. Forever.

Chapter 28

Shane didn't know much about the studio Chloe worked for, but they damn well had shown up when it counted. By the time he and Wyatt had made it to the airfield, the flight plan had been filed, the jet was fully fueled, and had a pilot who was also a law enforcement officer was ready to take them wherever they needed to go. On the jet, they'd been sent maps of the Wilmington pier, where Travis's boat was docked. Zac confirmed that Travis had made plans to leave today.

They'd also sent information about Noah Kent, who wasn't Noah Kent at all. The real one had been a twenty-one-year-old junior at North Carolina College when he'd died of cancer fourteen months ago. Evidently, Nathan Abittan, Noah's neighbor around the same age, had assumed Noah's identity and used it to get the internship on *Day's End*.

Nathan Abittan had both a mental health record and a father who was serving life in prison for murder and was the leader of a cult. He would've shown up on any search Linear Tactical did concerning the stalker, but Noah Kent, straight-A student with a crystal-clean record, had not.

Nathan/Noah had definitely been planning to kill Chloe for the evil he believed was being delivered by the show. Ironically, if Travis hadn't arrived when he had, and kidnapped Chloe for himself, she would've already been dead at Noah's hands.

That didn't mean Shane was going to allow Travis to leave with Chloe.

A storm had covered the area, making for a turbulent descent and landing and costing them further time they couldn't afford. But at least the studio had a car waiting when Wyatt and Shane arrived.

And the boat was still at the pier. If Travis was planning to get Chloe out this way, he hadn't done it yet.

The Wilmington police had been notified and wanted to help but were spread pretty thin due to problems of their own. Sending in an entire SWAT team based on unconfirmed intel hadn't been possible, but they had sent two squad cars. The officers who were watching had been asked to keep their distance from the pier. Shane had no doubt Travis would kill Chloe rather than letting her go free if it came to a showdown. Stealth was their best option. And fortunately, it was something both he and Wyatt understood.

"Locals just reported in that there's been no movement on Travis's boat. The storm is making it difficult to get any sort of visual, particularly because there are multiple access points to the docks."

"They have to hold back, Wyatt. If they rush in, he's going to kill her. He's obsessed with her. If he can't have her, he won't want anyone to."

Wyatt nodded as they pulled up at the pier and exited the car. "Then you and I go in together, no one else. It's almost like having the band back together."

"Except we're missing the other two-thirds."

JANIE CROUCH

Wyatt winked at him. "We both know Zac and the others were just dead weight we carried."

Having Wyatt here—any of the Linear Tactical guys—made a difference. Made what might have otherwise been a hopeless situation possible. Wyatt's presence helped Shane stay focused and frosty. He would get Chloe out. Away from this madman. Because Shane couldn't imagine a world—*his* world—without her.

Shane nodded. "You head around the back in case—"

"Westman, we have eyes on the suspect." The radio in Shane's hand that allowed them to communicate with the police interrupted his words. "He has someone with him, and he's definitely heading around the back pier."

The back pier wasn't the shortest way to Travis's boat, but it was the least visible.

"Hold," Shane said into the radio. "Do not engage."

He and Wyatt began running toward the pier.

CHLOE STUMBLED as Travis grabbed her by the arm and marched her toward the pier. The drugs were still in her system, making everything hazy. It was storming; the afternoon sky darkened almost like it was night.

Travis had tied her hands behind her back and gagged her with some sort of scarf. He'd pulled a windbreaker over her head and moved hair around her face to make it less noticeable.

"Stay quiet. If you yell, and someone comes to investigate, I'll be forced to kill them. You don't want that on your conscience, do you?"

No, she didn't, but she didn't want to get on that vessel with a lunatic either. The docks were empty, everyone somewhere else because of the storm. Chloe couldn't see anyone she could scream to even if she was able.

He walked her quickly toward the boat slips, angling her toward one of the last locations, where a large sailboat floated serenely in the water. Chloe stumbled, half because of the drugs he'd given her, half because this was it; she was out of time. She had to fight now, or she'd never get away. But how could she? Both hands were restrained behind her back; she was gagged and dizzy.

"We're almost there, sweetheart. Our new life. Can you imagine what we're going to share, Chloe? The two of us? Together. Forever."

Together. Forever.

She waited for the fire in her brain at Travis's purposeful mental attack, but it didn't come. Travis stopped and yanked her arm so she was closer.

"You're mine, Chloe."

Mine!

She knew he was trying to hurt her, to control her. And although she could hear his thoughts, they didn't burn. The pain was missing. All she could feel was . . .

Coolness.

Chloe's eyes shot around, her relief almost staggering her. Shane was here somewhere in this storm. He had found her. Was shielding her mind just with his very presence.

Travis glared at her. "You're mine, Chloe. Forever."

Mine. Forever.

Should she fake it? Pretend like it hurt to give Shane more time to make a move?

Travis grabbed her arm, shaking her. "What's going on? Is it the drugs? Are they affecting our connection?"

She could feel the coolness getting stronger. Shane was close.

She just shrugged.

Pain bit through her face as Travis backhanded her and then immediately pulled her up by both arms so they were nose to nose. "You will not keep me out, Chloe. I have ways—physical ways I didn't want to use because they would hurt you so badly—but I will make you connect with me." He began dragging her toward the boat once again. But this time Chloe resisted, pulling against him.

Fury blanketed Travis's features as he reached under the windbreaker's hood to grab her hair and yank her forward. Evidently stealth wasn't important now.

"I'm not going to let you take her, Travis."

Shane. Chloe closed her eyes in relief.

Travis immediately turned toward him, using Chloe as a shield, and pulled out a gun Chloe hadn't even known he had. Travis yanked her onto the gangway over the water, keeping himself tucked behind her as the two men stared each other down.

"You have no idea what she is. What she and I could be together." Travis spat the words. "She belongs with me, West-man. She is the one who will finally help me fulfill my destiny."

"Well . . ." Shane was cool and steady as always. He took a step forward, weapon still raised. "Why don't we go sit down and talk about this, the three of us? There may be a way for Chloe to help you fulfill your destiny without stealing her away from everything, Travis. She's more likely to help you if she's doing so willingly."

"No!" Travis's near hysteria echoed now, and he was waving the gun around wildly. "She's blinded by you. Can't see me for what I really am."

He took another few steps backward, dragging Chloe with him until they were farther on the gangplank, almost to his boat.

"Travis, just put the gun down. There's nowhere to go.

The police are here; you can't get out. But there's no need for anyone to get hurt."

"I'm afraid someone will indeed have to get hurt," Travis muttered in Chloe's ear.

Chloe realized he was no longer waving his gun so wildly. He was taking aim at Shane, ready to shoot. Shane, who was completely out in the open with no shot of his own because of her.

Travis was going to kill him.

She did the only thing she could: threw all her weight into Travis to knock him off balance, but she heard a gun fire anyway.

Then Travis crumpled onto her. He'd been shot from a different angle, somewhere behind him, not by Shane. Blood was pulsing from the exit wound in his chest as he grabbed her shoulders. His eyes fastened on hers as he and Chloe hit the railing of the gangplank together. She could feel his blood spilling on her body, blending with the heavy rain.

Travis looked over toward Shane, then back at her. He ran his fingers, now bloody, down her cheek. "We're destined to be together. Even if it's in death."

Before Chloe could figure out what he meant to do, he threw all his weight forward over the railing, dragging her with him. She could hear Shane yelling for her as she fell with a splash into the dark water of the harbor.

The freezing water stole Chloe's breath. Darkness and cold surrounded her, making orientation impossible. She fought to free herself from Travis's grip, but with her arms restrained behind her back, there was little she could do. He didn't fight, just wrapped his arms around her as they sank deeper and deeper.

Chloe's lungs screamed for air. She bucked and twisted, finally succeeding in getting Travis's body off her. He wasn't moving, but in death had dragged her down far enough to do what he'd set out to.

Air. She had no air. She kicked as hard as she could, *kept* kicking, but it wasn't enough. With the weight of her water-logged clothes and shoes, she couldn't get to the surface. She wasn't even sure she was going in the right direction any longer.

She wasn't going to make it. Could feel herself sliding back down and couldn't fight any more. She stopped and focused her mind on Shane. Let the coolness that always surrounded him drive out the terror in her mind. She linked herself to his cooling presence and closed her eyes.

And drowned.

~

SHANE DOVE under the water of the harbor again, searching for Chloe.

It had been only moments since Travis had pulled her into the dark water, but they were running out of time. *Chloe* was running out of it. Shane had found Travis's body in the depths but hadn't been able to find her. He didn't even bother dragging Travis up; he just pushed him aside and kept searching for Chloe.

Then he felt it. A connection to her mentally, like she was reaching out to him, pulling on his mind, his focus, his cold. Not to hurt him but to pull it into herself. Shane felt their link just for a split second.

And then it was gone.

Chloe was gone.

Shane dove wildly again, anguish tearing at him, ripping through the ice that had kept him focused. He couldn't lose her. Not now, when they'd really just found each other.

But the black water seemed to swallow everything whole.

Shane wouldn't give up. No matter what, he would keep searching for Chloe. He dived again, but in the opposite direction from where he'd been searching. He stretched his arms out as far as they would reach, hoping to feel her, since there was no way he'd be able to see her. He swam around until the need for air once again forced him upward.

And that's when he felt something hit his ankle. He immediately spun around in the water.

Chloe.

But she wasn't swimming. Wasn't moving at all.

Shane grabbed her lifeless form and began dragging them both toward the surface. As he broke through, drawing in much-needed air, he realized Chloe wasn't doing the same.

"Shane!" Wyatt shouted from the dock before diving into the water to help him.

They had to get her to the pier so they could start CPR. It wasn't too late. She hadn't been in there that long.

It couldn't be too late.

Shane and Wyatt swam with Chloe over to the pier, where the police officers helped them get her out of the water and ripped the gag off her mouth. Chloe still hadn't moved, hadn't coughed. Hadn't breathed.

Somebody cut the zip tie off her hands so she could lie flat on the ground. Both officers immediately began CPR, one giving breaths, the other chest compressions, as Shane climbed up beside them.

In the pale light of the poorly lit pier, Chloe's skin had a horrible bluish tinge to it. He didn't know if it was from cold or lack of oxygen. All he knew was that he wouldn't allow it. He would not allow Chloe to leave him.

She'd needed Avalanche before. To find her. To rescue her. Now she needed Shane. He thrust away all the emotional ice he'd used to keep things from touching him too deeply, from feeling too much, and reached out to her.

With his mind. With his heart. With every bit of heat he had inside him, he reached out to Chloe.

He kneeled beside her. "Come on, peanut. Don't you give up. Not now, not when we've just found each other and we know how perfect we are." Shane didn't care if Wyatt and the other officers heard.

"I felt you take my ice, Chloe. Now you take my heat, do you hear me? You let go of the ice, and you take the heat." He knew his words must sound ridiculous to the others, but he wouldn't stop.

Because damn it, he was not letting her go.

"Fight, Chloe. I know your brain can hear me. Use that survival instinct so ingrained in you and *fight*," he whispered into her ear. "Leave the ice and follow the heat. I did. It was all I could do around you."

Chloe's whole body seemed to convulse, causing the officers to stop the CPR and pull back. They turned her to the side as she vomited half the harbor. Finally, she rolled onto her back of her own accord. Although she shivered, her skin had lost much of its blue tinge. One of the officers took off his jacket and pulled it around her; another stood to call in what was happening.

Shane just lay down on the dock and pulled Chloe on top of him, crushing her head to his chest.

"Your ice is gone," she whispered. "I can hear all the voices I normally can't when you're around."

"I had to let it go to get you back."

She nodded against him. "I followed the trail of heat you were sending out to me. It brought me back."

Shane closed his eyes. None of this made any sense, but he didn't care. He only cared that Chloe was here, in his arms, alive.

"I'm going to need you to get the ice back, Avalanche," she

murmured. "It's nice to have someone shield me from the voices."

"I don't know if I'm ever going to be able to be icy around you again, peanut. I think you might have broken me."

She shifted her head and kissed his chest. "Okay. You build a wall of ice to keep everyone else out, and you and I will live around our heat."

He wouldn't have it any other way.

Epilogue

A few months later—Christmas.

EVERYTHING HAD CHANGED for *Day's End*.

The show had lost Alexandra, who'd been arrested for obstruction of justice and fraud, and was awaiting trial. She probably wouldn't do any real jail time, but she wouldn't be working on the show again either. Chloe had written a scene where Tia Day, Alexandra's namesake, had been killed in an epic magical battle between two sets of paranormal creatures.

Tia Day would return, reincarnated. Because Tia's fighting spirit would never die. But she wouldn't return in the form of Alexandra. That Tia was gone for good.

Chloe felt sorry for Alexandra in a lot of ways, since the woman had only been looking for attention. But a judge had decided she would be charged, so there wasn't anything for Alexandra to do except hire a firm full of lawyers, which she did.

Losing Noah and Travis was a double blow for the show,

since, despite everything, they'd been important members of the team.

Moreover, they'd lost Nadine. She'd never quite recovered from Travis's betrayal. She came in to the set every day and did her job, but her heart obviously wasn't in it. Chloe ached for her sweet friend, who had been betrayed so badly.

She'd tried to talk Nadine into coming with her to Lake Tahoe for Christmas, where she was meeting her sisters. Adrienne and Paige loved Nadine and wanted her there. Their husbands and Adrienne's three-year-old son did as well. Shane too.

But Nadine just wanted to be alone. Her wounds—physical, emotional, and mental—would take time to heal. Chloe would give her that.

Plus, Chloe had her own problems to worry about.

Day's End wasn't the only thing changing in Chloe's life.

She heard the back door slide open behind her. Could hear the men inside—Adrienne's husband, Conner, and Paige's husband, Brett, playing with Adrienne's son, Vince —felt the presence of her sisters as they joined her out on the balcony of the house they'd rented outside of Lake Tahoe.

Tomorrow was Christmas. Snow already blanketed the area and, except for Nadine missing, Chloe was surrounded by the people she loved most in the world. Could literally feel their love encompassing her, the same way her sisters' arms crossed behind her back as they came to stand on either side of her.

Triplets. Separated for most of their lives but together now.

"Shane wants to know if you're doing all right," Paige, the gentlest of the three of them, said.

Chloe nodded. "Just thinking about things. About change, both good and bad."

Would Shane think the change she was about to throw on him was good or bad?

"That man loves you, Chlo," Adrienne said, squeezing her waist. "I don't need Conner to leave so I can use my ability to see that."

Chloe smiled and leaned into her sister. "I know."

He'd stayed, even after the security job for the studio was over. He was now running the North Carolina branch of Linear Tactical and living in his grandmother's house permanently. Chloe was there most of the time too.

That didn't mean he was ready for this.

"What's wrong, Chloe?" Paige whispered.

"Yeah, you tell us your news, we'll tell you ours," Adrienne said. "Is it about the show? Is it ending?"

Chloe shook her head. "No, they're willing to see how the new season does. To be honest, everything that happened has so much interest targeted on the show, the studio knows they'd be idiots to shut it down now. I've got ideas . . ."

Both women on either side of her laughed. "Of course you do."

These were her sisters. She had to tell them. They wouldn't judge her.

"I'm pregnant," Chloe whispered.

She felt their arms slide away from her, not in rejection, but so they could look at her more closely.

"Are you being serious?" Adrienne asked.

Chloe nodded. "I'm three months along. I went to the doctor last week. Hilariously, the baby is due June 21. Our birthday." She laughed weakly and gave a mock celebration waving of her arms. "Happy birthday to me! Doctor thinks it's a girl."

Paige reached over and slapped Adrienne on the arm. "You told her. That's not nice, messing with me like that."

Adrienne laughed. Like out loud, belly laughed right there

in the middle of the snow. "I swear on little Vince's life, I did not. But given us, I'm not surprised. Even with how weird it is, I'm not surprised."

"Told me what?" Chloe asked. "What's weird?"

"It was supposed to be part of your Christmas present tomorrow, but I guess we'll tell you now." Paige shrugged, smiling. "Brett and I are going to have a baby girl also."

Adrienne held up her hand. "And baby number two on the way for me. Girl."

Chloe could feel her eyes getting wide. "When are you due?"

They were both grinning from ear to ear as they said it. "June 21."

All three of them were a tangle of limbs as they hugged one another.

Triplets.

≈

"Is it safe for me to come out here?" Shane asked a few minutes later as Paige and Adrienne went back inside.

"Only if you promise to come over and keep me warm, Avalanche," she said, smiling as he opened his jacket and enveloped her in it, her back to his chest. Wrapped in his warmth, she could feel herself heating from the inside out.

Certain inner parts more than others.

His emotions may cool her brain and all the chaos that lived there, but his touch would always heat her body.

"Looked like it was quite a celebration out here." His lips, warm and soft, brushed across her neck with the words. Her head automatically fell over to the side to give him better access. And she sighed as he began to work his hands up and down her body under the coat.

"My sisters have big news to share."

He nibbled on her neck. "I have big news to share too."

Chloe spun around so she was facing him. "You do?" Was he leaving North Carolina? Moving to the Linear Tactical headquarters in Wyoming?

God, could she live there? With all that snow? Were there any towns? What about *Day's End*? Maybe she could commute. Did they even have airports in Wyoming? Maybe if she sold her house in Los Angeles she could afford her own jet.

"Chloe."

She realized he'd said her name more than once. She blinked up at him. "I'm sorry. I was thinking."

He chuckled. "I could see that. Do you want me to tell you my news or just let that imagination of yours run away with everything?"

"You, please. Go ahead." She braced herself.

He took a deep breath. "I'm sorry. I can't continue to live with you in my grandmother's house like we've been doing."

Oh God. He *was* moving to Wyoming.

"I—I see." She couldn't tell him about the baby now. It would be . . . entrapment.

He ran a finger down her cheek. "I doubt you see at all. My grandmother liked you. Got involved with your show to get to know you better. I have no doubt she planned to set us up when I got home. But I didn't make it in time."

Despite his soft words, she couldn't shake the dread.

"But she wouldn't want us living there together, Chloe," Shane continued. "I have no doubt about that."

"She wouldn't?"

"No." His coat dropped from around her, and she felt the chill just as much on the outside as she did the inside. "So we can't keep doing that."

Chloe nodded. It had to be the pregnancy that had these damn tears threatening. "Okay. I can move. Get my stuff out."

"I have a better idea."

"What?"

Shane dropped down to one knee. Once he did, she could see her entire family pressing up against the sliding glass door to watch. Adrienne's husband, Conner, stepped to the side to let someone else see too.

Nadine.

She smiled and blew Chloe a kiss, then pointed for her to give her attention back to Shane.

"We have an audience," she whispered.

He just smiled, that grin that stopped her heart. "I know. I waited until Nadine got here because I know how important family is to you. My family—all the Linear Tactical guys—are arriving the day after tomorrow. We'll have *all* our family here."

Even on one knee, his head was up to her chest. She ran her fingers through his hair. "You said something about a better idea than me moving out?"

"Yes." He pulled out a ring. "The only way Grammi would want us living in that house is if we were married."

She smiled. "So I guess we should do that."

"I know one of the earrings she gave you was lost in all the crazy. But when I saw the one you left me on Travis's countertop, that was the second I knew I needed you in my life forever, Chloe. I had a ring made from that earring so that every time we look at it we'll know what my Grammi knew from the start: that you and I were meant to be. She even played the role of a zombie to make that happen."

He took out the ring, and Chloe just stared at it; diamonds surrounded the small ruby in the center. It was gorgeous. Perfect.

Just like how Shane was for her.

"I love you." It was the first time she'd said the words to

someone who wasn't family. She never thought they would feel so right coming off her tongue.

"You are my whole life, Chloe. I love you with a heat I never thought was possible in my frozen heart. You accept Avalanche as part of who I am. Embrace it, even. I never thought I would find that."

"If you can accept the voices in my head, I guess the least I can do is accept all of you."

He smiled. "Will you marry me?"

"Yes." He slipped the ring on her finger.

She could hear the cheers from behind the door even as Shane stood and pulled her in for a kiss. They were both breathing hard as they pulled away.

"I guess for once I got to surprise you. I think I like being the supriser rather than the suprisee, peanut."

Chloe just smiled, his love heating her from the inside out. Her life was more perfect than she ever thought possible. And would be even better by this summer.

"Well, speaking of surprises . . ."

THE END

Don't miss *Primal Instinct* and *Critical Instinct* – both available now.
Be sure to check out Janie's other series:
Omega Sector (4-book series)
Omega Sector: Critical Response (6-book series)
Omega Sector: Under Siege (6-book series)

Acknowledgements

As the old saying goes: it takes a village to raise a book. And this one would've never happened it if weren't for so many people.

First and foremost, Stephanie Scott, without whom there is no Janie Crouch, author. From the very beginning you have stood by my side, offering support, encouragement, and correct punctuation and grammar. You have never once faltered in knowing the exact right thing to say to me, even when I'm making very little sense. And I love when you start threatening to beat up people who give me bad reviews—them peeps better watch out. Woman, if I loved you any more I would turn into a pile of goo. Thank you.

To my beta readers, editors, and proofers: I hand a book to you in a slightly embarrassing shape, and you give it back to me so much better than I would've ever thought it could be. Elizabeth Neal, Marci Mathers, Aly Birkl, Lynn Brooks, Mary Lawson, Fedora Chen, and Samantha Wallace . . . I'm blowing all the kisses in my heart your way. You gals rock.

To the Tia Troopers . . . I have to write these acknowledgments before I know how much we actually raise for donation, but no matter what the dollar amount is, *we have done our part to stomp cystic fibrosis*. I have been amazed as literally dozens of authors and companies, some of whom don't know me at all, and none of whom know Tia personally, have stood with me in attempt to raise awareness and funds to fight CF. I can't list them all here, but a very special thank you to:

- Regan Black, who posted about the Tia Troopers on social media more than any other single person, including me.
- Joanne Rock, who gave and gave and gave to help our fight against CF.
- Tyler Anne Snell, who offered to name a character after people who bought this book, to help get us to our goal.
- Kobo Writing Life, Deranged Doctor Designs, Bad Boy Update, Hot Stuff Romance, Social Butterfly PR, and Bargain Booksy . . . all who donated advertising space or services to help raise money to fight CF for no recognition or gain.

Tia Troopers everywhere, my heart is humbled by your generosity. *We helped stomp CF!*

And to Tia and the entire Cordell family: it's easy for me to give time and money when at the end of the day I can walk away from CF. You can't, and yet your constant strength, dedication, and faith amaze me. I stand in belief with you that God will heal Tia of this disease. Until then, we will fight until CF stands for Cure Found.

About the Author

"Passion that leaps right off the page."—*Romantic Times Book Reviews*

USA TODAY bestselling author Janie Crouch loves to read—almost exclusively romance—and has been doing so since middle school. She cut her teeth on Harlequin Romances when she lived in the UK as a preteen, then moved on to a passion for romance suspense as an adult. She is a winner and/or finalist of multiple romance literary awards including the Golden Quill Award for Best Romantic Suspense, the National Reader's Choice Award and the coveted RITA Award by the Romance Writers of America.

Janie recently relocated with her husband and four children to Germany (due to her husband's job as support for the US military), after living in Virginia for nearly twenty years. When she's not listening to the voices in her head (and even when she is), she enjoys traveling, long-distance running, movie-watching, and trouble-making of all kinds.

Her favorite quote: "Life is a daring adventure or nothing."—Helen Keller.

www.janiecrouch.com

Made in the USA
Monee, IL
26 February 2024

54123725R00151